CONFESSIONS
THE
PRIVATE SCHOOL
MURDERS

JAMES PATTERSON is one of the best-known and biggest-selling writers of all time. He is the author of some of the most popular detective series of the past decade – the Alex Cross, Women's Murder Club and Michael Bennett novels – as well as the Maximum Ride novels and *Confessions of a Murder Suspect*, and he has written many other number one bestsellers including romance novels and stand-alone thrillers. He lives in Florida with his wife and son.

James was inspired by his son, who was a reluctant reader, to also write books specifically for young readers. James is a founding partner of Booktrust's Children's Reading Fund in the UK. James Patterson has been the most borrowed author in UK libraries for the past seven years in a row.

Also by James Patterson

Confessions series
Confessions of a Murder Suspect (*with Maxine Paetro*)
Confessions: The Paris Mysteries (*with Maxine Paetro,
to be published October 2014*)

Maximum Ride series
The Angel Experiment
School's Out Forever
Saving the World and Other Extreme Sports
The Final Warning
Max
Fang
Angel
Nevermore

Daniel X series
The Dangerous Days of Daniel X (*with Michael Ledwidge*)
Watch the Skies (*with Ned Rust*)
Demons and Druids (*with Adam Sadler*)
Game Over (*with Ned Rust*)
Armageddon (*with Chris Grabenstein*)

Witch & Wizard series
Witch & Wizard (*with Gabrielle Charbonnet*)
The Gift (*with Ned Rust*)
The Fire (*with Jill Dembowski*)
The Kiss (*with Jill Dembowski*)
The Lost (*with Emily Raymond, to be published November 2014*)

Homeroom Diaries
Homeroom Diaries (*with Lisa Papademetriou*)

Graphic novels
Maximum Ride: Manga Volumes 1–8 (*with NaRae Lee*)

For more information about James Patterson's novels, visit
www.jamespatterson.co.uk

Or become a fan on Facebook

CONFESSIONS

THE PRIVATE SCHOOL MURDERS

JAMES PATTERSON
AND MAXINE PAETRO

Published by Young Arrow, 2014

2 4 6 8 10 9 7 5 3 1

Copyright © James Patterson, 2013

James Patterson has asserted his right under the Copyright, Designs
and Patents Act 1988 to be identified as the author of this work

First published in Great Britain in 2013 by
Young Arrow
Random House, 20 Vauxhall Bridge Road,
London SW1V 2SA

www.randomhouse.co.uk

Addresses for companies within The Random House Group Limited can
be found at: www.randomhouse.co.uk/offices.htm

The Random House Group Limited Reg. No. 954009

A CIP catalogue record for this book
is available from the British Library

ISBN 9780099567387

The Random House Group Limited supports the Forest Stewardship
Council® (FSC®), the leading international forest-certification organisation.
Our books carrying the FSC label are printed on FSC®-certified paper.
FSC is the only forest-certification scheme supported by the
leading environmental organisations, including Greenpeace.
Our paper procurement policy can be found at :
www.randomhouse.co.uk/environment

Printed and bound in Great Britain by CPI Group (UK) Ltd

PROLOGUE

1

It hasn't been all that long since my last confession, but I already have so much to tell you. Fair warning: Most of it isn't very pretty.

My story starts with the catastrophic deaths of Malcolm and Maud Angel. They weren't just those wealthy New York socialites you read about in the *New York Times*.

They were my parents. Dead. They died in their bed under freakish circumstances three months ago, leaving my brothers and me devastated and bankrupt.

Not to mention under suspicion of murder.

We were eventually cleared of the crime—once I uncovered key evidence in the case. So, my friend, what do you think are the chances of another shocking, grisly crime happening in my life? Oh, about a hundred percent, and I can say that with total confidence.

Because it's already happened.

My brother Matthew has been charged with killing his twenty-four-year-old actress girlfriend, Tamara Gee, and her unborn child. Just to make things that much more scandalous, after my parents' deaths, Tamara announced to the press that she had been sleeping around—with *my father.*

Good times.

That brings me to today, which really isn't the best time to be reminiscing about the past. I had to put on a positive face for Matthew, who I had come to visit.

In *prison.*

Deep inside the infamous New York City jail known (for good reason) as The Tombs, I held my breath as a beefy guard led me down a long gray cinder-block hallway that was pungent with the reek of urine and male sweat and deposited me in a folding chair outside a Plexiglas cell.

"Wait."

So I did. And immediately began to nervously toy with the buttons on my peacoat. Matthew's trial was set to begin in just a few days, and I was here to bring him bad news. His so-called airtight alibi for the night of Tamara's murder had just completely imploded. I felt sick to my stomach just thinking about what could happen to him and, in turn, what might happen to what was left of our family.

My hands were shaking. I used to be the picture of calm in any and all situations, but these days I was feeling so raw that it was hard to remember how the numbing pills my parents had given me every day of my life kept my emotions in check.

I heard the echo of footsteps approaching from somewhere behind the concrete walls. Still no Matthew. Hinges squealed and metal scraped against stone. A door slammed shut and locked. Each sound was more hopeless than the last.

Finally the door at the back of the Plexiglas cell opened, and Matthew shuffled in with a uniformed guard right behind him.

You might remember when Matthew Angel won the Heisman, how he bounded up onto the stage with a self-satisfied grin and lifted the heavy trophy over his head while camera flashes popped. Maybe you've seen him returning kickoffs for the New York Giants, spiking the ball in the end zone and raising his fist to the sky. At the very least, you probably know him as the dude in the soup commercial. Matthew Angel has always been the guy every

Pop Warner grade-schooler wants to be: a heroic rock-star jock, all muscle, smiles, and thoroughbred speed. A football god.

That person was now unrecognizable. Matthew had been transformed into a brooding hulk in an orange jumpsuit, wrists cuffed to a chain around his waist, shackles around his ankles.

My formerly cocky brother was too embarrassed and miserable to even look at me as the guard put a heavy hand on his shoulder and forced him into a chair before uncuffing him.

My eyes filled with tears. It was a feeling I was still getting used to.

Matthew managed a half smile, then leaned close to the grill that was set into the glass wall. "Hey, Tandy. How're you? How're the guys?"

Our brothers, Harrison and Hugo. Even in the throes of this misery, Matthew was thinking about them. About me. One tear spilled over. I wiped it away before he could look up and detect any weakness.

I took a deep breath. "Matthew, there's something I have to tell you."

2

"*It's about your friends, Matty,*" I said through the grid. "The ones who swore they were playing poker with you when Tamara was killed. They say they lied to protect you, but now they've had some kind of crisis of conscience. They told Philippe they're not going to lie under oath."

I held my breath and waited for the inevitable explosion. While Matthew had a polished and shiny rep in public, we inside the Angel family knew that at any given moment he could go nuclear. *Prone to violent outbursts* was the clinical phrase.

But today my brother simply blinked. His eyes were heavy with sadness and confusion.

"I might have done it, Tandy," he finally mumbled. "I don't know."

"Matthew, come on!" I blurted, panic burbling up inside my chest. "You did *not* kill Tamara."

He leaned in closer to the grid, his hand flattened against the glass so that his palm turned white. "The guys are telling the truth, Tandy. We only played poker for a couple hours. I wasn't with them at the time when the medical examiner says Tamara was killed."

I pressed my lips together as hard as I could to hold back my anger. Not to mention my confusion and abject terror. "What? Where did you go?"

He shook his head. "I don't even know. Some bar? I got hammered and somehow made it home. It's pretty much a blur." He pressed the heels of his hands into his temples and sucked in a breath before continuing. "All I know is that I got into bed with her, and when I woke up, she was dead. There was blood all over me, Tandy. Blood everywhere. And I have no memory of what happened before that."

I stared at him, wide-eyed. For once in my life, I had no idea what to say.

But then, it wasn't completely out of the realm of possibility. Back when Tamara was killed, he was still on Malcolm and Maud's little Angel Pharma concoctions—

special cocktails whipped up at the drug company my father founded—which made him prone not only to violent outbursts and manic episodes but also to blackouts.

I looked down at my hands. They trembled as I gathered the guts to ask a question I'd needed the answer to for weeks.

"Why didn't you tell me Tamara was dead, Matty?" I hazarded a glance at his eyes. "You came home that day. You spent the whole afternoon with us. You never once felt the need to say 'Oh, hey, guys, I kind of found Tamara murdered this morning'?"

Matthew pressed the heels of his hands into his eye sockets. "I was in shock," he said. "And I was terrified, okay? I didn't know what had happened. And you guys were already being put through the wringer by the DA, thanks to Malcolm and Maud. I thought...I thought..."

Suddenly he slammed his hand against the glass and the whole wall shuddered.

"Watch it!" the guard barked.

"You thought *what*?" I asked quietly.

He shook his head. "I think I thought that if I just ignored it, somehow it would all go away. I didn't want more scrutiny placed on us." His eyes were wet as he finally looked me in the eye. "Maybe I did do it, Tandy. Craziness runs in our veins, right?"

"Not in mine, Matty. Not anymore." I took a breath. "I don't do crazy these days."

"Oh, you do crazy just fine."

Then, out of nowhere, Matthew burst into tears. I'd never seen him cry once in my entire life.

"I was drunk. I don't know how else I could have done it," he said between sobs. "If I could see the apartment again…maybe…if I could go back there, maybe it would come back to me. God, I wish I could just get bail. Have you talked to Uncle Peter? Can't he find the money somewhere?"

I shook my head, my throat full. "We're totally broke, remember? And your bail is five million dollars." I pressed my palm to the glass at roughly the same angle as his, as if the connection brought us closer. "Please don't keep saying you might be guilty, Matty. It can't be true."

The door behind him squealed open. "Time's up," the guard said.

"I'm sorry, kiddo." Matthew shot me what looked like an apologetic smile as he was pulled away. The door slammed behind them and I just sat there, stunned.

"You taking up residence or what?" the guard standing behind me said. I got up and walked briskly down the hall in front of him, pretending I wasn't completely broken inside.

When I emerged from The Tombs, the bright sunlight hit my eyes and they burned. I squinted as I hailed a cab on Baxter, then slammed the door so hard the whole car rattled.

"Please take me home," I said to the cabbie.

He drilled me through the rearview mirror with his hard black eyes. "You want me to guess where you live?"

"The Dakota," I barked, in no mood. "Just go."

The cab leapt forward, and we headed uptown.

CONFESSION

There's something I've been avoiding. Something I haven't admitted to anyone. I've barely even admitted it to myself. But this is a confession, so I'm confessing. Here goes.

I'm not entirely sure how I feel about this whole having-emotions thing.

I know, I know. I'm the one who freaked out when I realized that the multiple pills my parents had been feeding us kids every morning were, in fact, high-test Angel Pharma mood-, mind-, and body-altering drugs. I'm the one who demanded that Harry go cold turkey with me so that we could take back control of our lives, our heads, maybe even our souls.

But those pills tainted our very essence—everything that made us human. I mean, when I saw my parents' dead bodies lying twisted in their bed, I didn't even cry. I didn't feel anguish or loss, I just felt angry. Anger was the only emotion the Angel kids were occasionally allowed to feel. Probably because anger produces adrenaline and adrenaline can be very useful. Whether you're tearing down a professional gridiron with two three-hundred-pound defensive ends on your tail, playing Mozart at Carnegie Hall, working complex calc problems at a desk, or navigating the wilds of uncharted jungles, adrenaline is a good thing to have on your side.

And of course, Malcolm and Maud knew that. They formulated our daily uppers and downers for optimal performance. They rewarded excellence with extravagant prizes called Grande Gongos and responded to failure with extreme punishments called Big Chops. And all emotions, like empathy, sadness, even *joy*, were failures. Pointless. Not for their little protégés.

Until Malcolm and Maud were gone. And I started making decisions for myself.

Now it's three months later, and yeah, I'm feeling things, all right. I'm feeling sorrow and excitement and nervousness. I'm feeling happiness and uncertainty and self-doubt. There's even a little bit of hopefulness sometimes. It's all emotion, all the time, and to be honest, sometimes I just want to down a whole mess of those pills again so I can have a little peace.

But the worst of all these new emotions is the fear. I can't stand feeling fear. And these days I'm afraid *all the time*. I'm afraid for my brother Matthew and what will happen to him. I'm afraid for my little brother, Hugo, and my twin brother, Harry, and what it will be like if we're thrown out of our apartment and tossed into foster homes and public schools. I don't even want to know what would happen if either one of them was faced with an actual bully. Harry would probably dissolve into a blubbering ball on the floor and get his butt kicked, while Hugo would probably—no, *definitely*—Hulk Out and tear whoever it was limb from limb. Then I'd have *two* brothers behind bars.

And of course I'm also terrified that I may never see James again.

James Rampling. The only boy I ever loved, and the one person (besides my older sister, Katherine, who died years ago) I could trust with all these emotions…if I had any idea where to find him.

That might be the worst fear of all—that I'll never get to experience true love again. The very thought makes my stomach clench, my heart pound, and my mind race.

See? Fear. I can't stand it. And if things don't calm down soon, it might be the one emotion that'll convince me to go back to being Maud and Malcolm's good little robot. To go back to the drugs.

To go back to being numb.

1

DEAD RECKONING

The cabdriver used both of his big fat feet when he drove, jamming on the brakes and the gas at the same time, making me sick. As the cab bucked to a stop at the light at Columbus Circle, my iPhone rang. I grabbed it from my bag.

C.P. Thank God.

After a lifetime of other kids thinking I was all robotic and weird, I actually had a friend at school. Claudia Portman, known as C.P., was a tarnished Queen Bee who was dethroned last year when she cheated on her finals and was ratted out by her clique-mates. Because of a massive donation by her parents to our school, she got to stay for our junior year, but she'd dumped her friends and become a self-defined loner until the day I was cleared of my parents' murders and she'd sat down with me at lunch. "Move over," she'd said. "We criminals gotta stick together."

And even though I wasn't a criminal, I laughed.

"Hey, T!" she said now by way of greeting. "Did you read it?"

"Read what?" I asked, still distracted after my conversation with Matthew. Hordes of people streamed out of the subway and crossed in front of my taxi.

"You know *exactly* what I'm talking about," she semi-whined. "Come on, Tandy, get with the program. I *need* to discuss this atrocity against the written word with someone!"

Right. The novel was another super-sexy purple-prose page-turner that was sweeping the planet in dozens of languages (some of which I'd already mastered). C.P. had downloaded the ebook to my tablet, but I had immediately deleted it, hoping she'd forget to ask what I thought. It wasn't exactly the kind of thing I enjoyed reading.

Suddenly, the driver stomped on the gas and the cab lurched forward, sending my stomach into my mouth.

"I'll get to it soon," I told C.P., "but you know it's not really my thing." We took a turn at roughly Mach 20, and I was glad I hadn't eaten since breakfast. "I'm almost home. Can I call you later?"

"Sure! But only if you've read at least fifty pages!" she replied.

I rolled my eyes and hung up.

Twelve nauseating blocks later, I paid the driver through the transom and disembarked on the corner of Seventy-Second and Central Park West, where the Dakota reigned. We lived at the top of the infamous co-op—infamous for housing the social elite and for being the site of a few high-profile murders over the last half century or so. Our apartment was nestled right under the intricate Victorian peaks and gables.

Our parents had been anything but Victorian in their decorating choices, though. They'd filled our home with everything from a winged piano to a UFO-shaped chandelier to a coffee table full of pygmy sharks (since freed), and dozens of other priceless—and strange—contemporary art items.

I huddled into my coat with the collar up, my face down, trying to evade the many photographers lined up near the gate so I could slip right through, but I never even got there. Harry blocked my way, his dark curls tossed by the frigid wind.

"Tandy, you're not going to believe this." He grabbed my arm and steered me down the sidewalk, holding me close to his side as we automatically matched our strides. "Adele Church. She's dead."

I turned to look at him. There wasn't a trace of mirth on his boyishly handsome face. Not that I was surprised. Harry wasn't a jokester or a liar. He wasn't even much of a storyteller.

"She can't be," I finally said. "I saw her this morning."

"She was shot about five minutes ago, Tandy. She's in the park. Her body, I mean. It's still there."

The whole world went fuzzy.

This was not happening. Not again.

2

"How did you—" I asked my brother, my mouth dry.

"No one told me," he said, digging around in his pocket. "I took this."

Harry showed me the picture on his phone. My already weakened stomach clenched, and I grabbed his arm to steady myself.

"Sorry," he said, gritting his teeth. "Should have warned you it was ugly."

"It's okay," I told him, clearing my throat. I turned and started for the park. "Let's go."

We sprinted across the broad expanse of Central Park West against the light and entered the park by a blacktop pathway. Harry steered me to the right, just past the pretzel cart Hugo lived for, and we ran the thirty yards through a tunnel of shade trees to John Lennon's memorial in Strawberry Fields, darting around strollers, joggers, and Rollerbladers.

It was clear where Adele's body was. The vultures were already circling. And by *vultures*, I mean press.

I elbowed through a group of Korean tourists wielding their camera phones and wedged open a sight line to the famous mosaic with the word *Imagine* set into the middle of a triangulated path.

Adele Church's body was right there, at dead center.

The blurry photo on Harry's phone had in no way prepared me for the reality. Adele was lying on her back as if she'd fallen from the sky. Black bullet holes had punched through her chest and stomach, and her white-and-pink plaid coat was drenched with blood. I was close enough to read Adele's expression as stark disbelief even as her wide-open blue eyes went dull from death.

Bile rose up in the back of my throat, bringing tears to my eyes. I turned to Harry and pressed my face into his shoulder, biting down hard on my lip as I tried not to cry.

This was one of those moments. One of those moments when I would have given anything not to feel. I couldn't wrap my brain around why anyone would want to kill sweet, totally innocuous Adele. I wanted to strangle every member of the growing crowd of tourists who were angling to get a better view of her poor broken body.

Most of all I wanted to scream at her to just *get up*. That this couldn't have happened. Not to someone I knew. Not to someone our age.

Not to one of the very few people at school who were occasionally nice to me.

"Take a breath, Tandy," Harry whispered, which was odd, considering he was usually the one on the verge of a nervous breakdown, not me. "Focus on something else. What do you think happened to her?"

Harry knew me so well. Piecing together evidence would focus me. It would make me feel like there was something I could do. I was all about productivity.

I turned to look at the body, trying to force myself into cool indifference, and drilled down deep into my analytic left brain.

"There's a lot of blood," I said under my breath. "She didn't die instantly. Three shots and her heart was still pumping after at least two of them. She knew what was happening. She knew she was—"

I paused and cleared my throat. I didn't want to go there.

"I wonder if she saw the shooter."

Harry frowned ponderously. He was about to ask me

something when police sirens blew in bursts, startling everyone. The crowd separated as cruisers and unmarked cars streamed onto the scene of the crime. When the first cops to arrive got out of their gray Chevy, I froze. It was Sergeant Capricorn Caputo and his partner, Detective Ryan Hayes—the two cops who had been first on the scene of my parents' deaths.

Sergeant Caputo was tall and gangly, with a severe jawline, slick black hair, and an all-black wardrobe. Plus he was a total ass. He prided himself on being the tough guy, and his behavior could skew anywhere from rude to downright mean. Still, if you were as observant as I was, you might notice the checkered socks showing under the cuffs of his pants, which took the edge off his hard-core persona. While Detective Caputo was a general pain, he was focused. He lived his job.

His partner, Detective Hayes, was the opposite: a solid man, competent and kind, the sort of guy who put you totally at ease. Hayes was a good soul, and I was glad he would be on Adele's case, too. Even though, technically, he hadn't solved our parents' "murders."

I had.

"Sergeant Caputo!" I called.

He spotted me and narrowed his beady eyes, never taking them off my face as he picked his way carefully around Adele's body. "You're under arrest, Taffy."

Caputo had no problem remembering my name, but he loved to mess with me.

"Wow. Still going with that joke, huh? It stopped being funny about three months ago."

His gaze flicked over Harry, then back at me. "Please. You don't have a single funny bone in your entire skinny body."

I sighed. "So do you want to know what's going on here, or do you want to waste some more time coming up with lame nicknames?"

"You know this girl?" he asked, interested.

"Her name is Adele Church," I told him.

"We went to school with her," Harry added.

"What else do you know about Miss Church?" Caputo asked, flipping open his notebook and scribbling down her name.

"She was a sweet person," I said. "She lived up on Seventy-Ninth, I think. Her older brother graduated last year."

"She played the flute," said Harry. "And pretty much kicked ass in sociology."

"Any idea why someone would want to hurt her?" Caputo asked.

We heard more sirens with deeper whooping sounds as the coroner's van arrived. More cops were getting out of cruisers, stringing a yellow-tape perimeter around the body and shooing the onlookers back.

"Everyone liked her," I said. "I think she saw her killer, though. Maybe she knew him."

Caputo's face flattened with unsuppressed scorn. "I've got no time for your amateur-night theories, Tallulah."

"You know better than that, Caputo." I gave him my card. "I want to help."

He glanced at my card and scoffed. " 'Tandy Angel, Detective. Mysteries Solved. Case Closed,' " he read. "I was wrong. You're actually hilarious, T-bone." He glanced from me to Harry and pocketed the card. "Nice seeing you."

"You should call me," I shouted after him as he turned away. "Consultations are free for all clueless detectives named Caputo!"

He just kept walking.

"That man is going to break into our apartment and kill you in your sleep, you know," Harry said.

I smirked. "I'd like to see him try."

CONFESSION

I may have seemed confident to Caputo and to Harry while I was handing over my card, but I wasn't. In fact, the second my card touched Caputo's chalky, dry fingers, something inside me swooped, like the way your heart feels when you jump off a bridge with nothing but a bungee cord tied to your feet.

Because that was when I realized: Maybe I *wasn't* a good detective. Not anymore.

Yes, even Capricorn Caputo would have to admit that without me, the mystery of my parents' deaths might never have been solved. But that was then. When I was still full of Num, Lazr, Focus, and other secret Angel Pharmaceuticals concoctions. Now that I was off the drugs, I was *feeling* everything, but did I still have the sharp and rational mind of an ace detective?

My grades seemed to indicate that I did. But anyone could get straight As. Most of the kids I knew were technical geniuses, if you believe in IQ scores. Even C.P. Probably even Adele. But something had been going on lately that was starting to seriously bother me.

I was having these dreams. Dreams about James. And whenever I woke up from one of these dreams, I had a hard time figuring out whether it was really a dream, or if it was actually a memory.

That's my deepest, darkest secret, my friend. I think my mind was starting to play tricks on me. And I had a feeling I knew who to blame. My parents. And Fern Haven. And that awful Dr. Narmond.

But that's a story for another time.

3

I looked at Harry as we walked back to the Dakota. Harry and I were both dark-eyed and dark-haired, and we were fiercely loyal to each other. Two people couldn't be tighter friends and confidants than we were. Still, I wished we had that twin telepathy thing you always hear about, but we didn't. Probably because aside from the superficial physical traits and the aforementioned loyalty, we couldn't have been less alike.

Harry was quiet. He was mopey. He had this tendency to slouch. He was asthmatic, and he slept long and late every day when he could. Harry was also kind.

Yes, much to my parents' disappointment, Harry was born an emo, and even though he was a world-class

27

pianist who could bring an audience at Lincoln Center to tears, Malcolm and Maud described him as sensitive, sentimental, and weak. He had never won a Gongo or gotten a chop, and not even a billion emotion-quashing pills had ever dimmed a single ray of his brilliance.

According to me, he got major points for that.

I was Harry's flip side. I was up at dawn. I sometimes cooked elaborate breakfasts of apricot-and-chai oatmeal and fresh-squeezed orange juice before anyone else was even stretching their arms above their heads. I lived for a complex chemistry experiment and checked over my dad's financial books for fun—at least I had, back when he let me. I was known for being high-strung, and occasionally my sharpness was interpreted as, well, rudeness. I never danced around anything when I could cut to the chase, and no one had ever called me kind.

My parents gave me major points for *that*.

I'd also studied forensic science as a hobby since I was about six years old and had solved every mystery I'd ever read or seen on TV since I was eight. Now I just hoped I still had that talent. That quitting the drugs hadn't taken it from me.

Harry held the gate open for me, and we slipped inside the courtyard, ignoring the camera flashes popping all around us. Instead of thinking about me or Harry or Matthew, I thought about Adele. Adele, who listened well and laughed easily. Adele, who played in the orchestra and wore pink constantly and hung photos of composers and film directors in her locker. She could have gone on to do anything, be anyone, have a great big life.

Now she would never have another day. Another minute.

Call me crazy, but I wanted—no, I *needed*—to do something about it. I just hoped that the new and maybe-improved drug-free me still could.

I put my key in the lock of apartment 9G, the duplex where Harry, Hugo, and I had once lived with our parents but now suffered daily with our horrible uncle Peter until the courts decided what was to become of us. But before I turned the knob, the door opened, and a tall, dark, and drop-dead-handsome man of maybe fifty said hello.

My shoulders coiled. Stranger in my apartment equals not good. "Who are you?"

"I'm Jacob Perlman," he said calmly. "Call me Jacob. Peter has brought me in as your guardian."

Harry gave Jacob a dubious look. "I thought Uncle Peter was our guardian."

"He was. Now I am," Jacob said, his brown eyes free of guile. "Would you like to come in?"

"To our own home?" I snapped. "Sure. Thanks."

Jacob smiled slowly and stepped back to let us through. Harry, sensing that I'd flipped into set-to-pop mode, quickly disappeared down the hallway and into his room.

"Peter installed a stranger in our house to look after us?" I said, looking up at Jacob and noting the small scar near his ear, the perfect hairline, the razor-sharp shave. "Is that even legal?"

He smirked. "Tandoori, right?"

He had an accent I couldn't quite place, which was odd considering I'd been most places and spoke most languages. The wrinkles fanning out from the corners of his eyes looked like squint lines more than laugh lines. He was lean and muscular, but not like he'd been working out in a gym. More like he'd had a physically demanding life.

"Yeah, that's me," I replied. "Where's Uncle Peter?"

Jacob folded his hands in front of him. "He didn't say."

Great. So not only had he left a stranger in our house, he'd left him here alone. How was I supposed to know this guy was even who he said he was? There could be a team of ninjas hanging out in the kitchen just waiting to gut me.

Considering my family's history, it wasn't much of a stretch.

"You won't mind if I just...give him a call," I said, angling one foot toward the still-open door.

"Feel free," Jacob said. He was so sophisticated and smooth that the UFO chandelier hovering over his head—the one that had decorated our foyer my whole life—looked suddenly out of place.

He was a man of few words. That, at least, I liked. I speed-dialed my uncle, hating with every fiber of my being that I had to consult him on anything.

Uncle Peter was my father's totally despicable brother. He was intolerant and so rude that he made me seem like Miss Manners. In fact, we all hate him and call him Uncle Pig, sometimes to his face.

Peter had moved into our house when my parents died, had taken over my sister's room, which had been strictly off-limits up to that point, and had started treating the Angel kids like the dirt under his grubby fingernails.

He picked up on the fourth ring. "Yes, Tandoori, Jacob is your new guardian. Yes, it's legal. If you'd like to see the paperwork, ask him. I'm busy."

He hung up before I could even get out a word. Jacob raised an eyebrow. I cleared my throat.

"All right, then," I said grudgingly. "Looks like you're legit."

"I'm glad of that," Jacob told me. "I'd like to have a family meeting. Shall we gather in the living room in, say, twenty minutes?"

A family meeting was actually in order. I had to report on my awful conversation with Matty. But I wasn't sure yet that I wanted to include Jacob Perlman in *that*.

"Where will you be staying?" I asked him as we turned toward the living room.

"I'll move into Peter's room."

"Don't call it that," I snapped. "It's Katherine's room."

"I apologize," Jacob said immediately. "Katherine's room."

I narrowed my eyes at him. "I have some work to do."

"Twenty minutes," he reminded me.

"I'll be there."

I stalked off to my sky-blue bedroom, with its leafy ninth-floor view of Central Park and shelves of sea coral. If I stood at the windows and got up on my toes, I could just about see where Adele Church's body had been lying, her dead eyes turned skyward.

I flopped down on my bed and called C.P.

"You read it? Tell me you read it," she said hungrily. "Wasn't it just *awful*?"

"Actually, I haven't had time," I told her. "C.P.... Adele Church is dead. She was shot. They found her body in the park about two seconds before I got home."

"What?" C.P. demanded. "Are you kidding me?"

"No. I'm sorry. I just figured I should tell you," I replied.

"Oh my God." The tears were clear in her voice. "Tandy... oh my God. Do they know who did it?"

"Not yet," I told her. "But we'll figure it out."

"What's this *we* stuff?" she asked.

"I'll explain later," I told her. "And I promise, at some point, to read your latest favorite book porn."

C.P. sighed. "Oh, forget it," she said sadly. "All the fun's gone out of it now."

"Sorry," I mumbled. "I'll text you later?"

"Sure."

We hung up, and I rolled over onto my stomach, pulling my laptop across my bed to see what Google might turn up about Jacob Perlman. Uncle Peter had brought him into my house, so there was no way I was about to trust him without a thorough background check.

Turned out Google was full of Jacob.

And nearly every word about him was mind-blowing.

5

Jacob Perlman was a retired Israeli commando.

Yes, you read that right. A *commando.*

There was a whole *New York Times* profile on the guy. He'd rescued hostages from terrorists, disarmed and killed a suicide bomber he'd caught trying to blow up a marketplace, and evacuated a whole mess of kids from a school mere minutes before it was hit by a rogue Palestinian missile.

So basically, if anyone tried to mess with the Angel kids from now on, they were gonna get a beat-down. That much was comforting.

But why would a man who swatted down terrorists like they were houseflies want to babysit three bratty private

ol kids in New York City? And how did Uncle Pig
en know someone like him? Most of our uncle's acquain-
tances were as sniveling and pointless as he was.

I went next door to Harry's room, which was spacious
and modern, with one of his own amazing paintings of
angels adorning the ceiling. He was, of course, passed
out facedown on his king-sized bed. Harry needs a lot of
downtime to refresh his brilliant mind, but I thought it
was odd that he could sleep with the specter of Jacob Perlman looming.

I shook him awake, relayed my intel on Jacob, and
told him we were having a family meeting. Then I found
Hugo in his bedroom, sitting on his mattress on the floor
with his laptop on. After Malcolm and Maud died, Hugo
trashed just about everything he owned—the vintage toy
cars, his four-poster bed—and now only his Xbox, desk,
and chair were left standing. Hugo had the strength of a
full-grown man and wore his hair in long curls, Samson
style. He was upbeat and forgiving, and he exaggerated
every time he opened his mouth. He was also fearless. His
favorite person in the world, bar none, was our football
superstar brother, Matthew. Honestly, Hugo's behavior
when it came to Matty bordered on worship.

"Was Matty wearing one of those hockey masks so he
couldn't bite or spit?" Hugo asked, still typing as he spoke.

"Matthew is not Hannibal Lecter, Hugo." I sat down next to him on the mattress. "What're you up to?"

"I'm setting up a website," he informed me. "I'm going to raise money for his bail."

That was my ten-year-old brother for you. Always thinking. I reached out to ruffle his hair, then lay back on the mattress next to him and just listened to him type as I went over the bizarre events of the day.

Matthew, possibly a killer. Adele, dead for no apparent reason. A stranger running my household. Could my life get any more dramatic?

A few minutes later, Jacob paged us on the intercom, and we assembled in the living room: Harry and I taking up most of the red leather sofa, Hugo in the Pork Chair—a pink chair with hooves for feet that he loved—and Jacob perched above us on a kitchen stool he'd brought in for the meeting.

I wondered what Jacob thought of Maud's décor. She had favored huge pieces of artwork and had designed our place so that it looked like a hyperrealism exhibit at the Museum of Modern Art. It was all bold colors, life-sized statues, Pop Art canvases, and crazy kitschy furniture. We loved it. But then, it was all we knew. Somehow Jacob seemed like a guy who'd prefer a more minimalist style.

"First, I've e-mailed you the court order making me

your legal guardian," he said, looking directly at me. "And second, there is this."

He slipped a hand into the inside breast pocket of his khaki jacket and removed a four-by-six photo. He held it along the edges with both hands so we could see the faded color portrait of a woman in her fifties. Her hair was upswept. She wore a blouse with a deep neckline and a necklace of baroque blue pearls the size of melon balls.

I recognized her, of course. She was my father's mother, elegant and beautiful, a tough-love matriarch who had died before the Angel kids were born. But we still referred to her familiarly as Gram Hilda. A framed note and envelope from Gram Hilda hung on the wall of the staircase that led up to my parents' master suite. The note was handwritten, stamped by a notary, and was a companion to Gram Hilda's will. The letter was short and not too sweet.

"I am leaving Malcolm and Maud $100, because I feel that is all that they deserve."

Our parents had told us that Gram Hilda was very rich but didn't approve of their marriage for reasons they never explained. Even though she'd died just before their wedding, Gram Hilda's disapproval had been the inspiration to better themselves financially, and they had done it—without her help.

But wait a minute.

"Why do you have a picture of Gram Hilda?" Hugo asked, voicing my thoughts.

"Hilda expected that your parents would have children one day. She gave this photo to your father, who gave it to your uncle Peter, and he asked me to give it to you."

He turned the photo over, and I saw that a few lines had been written on the back in blue ink. Jacob read the inscription aloud.

" 'To my grandchildren. Hold yourselves to high standards. Do not disappoint yourselves or me. Hilda Angel.' "

"Yep. That was definitely Dad's mother," Harry said bitterly. I'm sure he noticed that she'd left out an important word before her signature: *love*. Or how about *best wishes*? We would even have appreciated a *sincerely*.

"And now," said Jacob, slipping the picture onto the table in front of us, "on to the real point of this meeting."

Jacob stood, took off his khaki jacket, and hung it over the high back of his stool.

"There will be house rules. Not too many, but they all must be obeyed."

Rules from a military commando. Would they include mandatory morning push-ups?

"Number one, you *must* keep your phones on and charged at all times," Jacob said. "Number two, if I call, you must answer. Number three, there will be no lying whatsoever. Even if it's a joke, anyone caught deviating from the truth will be punished." He paused and looked at us, hard. "Please don't test me."

Who the hell did this guy think he was?

"We don't lie," I told him.

"Well, Hugo does sometimes *embellish*," Harry said.

Hugo and I both shot him looks of betrayal. Harry turned up his palms.

"Here's why the rules are necessary," Jacob said, ignoring our aside. "I intend to protect you until you reach your majority. That's my job. And I can't do it if I'm misinformed. Understood?"

Silence.

"I'll take that as a yes."

Hugo leaned forward eagerly in the Pork Chair, looking up at Jacob. "Arm wrestle with me."

Jacob's eyes danced, waiting for a punch line. No one moved. "You're not kidding?"

"You just said not to kid," Hugo said. "Let's do it. Right here, right now."

To my surprise, Jacob smiled indulgently, got down on the Rothko-patterned carpet, and stretched out on his stomach facing Hugo, who assumed a similar, opposing position. They clasped right hands. Harry and I exchanged looks of mild amusement.

Stranger things have happened in the Angel household.

"Three, two, one, wrestle!" Hugo shouted.

Bam! Hugo's hand hit the floor, the whole thing over in five seconds. Hugo cursed under his breath. Jacob got up, smoothed the front of his shirt, and sat down on his stool. Hugo rubbed his elbow with stubborn respect in his eyes.

"Moving on," Jacob said. "You will each have fifty dollars a week for cab fares and lunches. You will have breakfast and dinner at home, where we will take turns preparing meals. So fifty dollars is more than you need—"

Harry sat straight up in his seat. "You must be joking. Have you ever lived in Manhattan, Jake? New York City is not cheap."

"Effective now, we're on an austere budget, Harry," Jacob replied. "Get used to it. You'll get your allowance every Monday morning, and it's your job to make it last. And finally, for now, I want you home every night by seven for dinner, in bed every night by twelve."

"What does any of this have to do with Gram Hilda?" Harry asked, glancing down at the picture.

"When it's time to tell you, I will do so," Jacob said. "No further questions? Good. Discussion closed. Feel free to see me if any questions do arise."

Our new guardian walked down the hall to Katherine's former bedroom, went inside, and closed the door behind him.

Harry, Hugo, and I shared a silent, impressed, maybe even hopeful look. All in all, Jacob Perlman had been polite and clear. Rules, we could follow. Someone who treated us with respect and dignity, we could handle.

Uncle Pig might have just done us the biggest favor ever.

7

"*I get it. The rules, I mean,*" Harry said finally. "He needs to keep tabs on us. That's his job. But I have one question."

"What?" I prompted.

"What's in it for him?"

"He gets to live in the Dakota?" I shrugged. "Plus Peter's paying him, of course."

Harry said, "He's going to be here until we're eighteen. That's a two-year job, right? But we'll probably be evicted for nonpayment in a couple of weeks. So when we're living in a refrigerator box under a bridge, what's Jake's plan for that?"

Hugo piped up. "Don't worry, bro. I'm going to write Matthew's biography. We'll get a big advance for the book, and then big bucks for the movie rights. I'm going to be Matty's agent, too, so I'm taking a cut for that. In a couple of weeks we'll be rolling in it." He kicked back with his feet on the table, his arms crooked behind him. Underneath his shifting weight, the Pork Chair squealed.

"You can't even spell," I pointed out.

"That's what editors are for," Hugo replied, grinning hugely.

"Does Matty know about all this?" I asked him.

"I'm working it out with Philippe," Hugo said, referring to our attorney, Philippe Montaigne. "I'm drafting a chapter outline right now."

"When you're not working on the website?" I asked, arching my eyebrows.

Hugo sat forward, his feet slamming heavily into the floor. "Man. I got a lot to do. I'll be in my room."

"First ten-year-old literary agent slash ghostwriter slash Internet-based freedom fighter in the history of the world," I said to the empty Pork Chair. "But I almost think he can pull it off."

"Of course he can," Harry said. "He's Hugo."

I smiled as loud guitar music shook the photos on the walls of the hallway. Hugo at work.

"I've got a composition due tomorrow," Harry said, rising from the sofa. "Are you okay?"

45

"Sure," I said, glancing across the room toward the windows that overlooked the park. "What could possibly be bothering me?"

A tiny line appeared in the center of Harry's forehead. "May I make a suggestion?"

I stood up as well. "All ears."

"Let Caputo be the cop," he said. "He's got a precinct and a forensics lab behind him. You're just going to get in his way."

"Do you even realize that if it wasn't for me the truth behind Malcolm's and Maud's deaths might still be a mystery?" I asked him.

"Memo to Tandy," Harry said, placing his hand on my shoulder. "Adele was not a relative, and she was killed with an actual gun. Murderers? They tend to not like the people who come after them. So I *suggest* you stay out of it, sis."

"You're probably right," I said with a sigh.

He eyed me shrewdly. "But it doesn't matter, does it?"

"Not really," I replied.

He shook his head and we parted ways. Him to his room and me to mine. I changed into a pair of my mom's silk pajamas—yellow with red poppies—and got into my king-sized bed, perfect for the restless thrasher I was. I plumped the pillows, stared out at the canopy of leaves across the street, and listened to the variously pitched sounds of traffic.

I thought about Adele, how she would never see another tree or hear traffic or kiss a boy or anything else. Right now she was on a slab in a cooler at the medical examiner's office waiting for the forensic pathologist to slit her open from clavicle to navel. My empty stomach turned.

What would Adele have done with her life?

Who would she have become?

Why did she have to die?

CONFESSION

Since I've been so busy listing all the negatives of being off the drugs, I've decided to share with you—and only you—one of the positives. I know what you're thinking. *There's a positive? Then what's she been whining about all this time?* I apologize if I've been in a morose frame of mind. But with all the deaths and the jail visits and the random strangers taking over my life, I'm hoping you can forgive me.

So here it is, the positive: I am starting to remember James. And I'm not talking about the weird dreams. I'm talking about actual memories. At least, I think they are. I hope they are. See, there were always little bits and snippets that I could recall, vague feelings, hazy shadows, flashes of a face or a knee or a hand. But now I was starting to see real 3-D images. I was start-

ing to hear his voice, sense his touch, smell his scent. I was starting to remember that I had been in love.

Not only that. I had experienced love at first sight.

There was a party one night about a year ago. A party I, of
course, had to sneak out to go to, Malcolm and Maud not believ-
ing in fun, as it were. It was exactly what you'd expect from the
children of the New York elite. Huge apartment, tons of break-
ables worth untold thousands, and at least a hundred kids drinking, smoking, and partaking of all kinds of drugs their parents
had definitely not formulated especially for them.

I hate to say "our eyes met across a crowded room," but they
did. But it wasn't just like "Oh, he's cute," or even "That's the hot-
test guy I've ever seen." It was like I knew him. And he knew me.
And we just hadn't seen each other in a really long time. Locking
eyes with James felt like coming home.

We made small talk about travel and school and our families,
but what I really remember was all the smiling. All the anticipation. All the skin-tingling uncertainty.

I had loved every minute of it.

And then it had happened. Just as I'd started to get that
awful, gut-deadening feeling that nothing could possibly come
of this—that it was too good to be true—James had leaned in
and kissed me. And I had felt it in every inch of my body.

Me: The girl who never felt *anything*. The girl who was on
so many drugs I'd barely cried when my favorite person in the

world—my sister, Katherine—had died. That was how I knew for certain that I was in love.

After that, sneaking out became a much more common occurrence. But here's the strangest, most unbelievable part of this: Aside from the clarity of our first meeting, I couldn't remember most of the time James and I had spent together.

Because when my parents did find out about us—because eventually they always found out about everything—they'd had my memory *purged*. Chemically purged, electrically rubbed out, scoured down to the bloody nubs.

My parents were rich and powerful and connected enough to know people who could do that. They'd not only taken me away from James physically, but done everything they could to make sure I'd never so much as dream of him again.

But I did now. All the time. Since I'd gone off the drugs, I was finally starting to remember, more and more each day, the details.

After all this time, I had real and tangible hope that one day I'd remember everything. And that once I remembered, I'd find a way to get James back.

8

The next morning, Jacob was actually up before me and
had laid out a huge breakfast of chocolate-chip pancakes,
eggs, sausage, and coffee, which resulted in Hugo's declar-
ing his undying love for the man. I, however, was kind of
annoyed that my morning ritual of breakfast making had
been brusquely taken from me without my consent. But
that didn't stop me from eating everything in sight. Which
made us late.

After thanking Jacob, Harry, Hugo, and I charged
up Central Park West and across the avenue at Seventy-
Seventh Street to our school, All Saints Academy. All
Saints is a privately owned, Gothic-style former church, all
massive stone walls, stained-glass windows, and soaring

roof lines. Our tiger parents had loved this school because of its small and very exclusive enrollment, but they'd also been obsessed with its headmaster, Timothy Thibodaux. The man was highly intelligent, even by Angel standards.

I had a like-hate relationship with Mr. Thibodaux. He was sharp, of course, but I didn't trust him. Not since he'd refused to let us return to school once we were under suspicion for our parents' deaths. Not *charged* with their deaths, just under suspicion. Yet he'd turned us away at the front door like a bunch of beggars in a Charles Dickens novel. At least he'd apologized for that slight a couple of weeks later when he'd been forced to take us back.

Even I had to admit that Mr. Thibodaux was good at handling the twenty kids in his class, nearly all of them privileged and untouchable. Harry and I, these days, were the exceptions. Our parents were dead and we were broke. But Mr. Thibodaux hadn't turned us away again—not yet, at least—because we were paid up through the school year. Next year, of course, I had no idea what would happen.

Harry and I were panting as we left Hugo at the door to the rectory, where the fifth graders had their classroom, and the two of us trotted up the front steps of the large stone church. We took a right turn off the narthex and climbed the stairway to the choir loft under the vaulted ceiling. This was our classroom, with its stunning long view of the nave and the altar.

Mr. Thibodaux was waiting at the top of the stairs. He wore an impeccably cut brown suit, green-framed glasses, and a mournful expression.

"I'm happy you Angels could make it," he said. And I actually couldn't tell if he was being sarcastic.

I noticed the grief-shocked faces of our schoolmates as Harry and I took our seats, and I gave C.P. a nod. We stowed our book bags and sat perfectly upright with our hands folded in front of us.

"Due to your incessant texting, I'm sure you all know that Adele Church has been killed," Mr. Thibodaux said. "I would be grieving at the loss of any of you, but Adele, in particular, was a very promising student, a talented musician, and a generally sterling person."

A few of the kids sitting behind me began to cry. Mr. Thibodaux noticed but went on.

"You may not know this, but my relationship with my students doesn't end at graduation. In a way, that's when it begins. I see all our graduates every year, and I am amazed at how each of them has grown. The brilliant ones don't always go straight to the top but take a winding and unique path. The slackers sometimes spring into action, and sometimes they turn slacking into a fine art.

"But whatever my students do, whomever they become as adults, I take pride and pleasure in knowing that we all crossed paths here, that we learned from one another here, that we helped one another become…"

He trailed off, and one of the girls behind me gulped back a sob.

"Adele lost her life, and we all lost her. We will never see her become who she was meant to be, but I know we will all always remember our dear, shining Adele."

Mr. Thibodaux crooked a finger in front of his lips, holding back tears as he looked across the room at an intricate stained-glass crucifixion scene in one of the windows.

"Please pray for Adele, keep her in your thoughts, honor her in whatever way you feel appropriate," he said finally, clearing his throat. "There will be a service for Adele this Saturday at St. Barnabas. Grief counseling will be provided here immediately. If you will all gather at my office door and form a line along the green wall, a therapist will see you forthwith.

"Class is dismissed."

Everyone slowly rose from their seats, but I was frozen in place. Harry looked back at me just as I started to shake.

"Tandy?" he said.

Grief counseling. The reason my parents had given for

sending me to Fern Haven. At the time I'd believed them, since I couldn't remember a thing from the months leading up to my incarceration. But they'd actually sent me there to have my memories wiped. To have James and everything we'd seen and done together plucked from my consciousness.

I would never trust a grief counselor again.

9

C.P. *stood at the end* of the line outside Mr. Thibodaux's office as I walked right by my classmates toward the side door. Harry was the only one missing, so I could only assume he was already pouring his guts out to the shrink. There weren't many things Harry loved to do more than talk about his feelings.

"Tandy? Where're you going?" C.P. asked me. She was wearing a zebra-print coat over a black dress, her short blond hair pushed forward over her forehead and her blue eyes wide.

"Outside," I said. "I don't need grief counseling." I clenched my fists inside my pockets. "By the way, have the cops interviewed you about Adele?"

C.P.'s brow knit. "No."

I looked down the line of students. "Have the cops interviewed any of you?" I called out to my classmates. They all stared at me, then at one another, blankly.

I sighed and turned to C.P. "Send them each out to me when they finish in the office, okay?"

She narrowed her eyes. "This was what you meant yesterday when you said *we*, isn't it?"

"Someone's gotta find out what happened to her. And clearly it's not gonna be the NYPD."

I waited on a teak bench in the courtyard between the church and the apartment building next door. It was one of those oddly warm winter days, and the sun felt good on my face. Harry was the first to come out, but he didn't even look in my direction. He just ducked his head and took off for the street, probably planning to go home or to the rehearsal rooms at Lincoln Center to take out his emotions on an unsuspecting piano.

Cliff Anderson was the next to emerge. He was a tall, square-shouldered son of a Wall Street tycoon with an ego bigger than Manhattan. He eyed me warily as he approached.

"C.P. said I'm supposed to talk to you...?"

"Have a seat."

He did, sitting as far away from me on the bench as possible without hitting the ground.

"I'm working with the NYPD on solving Adele's murder," I began.

"Seriously?" I'd piqued his interest. "That's...kinda cool."

"So, where were you when Adele was shot?" I asked him.

Cliff's jaw dropped. "You think I did it?"

"It's a standard question," I replied.

He glowered. "I was with my girlfriend at Dylan's Candy Bar."

I jotted that down.

"And your girlfriend's name?"

He gave it, the school she attended, and her phone number.

"Did you notice anything off about Adele lately?" I asked. "Was she worried about anything? Fighting with anyone?"

"She was depressed, actually," Cliff said, gripping the bench with both hands. "Her brother moved out to go to BU last semester, and the two of them were really close. Adele didn't exactly love her parents, you know? I think it was like the two of them against Mom and Dad, so once she was alone..."

I could imagine how much that would suck. If Malcolm and Maud had still been alive and all my brothers had moved out...wow. I wasn't sure I could have survived that.

"Thanks, Cliff."

Next up was Kendra Preston. She had transferred to All Saints this year, and I knew she still had friends at the Doyle School across town. I asked about her alibi, then got down to business.

"Do you know anyone who might want to do something like this to Adele?" I asked her.

"No, but did you know that two other girls our age have been shot to death in the last month?" she replied.

"What?" I gasped.

"Yeah." Her eyes were wide. "Scary, right? This friend of a friend from Doyle, Lena Watkins, died just outside her apartment a couple of weeks ago. They said it was suicide because she'd been depressed about a breakup, but everyone she knew was shocked that she would actually kill herself."

I wrote everything down as quickly as I could. "And the other girl?"

"Her name was Stacey Something-or-Other...Stacey Brown or Stacey Black or"—she snapped her fingers—"Stacey Blackburn! That's it. She went to Manhattan Day. There was a holdup at a liquor store in the Sixties and she was apparently in the way as the guy tried to escape."

"So three girls from three different private schools have all died of gunshot wounds in the past three weeks."

Kendra shivered inside her black coat. "Kinda makes you not want to leave the apartment anymore, huh?"

"It can't be a coincidence," I agreed.

If someone was actually targeting private school girls, then any of us—all of us—could be in danger. Had Caputo linked these three dots together? Or was this connection my very own bolt of lightning?

Either way, I had work to do.

10

I saved my money, and instead of catching a cab, I walked home from school as quickly as I could, cutting around joggers, bike messengers, jaywalkers, and eddies of lost tourists traveling against the flow.

Three dead private school girls. There had to be a connection. There just had to be. I couldn't wait to get to my private home office.

I opened the door to our apartment and passed under the UFO chandelier, then stopped in my tracks. Standing in the center of the living room was a tall woman with a sprayed helmet of blond hair, wearing a tight blue suit and very high heels. I could smell her heavy perfume from fifteen feet away.

It was strong enough to knock mosquitoes out of the air.

"Can I help you?" I snapped, getting a bit tired of finding strangers in my house every time I came home.

The blond woman tapped a few notes into an iPad before looking up.

"Oh. Hello," she said. Then she snapped a picture of Mercurio, our larger-than-life sculpture of a merman, which hung from a hook in the corkscrew opening under the spiral staircase.

"Excuse me," I said, taking a few steps into the room. That was when I saw that she wasn't alone. Uncle Pig stood in the corner, sporting his signature baggy Burberry and looking disheveled like always with his flyaway ginger hair.

He turned his tiny pig eyes on me.

"Oh, hello, Tandoori. Magda? This is my least favorite and only niece, Tandoori Angel, a psycho terror who is my late brother's daughter. Tandoori, this is Ms. Magda Carter. She's in estates and consignments."

"How fantastic for you," I said to the woman. "What the hell are you doing?"

"I'm pricing your possessions for the estate sale." She almost smacked her lips. "It's in two weeks, you know. So much to do, so little time."

My fingers curled into fists as she ran her gaze covetously over our parents' things—*our* things.

"Jumping the gun, aren't you, Uncle Peter?" I said. "The estate hasn't been settled yet."

Uncle Peter ignored me. Shocker. "Any questions about the artwork, Magda?"

"I think I've got it all," she said. "We're listing the piano, that darling little pig chair, the merman, and... this?"

She placed her palm atop Robert's head. Robert, the TV-watching Oldenburg sculpture in the living room.

My mouth went dry. As sick as it may have sounded to a normal person, Robert was like part of my twisted family.

"Definitely," Uncle Peter said with a sneer.

"Hey," I snapped. "Did you hear me?"

Uncle Peter jerked around as if he'd forgotten I was standing there.

"My apologies, Magda. Clearly my niece is out of sorts," he said. "You haven't seen the Aronstein flag in the master suite. Why don't you go upstairs and I'll join you in a moment?"

He waited as Magda clacked up the spiral staircase and then turned his beady eyes on me.

"Don't be so shocked, Tandy," he said in his most imperious tone. "You know that Royal Rampling is first in line to take over this twenty-million-dollar apartment, and the estate must document everything of value." Hearing the name Rampling coming from my uncle's mouth made me want to puke on his shoes. "Oh, wait. I remember now," he said in a cloying tone. "Mr. Rampling's son was a *special* friend of yours, wasn't he?"

Suddenly, a memory hit me with such force it almost knocked me off my feet—James and I happily cuddled up in a booth at a roadside McDonald's upstate. A troop of black-clad henchmen tearing us away from each other. And Uncle Pig. Uncle Pig standing in the parking lot, watching it all with a triumphant smirk.

"You were there," I breathed.

"I was where?" he asked.

"You were there!" I blurted, rage burbling up inside me. "At the McDonald's that day! When James and I were taken. When I was dragged to Fern Haven. You were there!"

Uncle Pig's face was blank. "You've never been inside a McDonald's in your life. Or any of those awful fast-food places, for that matter. If you'd ever consumed that processed poison, your parents would have had simultaneous coronaries."

I squinted, the memory quickly fading—going sideways, fizzling and shifting. Suddenly, James and I were on a beach. It was dark. It was dark and windy when the commandoes arrived.

"But I—"

Uncle Peter's face twisted in disgust. "Your parents really did screw with your awful little mind, didn't they?"

My throat clenched and I swallowed hard, but my mind had been turned to mush by the conflicting memories, by the confusion, by the humiliation. What really happened, and why did I suddenly remember things differently? There was no comeback to be had. I turned on my heel and swept out, trying to keep my head high.

He was still laughing as I stormed down the hall to my room.

CONFESSION

I wished my uncle would wander into a bad neighborhood, never to be heard from again. Or suffer a life-ending aneurysm. Or fall out a ninth-story window. I'd always believed he'd abused Katherine, and maybe even had something to do with her death.

There was no forensic evidence to prove that Uncle Peter had anything to do with either crime. Just my instincts. But my instincts had always been sharp.

He had, after all, moved into Katherine's room as if it somehow belonged to him.

It made me want to put my fist through a window actually, when I thought about it. That sounds frighteningly like something Matthew Angel would do, I know. So instead, I focused on Katherine.

Katherine Angel was my big sister, my idol, my best and closest friend—an even closer friend than Harry.

Katherine was hilarious, a prankster as well as a brilliant scholar, and if that wasn't enough, she was beautiful, too. She looked exactly like Maud when she was young. Sometimes, when we put photos of the two of them side by side, the only way to tell the difference was the style of their clothes.

My sister was sixteen when she died. We were told it was an accident, but I've never been sure. She was riding on the back of a motorcycle, her arms around the waist of her boyfriend, Dominick—a new boy we hadn't met, but whom, according to her letters, she was completely, mind-bogglingly in love with—when a bus rear-ended the bike and tossed my sister into oncoming traffic. Just like that, this person who had been so full of life, so adventurous and kind and seemingly untouchable, was dead.

The boy Katherine loved was never found. He simply picked himself up and disappeared. Kind of suspicious, no?

Maybe he was just terrified. Or felt guilty. Or both. Maybe Katherine's death *was* just an accident. But maybe, just maybe, her death had been arranged.

Yet another horrible mystery, for another horrible day.

But one thing is absolutely certain: I wished Katherine was here now. I wished I could talk to her about James and my muddled brain. I knew she would have found a way to make me feel better.

To make it all make sense.

11

It was dinnertime in apartment 9G at the Dakota—the eccentric, luxurious, very cloistered building with a gossip-column present and a sensational past—and I was in the kitchen, preparing tandoori chicken, the Indian dish for which I was named. Yes, I was named after a type of poultry preparation. My parents had been foodies with a weird sense of humor.

Harry had fired up the tandoor oven, and Hugo was vigorously washing the broccoli, his contribution to the rather ambitious five-dollars-a-head austerity dinner.

Jacob finished expertly chopping the carrots for the salad, laid his knife down, and cleared his throat.

"Children, there's something you should know," he

said. "There was a filing today before Judge Warren's probate court, and all I can tell you is that sometimes when a door closes, another door opens."

"What does that mean?" Harry asked, looking up from his history text.

"What does it mean, *literally*?" Jacob asked him.

"No, Jake. I understand the aphorism," Harry replied sarcastically. "What door is opening?"

Hugo shook the broccoli, creating a little local rainfall, and said, "I hope if a door is opening, it's not the one to this apartment, because I don't want to move."

Jacob took the broccoli from Hugo and put it in a steamer. "I would tell you..."

"But then you'd have to kill us?" I asked, eyeing the knife in front of him, wondering if he'd ever actually used one to kill a man.

"No, Tandoori. I would tell you, but it's just a filing," he replied, taking a sip of his sherry. "Let's wait a little longer and see if we have good news or bad. To tell you more would be cruel."

I walked over to the counter where Jacob was standing, picked up the bottle of sherry, and took a swig, staring into his eyes the entire time.

"Then why bring it up at all?" I asked. "Trying to let us know you have something over us?"

Jacob blinked and wiped his hands on his apron. "No. Of course not. You're right, Tandy. I shouldn't have said anything yet if I wasn't intending to tell you everything." He looked around at the boys. "I apologize."

I took another sip of sherry, and Jacob removed the bottle from my hand.

"That's enough." He set the bottle aside and reached for the knife again.

"Are you a spy, Jacob?" I asked him.

He sighed and smiled, cutting into a cucumber.

"Of course you are," I continued. "But a spy for whom? Uncle Peter? Or maybe the dead?"

"What a wonderful, vivid imagination you have, Tandy."

I narrowed my eyes. A vivid imagination or razor-sharp instincts? Only time would tell.

12

After dinner the four of us scattered like billiard balls, Hugo to his room and his manuscript, Harry to the piano in the living room, Jacob to Katherine's room. Once everyone was safely tucked away, I headed down the hallway to the room that had at one time been so secret, I hadn't even known it was there until after my parents died. I used the key I kept on a long chain around my neck to open the door, closed it quietly behind me, and hit the switch.

Light filled the room, illuminating my father's file cabinets and his glittering chemistry equipment. His graphs still hung on the walls, those colorful bars that had charted the effects of the pills on his guinea pig children. This had once been his lab, but now it was my office.

My very own PI headquarters.

I had kept the charts so that I would never forget what had been done to us, but I'd restocked the lab with my own equipment and books on forensic science.

I booted up my computer and had just typed the name *Stacey Blackburn* into the search engine when there was an urgent knock on the hidden door. I opened the lock, and Hugo barreled in.

"Not now, Hugo. I'm working."

"I'm here to help," he said. He went to the second computer and logged in.

"I thought you were working on Matty's biography."

"I'm taking five," he replied. "Tell me what you need."

I blew out a sigh and went back to my workstation. "Lena Watkins," I said. "Age about sixteen, lived on the Upper West Side, died last month of a gunshot wound."

Hugo bent over the keyboard and tapped a few keys. He knew how to hack into the NYPD computer system and get out without getting caught. It was a skill that could come in handy.

Hugo read, " 'Lena Watkins, Ninety-Second and Amsterdam, gunshot to the temple at close range.' Sound right?"

I nodded. "Witnesses?"

"No. Uh, her mother said Lena had been depressed. She was found dead with a gun in her hand, so..."

"They think suicide," I finished. "Send that page to me, okay, Hugo? I'll go over the rest myself."

My computer beeped, and I settled in to read. The first oddity that caught my eye was the fact that the gun was unregistered. An unregistered gun was a pretty weird thing for a wealthy sixteen-year-old Manhattanite to have in her possession.

"Lena *was* on antidepressants, but her parents said the pills were working," I said to Hugo. "Not only that, but she never talked about killing herself. She had been down but was coming out of it, and it says here that she didn't leave a suicide note. Which is kind of odd."

"If I offed myself, I'd leave a note," Hugo said, glancing at my father's charts on the walls. "Unlike *some* people."

"Tell me about it," I replied, facing him. "Also, get this: Lena had put a down payment on a new car and had gotten accepted early to Smith College. This doesn't really add up to suicidal depression. Not as I see it."

I turned back to the computer, but I could feel Hugo's eyes still on me.

"What is it?" I asked.

"You know I kind of idolize your ability to multitask, Tandy. But why don't you try saving Matthew before you go figuring out a whole mess of other murders? I mean, at least Matty's still alive."

I glanced at him sharply, feeling a thump of guilt and sorrow.

"Please?" he added, looking, for the first time in a long time, like a regular little boy.

Hugo looked up to Matthew the way I'd adored Katherine, so I didn't have the heart to tell him the truth—that Matthew himself thought he might be guilty. And that I had to focus on as many things as possible right now just to keep myself from focusing on *that*.

"Hey, I can do both," I said gently. "I promise."

Hugo rolled his eyes and started rummaging through a file drawer at the bottom of a cabinet. "Whatever."

Then, out of nowhere, he suddenly fell back and screamed.

"Tandy!" he shouted, scuttling back on his hands and feet like a crab, a look of sheer terror on his face. "Run!"

13

Hugo knocked over the computer stand, which crashed to the floor. I was already running to my brother's side, but something stopped me cold. It was oily and slick and was pouring onto the floor in a slithering black tube. Suddenly it stopped and reared up, a good twelve inches off the floor.

The thing unfurled a hood at the back of its neck. Hugo flinched. It was a snake. A cobra, to be more precise. And this cobra was pissed off.

"Don't. Move," I said through my teeth.

I knew a lot about snakes. For instance, I knew that any movement was guaranteed to agitate the cobra. I also knew that if it struck Hugo, neurotoxins would likely kill him before an antivenom could be found.

"*Tannnnnnndy!*" he cried. "*Help meeeeeee!*"

"I'm *thinking*," I replied, my heart slamming against my ribs. "Just don't move."

"You said that already," he replied.

The snake began to sway. A very bad sign. I grabbed my phone from my pocket and called Jacob. He answered on the first ring. I tried to stay calm, but my voice was in its highest register.

"Jacob, there's a snake in the apartment. A venomous snake."

"Where are you?" Jacob was all business. The cobra eyed Hugo like he was a piece of meat.

"In my office."

I heard fumbling. The sound of a door opening. "Your room?"

"No. My office. It's past my room on the other side of the hall. I'll open the door."

"*TandyTandyTandyTandyTandy.*" My fearless little brother was keening in terror.

"Hugo, I'm right *here*. Just stay still."

I dropped to all fours, keeping my eyes on the snake. It was only four feet from Hugo's right foot. He was wearing shoes, but his naked ankle was within striking distance. I knew the snake wouldn't attack unless it felt threatened, but that inch of bare skin still looked like a bull's-eye.

"Don't move, Hugo. Don't even blink. I'm going to drag you out of here," I said in a wobbly voice.

I moved toward Hugo, directly into the snake's sight line. My plan was to pull Hugo around the fallen computer stand and put that between us and the snake. As if the cobra could read my mind, it flattened and started to slither against the wall in my direction.

I heard Jacob coming along the hallway.

"Tandy!" he shouted, pounding the wall with his fist. "Tandy! Where are you?"

I glanced at the snake, terrified. All that noise couldn't be good. "Jacob!" Hugo screeched. "We're in here."

The door frame in the hallway was so well concealed, you could miss it even when you knew where to look. I crawled to Hugo and got right behind him, then rose to a crouch.

"Very slowly raise your hands up," I told him.

He reached back and I clasped his hands.

"It's looking right at me," Hugo whimpered. "Look at its *tongue*."

"Just don't look at it," I told him. "Pretend it's not there. We're just playing a game."

"Yeah, right."

I had begun backing up slowly, sliding Hugo with me toward the doorway, when suddenly it jerked open. Jacob hovered over us, and he was holding a very heavy-duty handgun.

"Where is it?" Jacob asked.

I pried one hand loose from Hugo's and pointed to the snake.

"You two get out of here," he said. "I'll handle this."

"You're going to shoot it?" Hugo shouted, scrambling to his feet. "Cool! There's no way I'm leaving now."

14

Jacob scowled. Yep. There was the commando I'd read about. Hugo's mouth snapped shut instantly.

"Go." Jacob directed his fierce gaze at us and said, "And, Tandy, call Pest Control. Now."

"Don't have to ask me twice," I replied.

Then I yanked Hugo into the hall.

"When I'm an adult, you can expect payback," Hugo said to Jacob. "And believe me, karma is a *peach*."

Jacob cracked a smile at Hugo, checked his gun, and slammed the door on us. I found the number for the New York City Department of Health and Pest Control, and after numerous rings, a woman with a languid voice answered.

"This is Officer Blum. How may I help you?"

"There's a venomous snake loose in our apartment."

I jumped at the sound of gunfire followed by breaking glass.

"Oh, *man*!" Hugo pouted, disappointed. I ran a hand over his hair in what I hoped was a conciliatory gesture. Crazy kid.

"Where should we send the unit?" the woman asked.

I gave our address. "How fast can you get here?"

"Say again?" said Officer Blum, alarmed. "You're in the Dakota?"

"Yes, we're in the Dakota." I gripped the phone and said, "I've ID'd the snake. It's a cobra. Maybe a forest cobra. Definitely deadly."

"I hope you've got nerves of steel, then, young lady. Don't make any sudden movements. You don't want to make that snake angry."

My office door opened, and Jacob came out holding four and a half feet of inky-black cobra. Its head was gone, but its body still twisted in Jacob's hand. My throat pretty much closed up.

Jacob brought the snake over to Hugo.

"Here's your snake, young man. Take a good look. I hope you never see one of these again. Now, bring me a bag, a broom, some rags, and the vacuum cleaner, please."

"Hello?" Officer Blum said. "Are you still there? Was this *your* snake? Was it your pet?"

"No way. Why would you think that?" I asked.

"I hate to tell you," she said, "but this is not the first snake loose in the Dakota today. In fact, it's the third. Pest Control is in your building right now."

I gripped the phone more tightly. "Are you kidding me?"

Jacob eyed me curiously.

"Do I sound like I'm kidding?"

"What the hell is going on?" I asked Officer Blum.

"No idea, but I'll tell the guys to come to your apartment next."

I grimaced as Hugo held out an open garbage bag and Jacob deposited the gory body in it.

"Actually, that's not necessary. This one is officially dead," I said to Officer Blum. "Maybe I should just bring it to them."

"Well, okay, then."

She told me the Pest Control officers were on the second floor and I hung up.

"Where are we going?" Hugo asked me as we headed toward the front of the apartment with the heavy bag full of dead snake.

"To find the Pest Control guys," I answered, slinging the bag over my shoulder. "Hugo, what were you actually looking for in Malcolm's file drawer?"

"Cigarettes," he said matter-of-factly.

"What?"

He lifted his shoulders. "I was looking for his stash."

Before I could demand why he would do such a thing, he added, "In movies about writers, they all smoke. I'm getting into character."

"Geez, Hugo." We paused in the foyer. "You want to stay four-foot-eight forever?"

"That's a myth about cigarettes stunting your growth," he said as I opened the front door. Then he shouted out to Jacob, "We'll be right back."

"Be back in five minutes," Jacob shouted back. "Five."

Hugo dashed across the hall and thumbed the call button until the elevator arrived. As we piled in, I turned over our latest drama in my mind. We didn't live near a zoo. And there were no indigenous snakes in New York City.

So why were there snakes loose in the Dakota?

CONFESSION

Remember when I said my greatest fear is that I might not experience true love again? Well, this might be an opportune moment to confess another pretty big fear.

I know a lot about snakes, vipers, and adders from all over the world. Why have I committed a snake encyclopedia to memory? *Know thy enemy*, that's why.

Snakes are the opposite of warm and fuzzy. They slither, they're sneaky by design, and, in case we weren't clear on this fact, they can kill you. Some snakes eliminate you so stealthily you don't even know you're dead until your blood coagulates and your heart stops cold.

Some snakes shoot you full of neurotoxins, wrap themselves around you, and squeeze out your life before consuming you whole, clothes, shoes, laptop, and smartphone, in one big package.

Most snakes eat only mice and voles and are the gardener's friend, but how do you know the difference in the space of a heartbeat? And that, I believe, is at the root of one's fear of snakes. It's a survival mechanism.

Some people are not just afraid of snakes, they're phobic. The technical term for a snake phobia is *ophidiophobia*, and people who have it dream of snakes, see snakes under every rock or rumple in the carpet, and freak out when they see snakes on TV.

When I see a snake, I automatically think of my uncle Peter, which makes me hate them even more. Because I imagine he could kill and feel about the same amount of remorse as a snake would.

Zero.

15

I tried not to think about the fact that the heavy plastic garbage bag in my left hand was packed with the fluid coils of a four-foot-long decapitated cobra.

Nothing to be afraid of, Tandy. Thanks to Jacob, it no longer has fangs.

When the elevator door slid open on the second floor, chaos greeted us. At least eight men and women in green jumpsuits were coming and going from open apartments while co-op owners clustered in small groups between the doorways.

I saw the elderly sitcom stars, Mr. and Mrs. Llewellyn Berrigan, in their matching striped pj's. The spectacular trombone player Boris Friedman, wearing tuxedo pants and a Grateful Dead T-shirt. And the long-divorced mul-timillionaire Ms. Ernest Foxwell, draped in a sheer yellow nightgown covered with a short mink coat and wearing ostrich-feather mules. Definitely gape-worthy.

Ms. Foxwell did not look amused. Neither did the opera singer Glorianne Pulaski, who was in aqua chenille and hair curlers, standing in her doorway, crying into her bedazzled iPhone.

Frightened and discommoded rich people can be pretty hilarious, I have to admit. In fact, Hugo cracked up at the sight of Mrs. Pulaski, but no one seemed to notice us. Not that I could blame them. There were venomous *snakes* loose in the building.

Jacob had said to be back in five minutes. As inclined as I was to follow his rules before, I was even more inclined now that I'd seen his gun—not to mention what he could do with it. So I just wanted to hand off the snake corpse to the proper official, ask several pointed questions about where they were in their investigations, and then get the hell home.

Finally, a man caught a glimpse of me and Hugo and did a double take. Baseball cap. Green jumpsuit. Badge. Snake-catching hook in hand.

"Please step out of the elevator car," he said. "We're shutting down the system."

"Oh my God. Snakes on an elevator," Hugo said in awe.

"Officer Blum from Pest Control said to find someone to give this to," I said, holding out the garbage bag. I swear it rustled. It moved.

"You're Tandy?" the man in a jumpsuit said. "I'm Officer Frank. Let's see what you've got there." He peeked inside the bag. "Whoa. Who shot this?"

"Our guardian," I replied. "He's got a license to carry weapons, of course. So what's going on?"

The guy eyed me shrewdly. "Why don't you tell me where you found this snake?"

Oh, so he was going to answer questions with questions, was he? I cleared my throat and put my game face on.

"My brother found it in a file cabinet in an interior room," I said, adopting a businesslike tone. "I believe he disturbed it."

Officer Frank's eyes flicked to Hugo. "You're lucky to be alive, kid."

Hugo was too busy staring at Mrs. Pulaski's hammertoes in her sequined slippers to reply.

"As to what's going on, we've found three poisonous snakes, counting yours, and no reason to believe we've got them all."

"May I see the other two?" I asked.

"Why?" Officer Frank asked curiously.

"Know thy enemy," I replied simply.

He frowned as if impressed with my logic. "I've got pictures of one of them," he said, pulling an iPhone out of his pocket. "Here you go."

The first snake was yellow, with scales standing up around its face. A beautiful eyelash palm pit viper.

"So many dark, warm places in this castle you live in," Officer Frank mused. "We're going down to the basement next and will set up some funnel traps. Uh, thanks for the snake, Tandy. And you, young man," he said to Hugo, "don't put your hands into dark places. That goes for your feet, too. Check your shoes before you put them on. Okay?"

"I'm never taking these off," Hugo said, gesturing at his feet.

It was clear that Pest Control had *zero* control over this snake infestation. There were ninety-three units in the Dakota, an idiosyncratic building with secret rooms, back staircases, tunnels, and mouse holes that were unchanged since the 1880s.

If snakes could hide inside our shoes, there were about ten million lovely little places for them to take up residence inside the walls.

Had someone decided to sic a pack of murderous snakes on the eccentric denizens at the Dakota? Or had our cobra been placed in 9G on purpose, with the other snakes merely a diversion?

Maybe I'm paranoid, my friend, but still, as you well know, my family has enemies. I couldn't dismiss the possibility that a deadly poisonous snake might have been planted in my office on purpose. That someone was out to kill me.

16

I woke up with my heart pounding like I was being chased by a herd of blank-eyed, gaping-mouthed walking dead. I'd had a bad dream, but of what? Dead girls? Snakes? The white rooms at Fern Haven?

As I clutched my blanket to my sides, I remembered. It was about Matthew.

Matthew's trial was starting today.

I rousted my siblings, and we chowed breakfast down while standing around the kitchen island. Then we pooled our resources and cabbed it downtown to the Manhattan Criminal Court at 100 Centre Street.

The streets were knotted with morning traffic. We spent long minutes sweating in the backseat of the cab, catching every single red light as commercial vehicles and herds of pedestrians blocked the roadways.

I was frustrated and mad at myself for oversleeping. What was with the new slumber-loving me? Was it another side effect of not taking my parents' drugs? And why today of all days? Philippe had warned me that if we were late, we would be barred from the courtroom until the lunch recess, and that just wasn't acceptable. I wanted Matthew to see that we were there to support him.

Our cab did the stop-and-go thing for several more minutes, and I thought Hugo might burst with impatience. When we were finally within walking distance of Centre Street, Harry paid the fare, and we leapt from the cab.

Together we ran toward the biggest building around. The courthouse was an imposing seventeen stories high, faced with granite and limestone, topped with an Art Deco ziggurat crown. It took up a full New York City block.

We zipped between the large, free-standing columns guarding the entrance and entered the swarming marble lobby, where we were funneled into a security line. A man with a wand checked us for weapons, and then we charged toward the elevator banks. As we crammed ourselves inside with a dozen others, Hugo pushed the button for the ninth floor.

I tried to gather strength from the proximity of my

brothers, but still, my newly awakened emotions were roiling. My feet tapped impatiently beneath me while I watched the numbers light up over the door in what felt like slow motion.

Today New York City's star prosecutor, Nadine Raphael, would give her opening statement, and then our family friend and attorney, Philippe Montaigne, would give his. Phil was a good lawyer and our family has trusted him for years, but criminal defense was not his area of expertise. Given our current financial constraints, we decided he was our best bet. But Nadine Raphael, on the other hand, was a Harvard-trained viper.

The elevator doors opened into a hallway that was jam-packed with lawyers and court workers by the hundreds. There was also a shifting phalanx of reporters jostling for a lead like a pack of hounds on the scent of a rabbit.

You have to understand: Our family was like raw-meat kibble for these oh-so-friendly, super-awesome, totally polite, not-at-all-invasive paparazzi. You can just imagine how many plays on words the brainiacs at places like TMZ had come up with for our name so far. *Fallen Angels*. *No Angels Among Us*. And my personal favorite, the one that almost inspired me to set the kiosk at the corner of Fifty-Seventh and Seventh on fire—the huge headline the *Post* slapped over Matthew's mug shot: ANGEL OF DEATH.

So when the pack of reporters spotted us, they attacked. What could possibly be more exciting for inquiring minds?

A reporter I had seen hanging around the Dakota was the first to speak. "Hugo. Hugo! Why did Matthew kill Tamara? What did he tell you?"

Hugo snapped his head around. "Matthew is innocent! Get it right."

Not that I didn't enjoy a good stampede, but I'd had enough. Harry, Hugo, and I managed to get through the heavy wooden door to the courtroom a split second before the bailiff slammed it closed. The slam echoed ominously.

We three younger Angel children stood at the back of the courtroom in one tight line as every single person in the gallery turned to stare. If things went as predicted, Matthew's trial would be nasty, tawdry, and totally fascinating for the public at large.

My poor brother. The media beast was hungry, and Matthew Angel was the appetizer, the main dish, *and* the dessert.

Harry reached for my right hand. Hugo reached for my left. I squeezed both.

The very least we could do was stick together.

17

The courtroom was paneled top to bottom in mahogany, had twenty-foot ceilings topped with carved gargoyles and angels, and was totally imposing. The twenty-two rows of high-backed benches, a lot like church pews, were almost completely filled.

My brothers and I made our way toward the front of the room, where railings and a gate separated the audience from the well, the enclosed area where the lawyers, the jury, and the judge would be putting on the trial.

The judge's bench was high above the courtroom floor, backed by flags and the New York State insignia. I looked at the table where Philippe and Matthew would be sitting;

it was empty. Across the aisle, Nadine Raphael's team was setting up at the prosecution table.

People in the fourth row slid over and made room for us. I gave the seat on the aisle to Hugo so that he could see the action. My usually boisterous, optimistic brother sat down, the picture of solemnity. I think he knew this was the center of the no-kidding-around universe.

Hugo straightened up and grabbed my knee when Matthew came in with Philippe. Whispers flew up from the gallery like pigeons.

There he is.

There's Matthew Angel.

Oh my God. He looks awful.

Do you think he did it?

Phil was handsome as always, shaved head, expensive tailoring, tidy with a capital *T*, an urban lawyer in command. My brother was wearing a suit that looked loose on him, and his expression sagged.

He didn't see us, but I hoped he could feel that his siblings had his back.

A lot of business was conducted in the next hour. Chubby-cheeked Judge Bradley Mudge addressed the people in the gallery. He told us the rules of order, and when the jury came in, he spent a long time instructing them on trial procedure.

I studied the faces and body language of the jurors and alternates. The people who would decide my brother's fate looked like a bunch of average Joes and Janes, none any more remarkable than the last.

But then I snuck another look at the prosecutor whose job it was to keep Matthew in jail, and goose bumps chilled my skin.

That woman was scary.

18

I craned my head to get a good look at prosecutor Nadine Raphael. She was almost six feet tall, with a powerful build, like an Olympic swimmer. Her broad shoulders and narrow hips were encased in a tight red Armani suit, and her black hair was short and swept back, tucked behind her ears, highlighting her beautiful, angular face. She could have been a modern-day Greek goddess—the severe and statuesque Pallas Athena, to be exact.

Ms. Raphael stepped out from behind the prosecution table and click-clacked smartly to the lectern in the center of the courtroom. About two hundred pairs of eyes followed.

She said hello to the jury, held up a photograph, and

launched her opening statement. I glanced at Harry and held my breath.

"This is one of the victims in this case, Tamara Gee. A sweet young woman of twenty-four, generous, funny, and if she looks familiar to you, maybe you've seen her on television or in the movies. But I don't want to focus on her career."

Sure you don't, I thought. *Reminding everyone of how universally beloved Tamara was won't help your case at all.*

"Tamara was a real person, a citizen of this city, an exemplary soul, and an expectant mother of the other victim in this trial. That victim was her unborn child. A child she called Trevor. A boy who never drew a single breath or opened his eyes. He died inside his mother's body.

"Until three months ago, Tamara lived with the defendant in the Village, in a nice apartment in an old building with an Italian restaurant downstairs.

"She liked to read mysteries until late at night, wake up early, and go for a run on the empty streets of Tribeca. And she was in love with Matthew Angel."

My mouth went dry. This woman was good at her job.

"Not surprising. Matthew is one of the most eligible bachelors in the country. But I'm not here to praise Matthew Angel. Let's just say that Tamara loved him and trusted him and was dreaming of the future, when she would have their baby.

"Sometime on the night of October twenty-second, or in the early-morning hours that followed, Matthew came home and went to bed with Tamara. According to his statement to the police, Matthew had been drinking. Had he also been brooding, harboring anger as well? Was he enraged that the baby Tamara carried might be his *brother*, not his *son*?"

Harry's grip on my hand tightened. I gripped him right back.

"We don't know what was in Matthew's mind. We only know that on the morning of October twenty-third, Mandy Shine, the housekeeper employed by Matthew and Tamara, knocked on the door, and when no one came to answer it, she went into the apartment, as was her custom.

"What she saw that morning caused her to run screaming into the street, prompting the doorman to investigate and immediately call the police."

Nadine Raphael spun on her designer heels, returned to the prosecution table, and exchanged the glamour photo of Tamara for another one. I tried to see it, but the prosecutor held it against her body.

Then she said, "This, ladies and gentlemen, is what Ms. Shine saw."

Nadine held up a horrible bloody picture of Tamara Gee lying faceup on a big white bed, a sheet covering her baby bump. Bright red blood was sprayed and spattered on every surface of the room, contrasting Tamara's pale skin and blond hair. I closed my eyes for a moment, feeling faint.

Jurors gasped at the sight of the grotesque tableau. The foreman, a large sunburned man, covered his eyes with the palms of his big rough hands. The brassy-blond woman sitting next to him doubled over and groaned. Another juror, a woman about Tamara's age, covered her mouth with her fingertips as tears filled her eyes.

"The defendant has no credible defense, ladies and gentlemen. He told the police that he had an ironclad alibi, that he'd been out drinking and playing poker all night long with friends, that when he got home in the small hours of the morning, he undressed and went to bed in the dark. That he didn't know Tamara was dead until he awoke the next morning to find her next to him, at which point he panicked and fled the scene. Why didn't he call the police? Why didn't he immediately seek justice for the love of his life?"

It was a good question. The very question I'd asked Matthew myself.

"Since that day, Matthew's alibi for the night in question has fallen apart. There will be no witnesses to tell you that Matthew Angel was out drinking or playing poker at the time when Tamara and their baby were killed.

"Here are the facts: Matthew Angel is a violent career athlete who believed that his girlfriend had been unfaithful with his own father. In fact, postmortem DNA tests have proved that the child was Matthew Angel's.

"But Matthew didn't know that on the night Tamara was killed. And this is what happens when Matthew Angel gets mad," Nadine Raphael said, rattling the photograph in front of the jury. "He kills the woman who loved him and the baby they made together."

I brought my fist to my lips and bit down hard to keep from crying out. *He couldn't have done it!* I wanted to scream.

"We will prove our case beyond a shadow of doubt. And we will ask you to find Matthew Angel guilty of two savage murders."

19

Hugo took in a big breath, completely filling his lungs. Seeing that he was about to yell, I clapped my hand over his mouth and held on.

I whispered into his ear, "If you as much as squeak, we will be thrown out of here. Blink once if you understand."

He blinked, and when he exhaled entirely, I let him go.

Judge Mudge peered down from the bench and said, "Mr. Montaigne. Are you ready to give your opening statement?"

Philippe said, "Yes, Your Honor."

I grabbed Harry's and Hugo's hands again. Phil stepped out into the aisle, and as he buttoned his gray jacket and walked up to the lectern, I felt a sudden rush of love for him. He was working to defend Matty knowing full well that whether he won or lost, he would likely not be paid a nickel for his time.

Matty did have his own money, separate from the lien against my parents' estate, but the Gee family had filed a civil lawsuit against him for wrongful death. Who knew if he'd have anything left once that was settled.

I shot a look at Harry, who put his arm around me and said softly, "Courage." I nodded and swallowed hard as Phil greeted the jury.

"Tamara Gee was a wonderful young woman, and Matthew Angel loved her very much," Phil began. "Even though Tamara told the press that she was having an affair with Malcolm Angel, Matthew's father, and that the baby she was expecting was not his, Matthew loved her.

"He loved her so much that whether or not the baby was his, he still wanted to marry her, still bought her a ten-carat heart-shaped diamond ring a week before her death. He still phoned her when he wasn't with her, and she still phoned him. We will introduce evidence to prove this. But for now, I want to tell you what happened the night in question, the night Tamara was murdered by an unknown killer for reasons we don't know.

"On that night, Matthew played poker with four of his friends, as he told the police, but he left earlier than he originally recalled, and instead of going home, as he first claimed, Matthew went out to a bar. He got, in his words, 'stinking drunk,' and sometime in the early hours, he came home. He didn't lock the door.

"He got undressed in the bathroom, then got into bed with Tamara. He never turned on the lights and he never kissed her good night. He passed out.

"The next morning, Matthew awoke and found Tamara, the love of his life and the mother of his unborn child, dead. At that point, Matthew Angel went into shock. He went into denial. He left the house and the gruesome scene the prosecution has just subjected all of you to, hoping against irrational hope that it wasn't true. That he hadn't seen what he had seen. Later that day, at home and surrounded by his loving family, he was arrested and charged with murder.

"The investigation stopped right there, ladies and gentlemen. But there are other possibilities. Was Tamara already dead when Matthew got into bed with her? Or was she killed while he was lying beside her, passed out drunk?

"To this day, the police believe that the defendant killed Tamara Gee and her unborn child, but here's the dirty little secret."

Phil paused for effect, and when I thought I would go

crazy from waiting, he walked to the jury box and put his hands on the railing. "The dirty little secret, folks, is that while Tamara was stabbed by a sharp object fifteen times, there was no murder weapon in the apartment.

"No murder weapon was found."

Point, Phil! He was every bit as dramatic as Nadine, but he didn't have to rely on shocking, grisly photos to stir up the jury. Phil had facts.

"There were no knives missing from the apartment, no knife in the apartment to match the victim's stab wounds, no evidence that Matthew had purchased any such knife. There is no proof that Matthew Angel had the means to commit this crime. There are no eyewitnesses to report having seen Matthew Angel commit this crime. Every single piece of evidence the prosecution will submit to you is circumstantial.

"What is true is that this is a classic case of the police rushing to judgment against a bigger-than-life individual without sufficient evidence. We suggest this: Someone came in and killed Tamara before or after Matthew came home, and he took his weapon with him.

"And what that means is that the real killer is alive and well, roaming the streets of New York City.

"Matthew Angel is guilty of getting drunk.

"But he's not guilty of murder."

20

After Philippe's opening, I pulled my hands up into my sleeves and wiped at my cheeks. Phil was *on.* If he ran the rest of this case with the same passion he'd brought to that opening, he'd win, no question.

Then the prosecutor called her first witness.

The housekeeper answered the questions while looking straight into Matthew's eyes, which was pretty damn brave. It also made it look like she didn't feel guilty at all about her testimony—that she believed every word she was saying.

So my heart sank to the floor when she said, "I believe Matthew killed Tamara."

Phil jumped up with an objection that was sustained,

but the damage was done. The jury members were already shooting one another wide-eyed looks.

Then Detective Ryan Hayes described Matthew's defiance when he and Caputo had come to the Dakota to arrest him. He said that Matthew hadn't cried. That he hadn't asked questions. That he had seemed unaffected by Tamara's death.

Well, in my humble opinion, Matthew was being judged by people who didn't know that he had been innocently taking Angel Pharmaceutical's special emotion-killing drugs for years.

Was it possible that the pills had not only numbed Matthew but had turned him into a cold-blooded killer? With the exception of Harry, everyone in the family had been labeled a sociopath at some time or other. If Matty hadn't been taking those pills, he might have reacted normally. He might not even be on trial for murder right now if he'd had the simple, God-given ability to show grief.

What had our parents *done* to us?

When court was adjourned for the day, I left Hugo with Harry and ran up the aisle against the tide of spectators and reporters heading for the hall to join the media circus undoubtedly already waiting outside. I reached Matthew and grabbed his hand. He spun around even as a guard was coming to escort him out of the courtroom.

"I just wanted to tell you we're here," I said.

He looked into my swollen eyes and tried for a bolstering expression. "Everything is going to be okay, Tandy."

I nodded as if I believed him, but, friend, I knew he was wrong. I just didn't know if he was lying to me or to himself. And then I heard shouting: "Matty, Matty!"

Hugo had broken away from Harry and was running toward Matthew, but he never reached him. Before he could throw himself over the barrier and into our big brother's arms, Matthew was dragged away by the guard.

"Don't worry, Hugo!" he shouted over his shoulder. "Hear me? I'll be home soon."

Hugo's chest heaved like he was about to start hyperventilating. All around us, people stared, and not in a kind or sympathetic way. I think the court artist was even starting to sketch us.

"Come on, you guys," Harry said, putting his arms around our shoulders. "Let's get out of here."

Of course, the press was waiting for us in a huge jumble in the hallway.

"Tandy! What did you think of the opening statements?"

"Does it bother you that your brother didn't seem to care that his girlfriend was brutally murdered?"

"Why aren't you kids in school?"

Obviously, I ignored them, and smirked when I saw

Hugo shoot them his famous middle-finger salute right before Harry bundled us all into the elevator. When we reached the lobby, the crowds of courthouse employees leaving the building unthinkingly surrounded us and we flowed anonymously out to the street.

I took a deep breath of the cool, fresh air, thinking it would calm me, but instead my stomach suddenly heaved. I looked around, desperate, and puked right there in the gutter.

"Tandy? Are you okay?" Hugo asked, alarmed.

I managed to nod as Harry helped me up.

A woman with a large croc handbag handed me a wad of tissues and said, "Shall I call someone?"

"Thanks, but I'm okay," I replied miserably, taking a deep, shaky breath.

"We're fine," said Harry, his voice breaking.

Yeah, right. I wondered if we'd ever be fine again.

21

Jacob Perlman was waiting for us on the red leather sofa in the living room. Along with his standard khaki shirt and pants, he was wearing his fierce no-nonsense look, and I had an idea why.

"Uh-oh," I said, coming into the room.

"Sit down, Tandy. All of you."

We arrayed ourselves around the coffee table that used to be a shark tank and was now just an empty five-by-five glass container with some dead algae clinging to the walls.

"Raise your hand if you went to school today."

He looked at us. The boys looked away.

"We went to court," I volunteered. "Matthew's trial started today."

"I'm aware of that. Now." Jacob crossed his arms over his chest. "Why didn't you tell me?"

"You might have said no," Harry said. "We didn't want to fight with you about it, and we especially didn't want to be overruled."

"I haven't seen my brother in a month," Hugo said passionately. "I had to see him. I don't care what you do to me. I'd skip school and do it again."

"So you lied by omission," Jacob said. "We talked about this."

I leaned forward in my seat. "But I—"

Jacob held up one finger to silence me. It worked. "When you didn't go to school, Mr. Thibodaux was concerned."

"Ugh," said Hugo.

"You're surprised, Hugo?" Jacob asked, raising an eyebrow.

Hugo hung his head. "No, sir."

"Mr. Thibodaux called me."

"Oh, man," said Harry.

"I take it you know where this is going?" Jacob said. "Well, I'll tell you, anyway. I called each of you. None of you answered. I tried again. Still nothing. And then, since your phones are supposed to be on at all times and you're always to answer when I call, I worried that something might have happened to you. So I called the police."

"We turned off our phones when we went into the courthouse," I explained. "You knew Matty's trial was today. Why not look for us there? We weren't missing nearly long enough for the police to begin a search."

"Given recent events, in particular the murder of a young woman *across the street from this building*, I didn't have time to hope you were fine and go down to the courthouse to check. Sergeant Caputo and I were extremely worried. Normally, he would wait forty-eight hours, but you kids are special friends of the Twentieth Precinct.

"The police canvassed this building. Several officers searched for you around your school. A squad of uniformed officers went looking for your dead bodies in Central Park."

Hugo said in a small voice, "Do you think maybe you overreacted a little bit? I mean, we went to court. Everyone should have known that. He's our brother. The trial is major news. Caputo's partner was even there. Testifying *against* Matty."

"You could have flipped on the news and seen our faces splayed all over it," Harry added.

"You disobeyed," Jacob said firmly. "You didn't tell me where you were. That is a *big* deal."

"I'm sorry," I said. "We're not used to reporting in yet, Jacob. We never had to before."

Jacob went on as if I hadn't spoken. He kept his voice even, which was almost scarier than if he'd gone crazy.

"The search was finally called off when, as you say, Harry, one of the officers saw your faces splayed all over the news. But not before thousands of tax dollars were spent and you aged me about ten years. You owe an apology to the NYPD and to Mr. Thibodaux. *I* don't want your apology. I want obedience.

"The three of you are grounded until further notice. School. Home. That's all. Tonight, after what I'm sure will be a very awkward dinner, you will go to your rooms."

Hugo said, "Jacob, just saying, maybe you take your military training too seriously."

"You think so? I've saved hundreds of people in my lifetime. How about you? Any of you ever save a life?"

Harry and I looked at each other. I'd never felt so intimidated.

"I didn't think so. I'll see you at dinner. We're having whatever is in a can or a jar. Keep your expectations low."

22

That was it? We were grounded?

One summer, Hugo got a Big Chop for talking back to Maud. He was sent to boot camp in Hawaii, where he harvested prickly pineapples for two months in the blazing sun and slept in a guarded barracks at night. He was *eight*. Grounding, for us, was nothing.

I gathered my brothers for a conference in Hugo's room. I said, "We have to talk."

"You don't even have to say it, Tandy," Harry said. "We screwed up. What if we *had* been kidnapped? There's some precedent for that. What was Jacob supposed to think?"

"Malcolm and Maud never worried where we were,"

Hugo said. He kicked at the knees of his tattered life-sized stuffed pony, a baby gift from Uncle Peter.

"They knew we could take care of ourselves," Harry said. "Jacob doesn't know that."

"Our parents were self-involved," said Hugo. "They only cared if we were insubordinate. Or if something we did came back on them."

"So what are you saying?" I asked Hugo.

"We don't expect people to care." He flopped down on his back, lying diagonally across his mattress with his arms crossed over his chest. "Jacob actually cares about us. *Us!*"

Like it was the most impossible thing to fathom. Which it kind of was.

"It's weird, but...I think you're right," I said.

"But how *can* he? He's barely known us for a week," Hugo said.

"Maybe he's suffering a loss?" Harry suggested.

"Maybe he doesn't have any kids of his own. Or maybe they died," Hugo said.

"Or maybe he *likes* us," I added. "Maybe he likes us and he *cares* and he's *responsible*. Isn't that enough?"

I let this very alien idea—alien to the Angel kids, at least—sink in. Then we went together to Jacob's door.

When he opened it, Hugo said, "Jacob, we're sorry we were so thoughtless."

"In our defense, we've never been held to account for our whereabouts during the daytime, but still," Harry said, "we were wrong. We'll never go off your radar again."

"Is there something we can do to make this up to you?" I asked. "Within reason, of course." I smiled.

Jacob put his hands on his hips. "What do you suggest?"

"I've got a hundred bucks," I joked.

"And I've got fifty," said Harry.

"You can't pay the man off! He's Israeli military!" Hugo said, wide-eyed.

"So we'll treat for a Chinese dinner out. How's that? If you'll accept our apologies, Jacob," I said.

Jacob cracked a small smile. "Apologies accepted."

Then he did the unthinkable. He hugged us. All three of us and Jacob in one big group hug. Even I was moved. But it was Hugo who started to cry.

Harry and I exchanged a look and backed off so that Jacob could hug Hugo and only Hugo. My little brother just sobbed into Jacob's chest. He let go of a whole world of pain that he'd been expressing in every way but sadness.

"I didn't understand I could hurt you!" Hugo cried.

"It's okay. I'm here for you," Jacob said. "I've got you now. We're all going to be fine."

23

My phone rang, jolting me out of a bottomless sleep.

I fumbled around at my bedside table and grabbed my phone. It was C.P., and it was barely light out. I rubbed the bleariness from my eyes and checked the clock. It was just after six thirty in the morning.

I answered on the third ring. "What's up?"

"Tandy," she whispered, her voice strained. "It happened again."

"What?" I asked, swinging my legs over the side of my bed, fully alert. "What happened again?"

"Look."

My phone beeped, and I opened the link C.P. had sent me. There, six inches from my still-gummy eyes, was a

breaking news story: TEENAGE GIRL FOUND DEAD IN CEN-
TRAL PARK.

Below the headline was a photo of a blond-haired girl
lying curled on her side on the Bow Bridge.

"Oh my God," I gasped, my free hand fluttering up
to cover my mouth. I brought the phone back to my ear.
"C.P....I can't even...did you know her?"

"No idea who she is. Who she *was*. They don't name
her in the article. But you can bet we'll find out before
school starts. I'm sure the entire Upper West Side is texting about it right now."

"Of course they are," I agreed, getting up and reaching
for a pair of jeans. My hands were shaking. "This is unbelievable. Another murder right across the street."

"Get up and get dressed," C.P. said. "I'll meet you
downstairs in half an hour."

"You sure you want to come to the dead zone?" I asked
bitterly, looking out the window across the park.

"Not funny, Angel," she replied. Then the line went
dead.

I dressed fast, then downed a cup of milky coffee and a
buttered roll. As I brushed my hair, I ran a search on the
latest murder.

I found a story on the news feed.

Marla Henderson, 17, was found dead at approximately 5:30 this morning on the Bow Bridge in Central Park. Bystanders at the scene say that Ms. Henderson appeared to have been shot. Police refuse to comment on an ongoing investigation.

Harry, Hugo, and I left for school together and found C.P. pacing outside the Dakota's gates. Her posture was tense, and her eyes darted everywhere.

"Guys, I need some girl time with C.P.," I told my brothers.

"Yeah," C.P. agreed, latching on to my arm like it was a life preserver. She looked Harry up and down. "Girl time. Girl blather. Just us."

Harry narrowed his eyes and shoved his hands into his coat pockets. He looked, somehow, disappointed. "Whatever you two are up to, don't get caught."

Harry and Hugo set off up Central Park West. As soon as they crossed Seventy-Second, I turned to C.P.

"We've got to make this fast," I said, thinking of Jacob, our talk last night, and my new vow to myself not to disappoint him again. "I can't be late. I mean it. I can *not* be late to school."

24

We made a mad dash across Central Park West and kept going over the blacktop path, taking a left through the glorious woods in the park called the Ramble, and then kept running toward the lake. It took about ten minutes from the time we left my corner to the moment we pulled up as close as we could get to the western side of the Bow Bridge.

Usually, the bridge is magical, a genuine and well-deserved tourist magnet. It spans and is reflected in the serene twenty-acre lake and looks like something out of a painting by Claude Monet. In warm weather, rowboats skim the water and sunlight glorifies the romantic boat-house restaurant, as well as the Fifth Avenue skyline.

Right then, the scene was anything but poetic.

The entire area around the Bow Bridge was blocked off by police cruisers and pedestrians standing four or five deep outside the crime-scene tape.

C.P. and I were at the edge of the crowd with all the other rubberneckers. We couldn't see the scene, but we soon realized we'd scored a prime spot. Right next to us, a reporter was interviewing the gray-haired woman in biking gear who had discovered Marla Henderson's body at dawn. She gripped the handlebars of her bike like she was afraid she might faint if she let go.

"I was out for my morning ride when I saw this young girl lying on the bridge, right over there, in this really awkward position, and when I got closer I could see that she wasn't breathing."

"So what did you do?" the reporter asked.

"I ran over to her, of course. I saw blood all over her clothing. I put my hand on her neck and her skin was cold." The woman covered her mouth with her pale hand, and I could see that she was trembling. "Oh. It was horrible. Horrible. Poor dear little thing. I called the police, and they were here in about five minutes. That's all I know."

My phone pinged—the Google alert I'd put on Marla Henderson, who was by now on her way to the medical examiner's office.

I read the alert out loud to C.P.

" 'Marla Henderson was shot by assailant or assailants unknown. Ms. Henderson was seventeen, a junior at Brilling Day, an all-girls school on West Ninety-Second Street. Mrs. Valerie Henderson, Marla's mother, told WXOX that she wasn't discovered missing until the call from police this morning.' "

"So she did go to private school," C.P. said, shuddering. "It's too real, Tandy. I mean, someone is killing girls just like us, practically right outside your door."

I shoved my phone back into my bag, questions colliding in my mind like a thousand tiny Ping-Pong balls. Had Marla's killer been waiting for a teenage girl to come through the park? Or had he been stalking this particular girl? Had Marla Henderson, Adele Church, Stacey Blackburn, and Lena Watkins been shot by the same person?

Were they all victims of a pattern killer?

"What's going on in that beautiful, twisted little mind of yours, T?" C.P. asked.

"I'm wondering if a serial killer is hunting private school girls who live on the Upper West Side of Manhattan."

"Stacey Blackburn was shot on Fifty-Ninth Street...."

"I know, and what I found online said she lived on Eighty-First and Central Park West," I told her, biting my bottom lip as I glanced around at the trees and the buildings, the clouds in the sky that seemed to graze the tops of the highest skyscrapers. "I wonder where Marla lived."

"Okay, that's the first full-body shiver I've ever had in my entire life," C.P. said. "At least, the first one that didn't involve a hot guy."

My phone buzzed and I yanked it out again. It was a text from Harry.

You've got twelve minutes.

"Sonofa—"

I grabbed C.P.'s hand and ran.

25

I was breathless and sweaty by the time I got to the choir loft. Harry gave me a withering look, but I knew he was just busting my chops. Mr. Thibodaux entered the room seconds after C.P. had found her seat and I'd stashed my books under my desk.

I did my best to focus and even ask appropriate questions at the appropriate times, but I kept seeing images in my head of Marla Henderson in a semifetal position on the bridge and Adele Church lying on the IMAGINE mosaic with bullet holes in her chest.

After school, trying not to think too much about disobeying Jacob again, I headed toward the Twentieth Precinct station house, a brown-tiled and granite-faced building on the pretty tree-lined block of Eighty-Second Street. As I entered the vestibule, I ordered my many splintered thoughts, mentally rehearsing what I wanted to say. On my right was a display of photos of officers from the Twentieth who had lost their lives on 9/11, and across from that, an honor roll of valorous officers across the decades.

I went up a couple of steps to the main floor of the station house, cut through the disheveled group of chatting middle-aged community organizers, and approached the clerk stationed behind a Plexiglas window. She looked up from her book and greeted me with a toothy smile.

"I need to see Sergeant Caputo," I told her.

"Oh, he's awfully busy, dear, like a dog chewing at his fleas. Why don't you leave him a note and I'll see that he gets it?"

"It's what I'd call urgent," I said. "I can wait."

Her expression turned sour. She looked me up and down. I was dressed entirely in black, including my nail polish. I got the feeling she didn't approve.

"Your name is?"

"Tandoori Angel."

"And why do you need to see Sergeant Caputo so urgently?"

"It's personal," I told her. "Just tell him who's here. Trust me. He'll see me."

I sat on a bench in the oak-and-linoleum waiting room and stared at the bulletin board across the way. Apparently, the city would pay a hundred dollars for any guns turned in, no questions asked. I thought of the gun Jacob had used to kill the snake, and the gun or guns used to kill all these innocent girls.

I gotta say, I definitely felt better knowing my guardian was armed.

"Tootsie Angel!"

I looked up to see Caputo standing over me with a steely look in his opaque dark eyes. I shot the toothy lady a triumphant look. She rolled her eyes and went back to reading her romance novel.

"What trouble are you into now, missy?" Caputo asked.

"Could we talk privately?" I asked, standing. "I have something personal to discuss with you."

"Anyone ever tell you what a pain you are?"

"No, sir," I said plainly. "Nobody ever has."

He snorted and said, "Okay, follow me."

Caputo didn't have an office. He worked in a bull pen, a horseshoe of gray desks against the windowed walls that faced the dark alley behind the building. Four detectives were manning their phones when Caputo rolled an extra chair around to his desk and indicated that I should sit in it.

I didn't waste any time.

"Detective, I've brought an apology from my brothers and myself, for all the trouble we put you and your colleagues through yesterday."

I handed him a small creamy envelope with his name in cursive letters on the outside. He placed the unopened note on the corner of his desk.

"That's it?" he said.

"No. I want to talk to you about Marla Henderson and Adele Church."

"What about them, Shandy?"

"They were both shot within walking distance of each other, and I think there may be a connection between them."

Caputo said, "They knew each other?"

"I don't know."

"So what's your news flash?" He tapped his thumbs together.

"Two other private school girls were also shot in the last month. Lena Watkins—"

"Watkins?" he interjected. "She was a suicide."

"Really? There was no suicide note. And why would she shoot herself on the street?" I asked. "Maybe you could look into that?"

No answer from Caputo.

"And then there's Stacey Blackburn."

He leaned back casually in his chair. "I don't know that one, Prissy."

"She was shot in a liquor store holdup in Midtown, but the robber wasn't caught. There's no way to tell if Stacey was really a victim of an armed robbery, or if she was executed—just like Adele and Marla."

I finally had Caputo's attention. He gave me the benefit of full eye contact, and I have to admit, I liked it. He was actually taking me seriously. Then he spun in his chair and typed into his computer. I saw that he was looking up Stacey Blackburn.

"The gun that was found in Lena Watkins's hand," I said. "Could you see if it's the same gun that was used to kill Stacey Blackburn?"

Caputo said, "No one compared those incidents, Tandy. A suicide and a homicide. Nope. They weren't run against each other."

I said, "I have a hunch—you get those, don't you, Detective? I've got a hunch that Lena and Stacey were shot with the same gun, but after the killer left it behind with Lena he had to get a new one. He then used *that* gun to shoot both Adele and Marla."

"Well, ballistics is still out on Henderson, not that I could tell you if there was a match. Thanks for stopping in. Oh, and thanks for the apology. I'll pin it on the bulletin board for all the guys to see."

Caputo stood up, all pale six feet of him. I stood up, too.

"Just tell me this. Were the bullets the same caliber?"

He gave me a long look. I made sure not to blink.

"Both girls were shot with a thirty-eight. Now, don't tell anyone I said so, Brandy. Or you and I are through. Clear?"

I walked home on autopilot. I was sure I was right. Someone had put targets on private school girls. But I was also sure that I'd gotten through to Caputo. He was going to look into my theory. I could feel it.

I was working with the NYPD. Unofficially, but still. I had contributed to the investigation, and if I turned out to be right, who knew what might happen next?

CONFESSION

I first met Caputo three months ago, the night my parents died. Harry, Hugo, and I were in bed. Samantha, my mother's assistant, was in her room, also asleep in bed. Matthew was living with Tamara way downtown, but he had a key and he knew the ins and outs of the labyrinthine Dakota.

When the police arrived, none of us knew that our parents were dead in their suite upstairs, and when questioned by the unsmiling Detective Caputo, we had no alibis except the unprovable "We were asleep."

The apartment was locked. There had been no forced entry.

So Detective Caputo jumped to the obvious conclusion that we were prime suspects, that one or all of us had killed Malcolm and Maud.

Not that I could blame him.

We all had the means, the motive, and the opportunity. Every one of us in that tight family circle had good reason to kill Malcolm and Maud, who were, after all, very complex people whom many have described as monsters. Even me.

Still, I wish I could have prevented their deaths. I miss them. I loved them and I think they loved us, in their own twisted way.

But here's a confession, my friend, and I tell you this with a true heart.

We're better off without them.

I think maybe now we have a chance of becoming who and what we were meant to be. And I can't keep Jacob's words from scrolling over and over through my mind.

"I've saved hundreds of people in my lifetime. How about you?"

I'm making a promise to myself, and also to you. I *will* save lives. I hope I will save potential victims of the Private School Girl Killer. And, if I can, I will also save Matthew.

And, of course, that's not all.

Wherever he is, whatever has happened to him, I will find James Rampling.

Don't worry, love of my life. I have not forgotten about you.

I was walking with James at the edge of the surf. The clouds blocked the moon and the stars, and the sky was coal black.

I started to tell James about the phosphorescence of the one-celled animals, and he squeezed my hand.

My heart caught. Dammit. This was supposed to be romantic and here I was giving a science lesson.

"I'm sorry. Sometimes I just start spouting this *stuff.*"

I could barely see his outline, but I knew his face so well. "I *love* listening to you spout," he said.

I laughed. "Seriously?"

"I want to spend the next ninety years listening to you. And I couldn't care less *what* you want to talk about, whether it's phosphorescence or what you ate for break-fast this morning. Sound like a plan?"

I pretended to consider. "Would we also eat and sleep?"

James laughed, and then the surf rolled in and covered our feet, so ice-cold it hurt. I squealed and danced away from the lapping waves, and James ran with me. He put his arms around my waist and hugged me hard. My breath hitched. It felt so good to be in his arms. It was where I belonged.

The surf rolled back, and James pressed his lips into the crook between my neck and shoulder. "I'd like to stay here forever," he said, kissing my skin. "Right. Here."

"Now, *that* sounds like a plan." I sighed.

He turned me around and pulled me to him, bending to touch his mouth to mine. His lips were soft at first, but then forceful and demanding. As he crushed me tightly against him, I shivered with excitement.

"Are you cold?" James asked.

I shook my head, unable, for the moment, to find my voice. He cupped my face with both hands.

"Because we can go home, if you want to."

There was a little house up in the dunes, *our* house, with three cozy rooms and a porch with a glider and a view of the ocean.

"Actually, I feel warm," I told him. The wind whipped

my hair as I fumbled with the tiny buttons on the long cardigan I wore over my little skirt. "Just being near you makes me feel warm."

That was when a roar came up like the sound of a typhoon. It was a heart-stopping, booming sound, loud and invasive, a noise that blocked out my very thoughts.

"What *is* that?" I yelled.

But before James could answer, the lights hit me from all directions, utterly blinding me. I reached out for James, groping against the brightness, but he was gone. From impossibly far away, I heard him call my name, then—

Nothing. Nothing but indistinct shouting and the crackle of handheld radios.

"James!" I screamed, still staggering, reaching out, trying to find him. "James! Where are you?"

And then a heavy sack fell over my head.

27

I sat straight up in bed, gasping for breath.

Oh my God. Had I been dreaming?

"Tandy? Tandy. What's wrong?"

It was Harry calling me from outside my door.

"I'm okay. I'm fine," I told him, still struggling for breath. The doorknob twisted, but the door was locked.

"Let me in."

"I'm on the phone with C.P.," I lied. "What time is it?"

"Six fifteen. Were you screaming?"

"Um...singing," I said.

"You scared the crap out of me!" he said through the door. Then he blew out a sigh. "You've got no ear. Whatever you were doing."

"Ha-ha."

I heard his footsteps clomp off down the hall, and I leaned back against my pillows, trying to remember my dream, but it grew more vague and slippery by the moment. I did remember the feelings, though, and those I could never have made up.

Was this dream of me and James on some beach, in fact, a memory? Or a fantasy? I closed my eyes and breathed, wishing I could trust my instinct.

This dream had felt real. It had felt so very, very real.

It was like James himself was inside me saying *Don't forget me.*

I shoved myself out of bed, my heart bounding around like an excited jackrabbit. If I was starting to remember, then everything was about to change. If I could remember James, remember what had happened to us, then maybe I could find him. Maybe, just maybe, we could be together again.

As I reached for my bathrobe and headed to my private bathroom, I could practically hear Harry scoffing inside my head—Harry's voice saying, *"Oh, God, Tandy, would you get a life?"*

But suddenly there was no point in having a life unless James was in it.

SHADOWS
OF THE
PAST

CONFESSION

In the same way I get obsessed with the details of a case I'm trying to crack, ever since I got off my parents' special cocktail of
drugs, I've been obsessed with the mystery of a single word:
love. I've read just about everything that's been written on the
subject. Poetry and literature, psychology and science. And I've
located one certifiable truth. Are you ready?

An emotional bond between two people can form in a fifth
of a second.

Think about that. You can't take in a breath and exhale it in
one-fifth of one second. You can't form a cogent thought in that
tiny amount of time. You can't even blink.

So I think I get it. I think love at first sight bypasses cogent
thought.

That is what that first moment was like for me.

And that first kiss? Forget about it. It was just a kiss in the way that an earthquake is just an earthquake. It was life-changing, mind-altering perfection. My first kiss with James was so defining that nothing my parents did could wipe it from my memory. Even now, even today, I could still feel the sensation of our lips touching. They couldn't take that from me.

But they tried.

A few weeks after I was released from Fern Haven, Maud told me that James and I had run away together. That was all she would tell me. No details, no reasons, no explanation of why she'd felt the need to tear us apart. Of course I tried as hard as I could to remember, to figure out why I'd done what I'd done, but in place of the images of James and me in each other's arms, all I could see was that white room deep inside Fern Haven. All I could remember were the treatments that were like blackouts followed by whiteouts.

By the time I was returned to the Dakota, my mind was filled with buzzing and snow, exactly like the static on a TV that's lost its signal. I couldn't remember where I'd been, what I'd done. At the time I couldn't even recall James's face or his name. Just a vague, shadowy, nebulous idea of him. And the pressure of his lips on mine.

Not that I told anyone that. Of course I didn't. Because I knew they would try to take that from me, too.

Dr. Keyes, my therapist, became my personal coach.

Dr. Keyes: "How do you feel, Tandy?"

Me: "I don't."

Dr. Keyes: "Good."

Someday I'd like to have a real sit-down with Dr. Keyes. She has a lot of explaining to do. But now that my memories are starting to come back, I'm putting aside my revenge plans. I'm focusing on the saying "Love will find a way."

I'm counting on it, because James and I were meant to be together. I know that what we had was the real thing, even without my bleached-clean and sanitized mind totally back to normal yet.

But where is he?

Where is James Rampling?

Is there a chance that wherever he is, he's dreaming of kissing me?

This is a mystery I must solve.

If I'm such a multitasking investigative genius, I ought to be able to figure it out.

28

When Malcolm and Maud found out what had happened between James and me, they took quick, decisive action to make sure we were separated. Not just separated. They wanted to be sure that James Rampling would never be able to come near me or our family ever again.

It would be quite reasonable to ask me, dear friend, if this forced separation happened in a small village in a time before electricity and running water and, oh, I don't know, rational thought. Because honestly. How could this have happened in New York City, in the twenty-first century?

Well, the Angels wanted it to happen, so it did.

Dr. Keyes told me my parents were terrified that my

relationship with James would derail all the grand plans they had for me, which in their opinion meant he would ruin my life. She said the best thing would be for me to forget him and move past this short, nearly devastating interlude. And she said her job was to help me obliterate the nightmare quickly. Thoroughly. Permanently.

But apparently she didn't do her job all that well. Because my memory is coming back. I know it is. That has to be what these dreams are—real memories trying to push their way through.

After my parents' deaths, I ransacked Maud's office and found a hidden newspaper article with this headline: SON OF STORIED FINANCIER, 18, DISAPPEARS UNDER MYSTERIOUS CIRCUMSTANCES.

Below the headline was a photograph of James.

Just the sight of him—the fully formed, non-nebulous, totally sharp sight of him—knocked the wind out of me. It also knocked any doubt out of me. At that moment, I knew. I knew for absolute certain that these little flashes I'd been getting, these memories and wisps of images, were real.

So I took the article. I buried it in a file of research on the effect of nuclear waste on sea coral and locked it away in my room.

Now I got out of bed and went to my desk, which was

right near my windows, facing the park. I pressed my left ring finger to the biometric plate at the side of the pedestal and the locks thunked open. I opened the file drawer.

I pawed through the file until my hand fell on the scrap of newsprint.

There, under the headline, the photo jolted me once again. His handsome face, his light eyes, his sweet smile, and the strong line of his jaw. And then I saw him leaning in toward me, sliding his fingers into my hair....

No. Not now. I had work to do. I forced myself to focus on the article.

> Royal Rampling, billionaire financier and father of James Rampling, 18-year-old student at the Park Avenue High School, who was reported missing this week, has contacted this paper to say that James is living abroad.
>
> Said Mr. Rampling yesterday, "James is perfectly well and is attending a private school in Europe, where he is devoting himself to his studies."

The article went on to cite Mr. Rampling's business expertise and the size of his fortune, but the last paragraph was dedicated to my mother.

On July 14, Mr. Rampling reported Maud Angel, founder and CEO of Leading Hedge, a New York hedge fund, to the SEC for securities fraud. He is further suing Mrs. Angel personally for $50 million.

Reading about my mother's supposed crime still knocked the air out of me. Philippe had explained to me that Maud was, indeed, in serious trouble before her death. She had invested heavily in Angel Pharmaceuticals, telling her clients that the company was solid when it was actually nearing collapse.

Furthermore, Maud had borrowed money and had issued false financial statements to hide losses, and when Angel Pharma's crooked books were exposed, Maud couldn't pay back her investors.

Royal Rampling was her most damaged client, so he had called her out. On the night my parents died, Rampling had been poised to bankrupt her. I was sure Maud detested him. So it was no wonder she didn't want me seeing his son. And maybe, just maybe, Royal Rampling didn't want his son seeing me, either.

It was about them, of course. Always. Always about them.

A white-hot fury seared through me so fast I almost

crumpled the precious article and its photo in my hand. But at the last second I stopped myself and instead flung the rest of the folder across the room as hard as I could, letting out a guttural howl. Papers fluttered to the floor. The folder smacked against my door. It wasn't all that satisfying, to be honest, but it was something.

Clenching my jaw, I grabbed my robe and walked into my bathroom, turning the hot water in the shower as high as it would go. Then I stood under the punishing spray as long as I could, trying to catch my breath, thinking about the Capulets and the Montagues.

But James and I were different from Romeo and Juliet. While Malcolm, Maud, and Mr. Rampling had succeeded in separating us, I wasn't dead.

All I could do was hope that James wasn't, either.

29

I *had once defiantly told* **Capricorn Caputo** that I slept like a stump. This was three months ago, during the days when arcane chemical compounds were both focusing and numbing my mind. Now my brain was free at last and fighting for a comeback. Which meant that that night, I couldn't sleep. I could almost feel the neurons seeking out unused connections, spanning voids, plugging in, powering up.

The glowing clock next to my bed read 1:14. I couldn't quiet my mind no matter how many sheep I counted or lines of poetry I recited or digits of pi I recounted.

Where was James? Had he bailed after we were separated or had his parents sent him somewhere? Was his memory wiped as well? Did he remember me at all? If he did, why hadn't he tried to get in touch? He must have had my phone number, my e-mail, my family's address, something.

And then, at exactly 4:30 in the morning, I sat straight up in bed. Maybe James had tried to get in touch with me but his messages hadn't gotten though. It wasn't like Malcolm and Maud to go to all that trouble to wipe my brain and then just let a letter or a text or an e-mail get to me. They were nothing if not thorough. Maniacally so.

If his texts or e-mails had somehow been blocked, the next logical thing for him to try would have been writing. Good old-fashioned snail mail.

I pushed myself out of bed, intent on searching Malcolm's and Maud's things again, but I paused. I'd already gone through all their stuff. If there had been anything in this house from James, I would have found it.

And then it hit me, like a smack to the forehead. Not everything we'd once had in this house was still in this house.

After Malcolm's and Maud's bodies had been removed and the crime-scene unit was wrapping up, the CSI people had carried off four cardboard boxes full of my parents' personal files.

Those files had never been returned.

I clutched the post at the end of my bed. Where were those boxes now? Had they been stored in some kind of evidence locker? Or even destroyed?

Panic gripped my insides, and I reached for my cell phone. I needed to go through the files. I was sure there was something important inside those boxes. A journal, or a letter exchanged by Maud and Rampling agreeing to the separation of their kids.

Maybe even a letter from James.

Those boxes held answers, and I'm all about answers.

That's one thing about me that hasn't changed at all.

30

My mind was revving like a race car engine as I joined my brothers in the kitchen that morning. I had left Philippe a message at 4:36 AM. So far, I hadn't heard back. I glanced at the clock on the stove. It was now 7:57.

I reached for the coffee and almost knocked it over. Harry gave me the squinty eye, trying to assess my body language and read my mood. After a couple of minutes of me fidgeting and his eyes getting narrower, he actually took away my coffee, emptied it into the sink, and brought me a glass of milk.

"What's with you?" I asked.

"What's with *me*? You're like a zombie on crack."

I rolled my eyes and said, "A zombie on crack. What would that look like, Harry?"

Hugo stuck his arms out in front of him, fixed his eyes on nothing, and took a few speedy laps around the dining table. He was still going at it when Jacob entered.

"I don't even want to know," our guardian said in a lighthearted way.

Harry and I laughed, and I was glad when Harry didn't press me on what I'd been obsessing about. At this point, I had nothing more than an idea—a hope. Even if the boxes were safe, I didn't know where they were, what they might contain, or if I could get my hands on them.

I drank my milk and ate my oatmeal while Jacob quizzed Hugo on the Spanish-American War.

Ten minutes later, Jacob stood at the front door and hugged each of us good-bye. I'd never been hugged good-bye in my life, and I started to squirm. I mean, group hugs after arguments are one thing, but this was a tad outside my comfort zone. Jacob, however, wasn't having it. He gripped my shoulders, looked me in the eye, and said: "Have a good day, Tandy. I'll be right here when you get home."

"Good to know," I told him. But inside, I did feel a little bit squishy. No one had ever promised me that before, either.

Hugo and Harry took their hugs and promises like men, and then we hightailed it to the elevator.

I got through the morning at my desk in the choir loft at All Saints, asked sharp questions, and even stood up to present my opinion of the effects of electronic communication on the teenage brain.

"Not good, but highly necessary."

But the whole time, a huge chunk of my mind was fixated on an image of four cardboard boxes.

At lunch, I sat on the stone front steps of the school with traffic whizzing by and texted Phil. He was in court with Matthew, of course, but he texted me back half an hour later, while I was in class.

Call me when you can.

I texted back.

Just tell me if u have the boxes

His text back was almost immediate.

Call me. Too long for text.

Ugh. I texted back.

So leave me a vm!!!!

By the time the dismissal bell rang, Phil *had* left me a voice mail. I clapped my phone tight against my ear and heard the murmur of crowds moving around him in the courthouse corridor, breaking up his words. I could just barely make out what he said.

"Sorry we keep missing each other, Tandy, but look. I have the boxes. They belonged to your parents, who were my clients. Without their express permission, I can't give them to you. I'm sorry."

I gripped the phone. "Sonofa—"

I called Phil again. His voice mail picked up, of course. I held the phone in front of my lips and shouted. "I want those boxes, Phil! Malcolm and Maud don't need their old files anymore, and as one of their heirs, I'm entitled to their stuff!"

Then I took a deep breath and called Jacob. "I'm stopping by our lawyer's office on the way home. I'm not grounded from our lawyer's office, right?"

"No. I think that's a reasonable place to go. Any chance you'll tell me why?" Jacob asked.

"Nope. But I'll be home for dinner."

Luckily, Jacob didn't argue. My destination on William Street was one of many featureless gray office buildings that form tall canyons shading the streets of downtown Manhattan. By the time I arrived at Phil's address, the elevators were disgorging personnel leaving work for the day. I hoped Phil's office wasn't already closed.

When I arrived on the twentieth floor, I followed the arrows until I was outside the glass door that read P. MONTAIGNE, ATTORNEY-AT-LAW. I pushed at the door and it opened. I exhaled a breath I hadn't known I was holding.

"Phil? It's Tandy."

And there he was, standing in the doorway to his interior office, looking at me with very sad eyes.

"Tandy, I can't do it. Can you just trust me on this?"

"Not a chance," I replied, gearing up for a fight. "Those boxes are mine."

He gave me this look like I'd just hauled off and punched him.

"I'm sorry, Phil. I shouldn't have—"

"It's okay," he interjected. "I have to tell you something about Matthew."

That brought me up short. Here I'd been obsessing about James and my love life and my supercontrolling mother and I hadn't even asked how the trial was going.

"What? What's wrong with him?" I asked.

"He wants to testify in his own defense, Tandy," Philippe told me. "If he takes the stand, it will be a disaster."

"How big a disaster?" I asked.

"I'm afraid if he takes the stand...we'll lose."

31

Philippe snapped on the lights in the conference room, and we sat in padded swivel chairs across from each other at the glossy blond-wood table.

I was sweating through my clothes and feeling sick over bulldozing my way into Phil's office and ordering him around, especially when he was concerned about my brother. I pictured Matthew lying on a narrow slab in his cell, his hands balled into fists, angry, helpless to do anything except commit suicide on the witness stand.

I said to Phil, "What can I do to help Matty?"

"I don't know, Tandy. Reasoning with him only makes him more belligerent, more entrenched. If there was a weak prosecution, his testimony *might* move the jury. But it's Nadine Raphael and she'll vaporize him. My guess is that he's having posttraumatic shock from so many deaths: your parents, Tamara, and his unborn son. I think he just wants to blow everything up."

A long silence followed as we both visualized the attack by the aggressive assistant DA and what would remain of my brother's defense when she'd finished detonating him.

I ached for my brother. He didn't deserve this. Any of this.

I wanted to see Matthew run down a field with a football tucked under his arm. I wanted to hear him laugh and see him bounce Hugo on his shoulders. I wanted him back in the apartment with the rest of us. A family.

I wanted him to be free.

Phil said, "Matthew is my problem, Tandy. I've had a chance to think about yours. You can look at those file boxes as long as you do it here, in this conference room, now.

"Tomorrow I'm sending the whole lot to climate-controlled storage along with your parents' other papers so that I will always have whatever I may need to protect you from future lawsuits. Agreed?"

I was so excited my fingertips tingled. "Yes. Of course."

"I'll be right back."

It felt like he was gone for hours. When he finally did

come back, he was pulling a dolly loaded with four cardboard cartons.

"Here's your one and only chance, Tandy. Make the most of it." He gave me a bottle of water, a notepad, and a box cutter, then left the room and closed the door.

Unfortunately, my one and only chance had a cutoff time. I'd told Jacob I'd be home by seven.

32

I had about forty minutes to go through the boxes and get
out to the street. And actually, with rush-hour traffic running up, down, and across Manhattan, I was cutting my
travel time close.

It was go time.

I lifted the first heavy box onto the conference table. I
sliced through the tape, pulled up the flaps, and peered inside.

Dozens of stuffed file folders proved, upon inspec-
tion, to be full of stock brokerage sell orders, buy orders,
order confirmations, and monthly statements. I opened
the second box and the third, finding similar bundles of
brokerage-house litter. These papers might be critical to
future legal actions, but they meant nothing to me.

I was looking for something personal. A journal, a confession, an envelope marked *To Tandy, re James Rampling*. But of course, that would've been too easy.

As I flipped through the file folders, I was starting to think that this whole thing was futile. But I couldn't quit until I'd searched the last box. I slit the tape on box number four, hoped there was anything in it other than financial files, then pulled on the flaps.

Damn. More files. But then something caught my eye. A blue folder with a white tab, different from all the green and tan. I tugged it out, and my heart all but stopped.

The typed tab read: FERN HAVEN: TANDOORI.

I shook as I pulled the folder into my lap. Did I really want to know what was inside? Did I want to know what had actually been done to me?

Answer: *Hell yeah.*

I flipped open the folder and hungrily scanned the pages. A barrage of frightening phrases jumped out at me. Phrases like *Experimental treatment. Test case 33. Psychotic break.* And my favorite, *Possible side effects include prolonged amnesia, inconsistent recall, hallucination, catatonia, coma, depression, suicide.*

Fantastic. My parents had wanted to eradicate their enemy's son from my life so completely, they were willing to risk my life for it.

Quaking with fury, I glanced at the closed office door. There was no way in hell I was leaving this folder in a box to be placed in storage. This was about my life. My health. I folded it in half and went to stuff it into my bag. When I did, a stiff cardboard envelope slipped out and fell to the floor at my feet.

I shoved the file into my bag and grabbed the envelope.

"What's this, Maud?" I muttered. "X-rays of my scrambled egg–style brain?"

Bracing myself, I opened the envelope. Inside were five postcards of European city scenes. I flipped the first one over.

To: Tandy Angel, the Dakota, 1 West 72nd Street, Apt. 9G, New York, NY.

All the blood rushed to my head. These postcards were for me? But I'd never seen them before. My eyes automatically darted to the signature.

Love, James.

Suddenly everything went gray. I stumbled back into the cabinet behind me and upended a glass vase, which crashed to the floor. Almost instantly, Phil opened the door.

"What happened?"

I covered the postcards with a file folder.

"S-sorry," I stuttered, glancing at the shattered glass near my feet. "I tripped."

"Are you all right?" he asked.

"Yeah. Not a scratch," I told him, though if he'd taken a closer look, he would have seen I was shaking like a leaf.

"I'll go get the dustpan." He closed the door again and was gone.

I ever so slowly moved the folder off the postcards, as if that cobra from my office was going to jump out and sink its teeth into me. The same tall scrawl covered each of the cards. They were all from James.

He was, in fact, alive.

And he'd been trying to get in touch with me all along.

33

There were no available cabs—anywhere—so I ran down the steps to the subway. After a bone-rattling fifteen-minute ride uptown, I exited on the north side of Seventy-Second and Amsterdam.

I walked as fast as I could toward the Dakota, and seven minutes later, I blew through the front door of apartment 9G with my five precious cards from James inside my bag, along with my Fern Haven file. I shoved my bag under the bench in the hall, then ran to the kitchen to help Harry with dinner.

I wanted to be alone as soon as possible, and as usual, Harry was on to me. In fact, he kept looking at me like I was wearing a boa constrictor on my head.

Which, given the recent plague of snakes, wasn't that far-fetched.

"Matty wants to testify for himself," I said as I put water on for the pasta. I wanted to focus on something other than James, and luckily—or unluckily—I had something pretty damn important to focus on. "Phil is scared. By law, Matty has the right to take the stand, even against his lawyer's advice, even if he will blow up his case."

"Someone should talk to him," Harry said, looking pointedly at me. It was pretty clear who he thought that someone should be.

Over dinner, Harry, Hugo, and I talked to Jacob about Matthew, telling stories of what he was really like and how the press was totally misrepresenting him. We even laughed over a few of Hugo's accounts of heroic Matty coming to his rescue. Like when Hugo had left the tub on to see if he could fill the entire bathroom with water and swim around in it wearing Malcolm's scuba gear. It felt good to laugh.

But once the dishes were in the dishwasher, all I could think about was being alone. I fled to my sky-blue sanctuary, locked my door, and took my bag with me into bed.

My hands shook as I handled the cards my parents had obviously confiscated from the mailbox downstairs, committing a federal offense to keep me from reading what was legally, morally, and ethically mine.

I put the cards in a neat stack in front of me and looked at the top card on the stack, a picture of Wengen, a village in the Swiss Alps. I turned the card over and saw that it was postmarked just a couple of weeks after James and I had been separated. He'd written it while I was still locked up in Fern Haven.

James had covered every bit of available space on the back of the card, even crowding his note into the address box.

He'd written:

Tandy, My e-mails bounce back. Your phone goes straight to voice mail. I'm going crazy not talking to you. You know my number. Please call me. I'm so worried about you, and I think about you all the time. I'm no poet, so I have to borrow the words of Alfred, Lord Tennyson:

"She is coming, my life, my fate; / The red rose cries, 'She is near, she is near;'/ And the white rose weeps, 'She is late;' / The larkspur listens, 'I hear, I hear;'/ And the lily whispers, 'I wait.' "

Love, James

My eyes filled with tears.

James was alive. He was alive and was out there somewhere thinking that I didn't care about him. That I'd cut him off on purpose. My heart felt like it was trying to twist out of my body at the thought.

After all this time, all this silence, he must hate me. What was I going to do? How was I going to fix this? I bit my lip as hard as I could and tried to *think*, not cry. Because crying wasn't going to do me any good.

I thought about that poem James used—Tennyson's "Maud"—and how my mother once forced me to handwrite the entire epic as a punishment. But those words, coming from him, felt so different now.... It was all too complicated to process. I couldn't think. I couldn't reason. I couldn't do anything until I finally gave in, flopped down on my bed, and let it all out.

Do you feel everything this way, friend? Is this what your emotional life is like?

I don't know how you can stand it.

34

After my emotional breakdown subsided and I'd blown
my nose a couple hundred times, I fanned the postcards
out on the bed, picture side up. The photos were of Stock-
holm, Rennes, London, Erfurt, and Wengen. I turned
them over again to be sure I hadn't missed the obvious.

There were no return addresses, but then, James had
been traveling when he'd written them, and he must have
thought I'd respond to him by e-mail or phone.

He couldn't have known that my parents had canceled
my e-mail account, assigned me a new phone number,
eradicated my Facebook page, and stolen my mail.

I took one of the cards into my trembling hand.

Dear Tandy,

I guess I should take a hint. You don't want to see me anymore and I understand. What we did was wrong. Your parents are furious. I brought so much trouble into your life. But still, I thought...at least I hoped...that you would at least write to me to say good-bye.

E. M. Forster wrote this in A Room with a View: *"It isn't possible to love and to part. You will wish that it was. You can transmute love, ignore it, muddle it, but you can never pull it out of you. I know by experience that the poets are right: love is eternal."*

I love you, Tandy. I wish I could forget you, but I can't.

Eternally yours, James

He'd written his e-mail address at the bottom with a note next to it in tiny letters: *Just in case.*

Because James had "taken the hint," he'd stopped writing months ago, and now I had no way to tell him that I'd been locked up at Fern Haven all that time. That my parents were dead. That I missed him and wanted to see him more than anything.

I grabbed my phone with both hands, took a breath,

closed my eyes, and wished as hard as I could that this would work. Then, for the first time since before my brain had been thoroughly washed and tumble dried at Fern Haven, I wrote an e-mail to James Rampling.

James. I just found out today that you wrote to me. If you don't hate me, please write back. There's so, so much I have to tell you. Love, Tandy

I launched the e-mail to the address James had provided and held my breath. A moment later, my phone beeped. Mailer-Daemon had returned my e-mail, "Addressee unknown."

Just like that. The e-mail address was all I had, and just like that, all I had was nil.

I threw my phone across the room. Then Hugo screamed.

"Help! Tandy! Harry! Jacob! Spider!"

35

"*Come on, Hugo!*" I shouted through the closed door as I retrieved my thankfully intact phone. "That's not funny!"

Hugo yelled, "Jacob!"

I pulled myself together and opened my door. At the exact same moment, Harry popped out of his room. His eyes widened at something I couldn't see, and he lunged for Hugo, wrapping his arms around him and dragging him back down the hallway.

I followed Hugo's trembling finger and saw something black and hairy and about four inches long, clinging to the door frame at eyeball height.

Hugo wasn't joking.

It was a spider, all right, and it was huge. From the

corner of my eye I saw another one skitter nervously across the floor. I clapped my hands over my mouth. First snakes. Now spiders. I leaned in for a better look at our new friend on the door frame and recoiled. Not just spiders. Deadly spiders.

Was this why our parents had forced us to memorize every species of every creature on earth? Just in case our cloistered apartment building was one day randomly attacked by exotic wildlife?

Hugo was still screaming when Jacob came loping down the hallway with a bath towel in his hands. He flicked the towel at the spider and, when the arachnid dropped, stomped on it with his desert boots.

"There's another one!" Hugo shouted. "What *is* it?"

"It's a Sydney funnel-web spider," I told him, sidestepping the crawling monster. "It's exclusive to Australia and one of the most venomous spiders on earth. They don't run away. They attack. Be careful, Jacob."

Jacob threw the towel again and again, but the spider evaded it and ran up his leg.

Hugo, Harry, and I all screamed, but Jacob just calmly flicked the spider off his leg, then ground it under his sole.

We all stood around him, bug-eyed and trying to catch our breaths. It was pretty incredible how one guy could be all touchy-feely one minute and bad-ass commando the next. Jacob was really growing on me.

"Do any of you know anything about this rash of creatures?" he asked. "Anything at all? Even the ghost of a suspicion?"

"They can't just be living loose in this building," I said. "They had to have escaped from someone's collection or something."

Jacob said, "Then this apartment must have a tunnel or some kind of access to wherever they've been living, and we don't know if we've gotten them all. Keep your eyes open. Shake out your clothes and your bedding. Tandy—"

"I've got Pest Control on speed dial," I said, lifting my phone.

"Good. Call them, and while we wait, let's gather in the living room," said Jacob.

"Excellent," said Harry. "Perfect time to have a family meeting. I think Tandy should tell us why she's been jittery, throwing things, and crying. *All the time.*"

36

Did I want a family meeting, my friend? About as much as I wanted a monster zit to sprout on the tip of my nose. But I was surrounded. There was no escape.

And the last thing I wanted was to be alone when the next Sydney funnel-web spider attacked.

After I hung up with Pest Control, we gathered in our living room. When clustered in the seating area, we had 360-degree views, so any big, hairy spiders would find it hard to sneak up on us.

I dropped down onto the shiny red sectional sofa; Jacob pulled up a dining room chair, and Hugo took the Pork Chair, crossing his legs and looking at me as if I was about to read him a story. Harry sat at the far end of the sofa and leaned toward me with his arms resting on his knees.

"You're the definition of a hot mess, Tandy," he said. "What, in particular, is stressing you out?"

"Do you really have to ask?" I asked. "Matthew is on trial for murder, several private school girls exactly our age are dead in the morgue, there are venomous creatures swarming in our apartment, and we're scheduled to be homeless in the very near future. Should I go on?"

"Yes," Harry said. "Go on. And tell the truth."

I threw a sigh that should have moved the curtains hanging across the room.

"It's personal, okay? And I'm not in any danger," I said, shooting a placating look at Jacob. "I have a right to my privacy, don't I?" I added in a wobbly voice.

I stood up and looked for a way out, my bedroom or the front door or a wormhole into another dimension, I didn't care. But I was confronted by three people standing up to head me off.

It was like they were staging an intervention.

"Tandy, sit," said Jacob. "Please? Sit down and tell us what's bothering you."

He seemed legitimately concerned, but I really didn't want to talk about James with Jacob. What if he thought it was trite? Some teenage girl moaning about a lost love?

The man killed terrorists. He shot venomous snakes. He squashed deadly spiders. Besides, when it came down to it, I hardly knew him.

Harry said, "Sit, Tandy."

"Sit down or else," said Hugo.

I laughed nervously at my little brother, then threw myself back down onto the couch.

"Well, Jacob, this is the whole terrible story. Are you ready?"

He said, "Don't be afraid. You're safe with us."

So I told him. I told him about James and my collision with true love. I told him about waking up in a white room in some kind of hospital, my head, actually my entire body, aching like I'd done the slalom course at the Winter Olympics. I told him about the buzzing snowstorm in my mind where my memories had once been. And then I filled him in on our startling discovery that the vitamins our parents had been feeding us since we were babies were actually specially formulated concoctions to help them control our bodies and minds.

When I was done, Jacob looked like he'd been slapped across the face.

"You poor girl. Fern Haven? Peter said you were sent to a spa."

"That's hilarious," I said flatly. "Unless spas are offering electroshock treatment, aggressive talk therapy, and mind-numbing pills these days."

Even Harry, who knew just about everything, went pale. He slid over and wrapped me in his arms.

"I could kill them," he said, clearly meaning Malcolm and Maud.

"Too late," I replied.

"Can you go on, Tandy?" Jacob asked me.

"Sure."

Once I'd started, I didn't feel like stopping. But I didn't want to linger any longer on the broken recollections of Fern Haven. So instead, I skipped ahead to the present.

37

Night was upon the city, but it was never really dark in the heart of New York. The streetlights below threw wide cones of light on the sidewalks, and traffic zoomed up and down the avenue, headlights blazing.

Jacob turned on the torch lamp behind the sofa and flipped the switch that lit the sconces along the windowed wall.

"Do you need anything?" he asked me. "Water?"

I shook my head. I was eager to move past my recent and painful past.

"After school today, I went to Phil's office and went through four big boxes that the crime-scene techs took away after Malcolm and Maud died," I told them. "I found the medical file from when I was at Fern Haven, and inside that, I found some postcards from James."

"Say that again," Harry said incredulously.

"I found five postcards from James that I'd never seen before," I said. "Our parents never gave them to me."

"Figures," said Harry. "Control freaks."

"That's putting it mildly," Jacob muttered.

"The good news is James loves me," I said miserably. "At least, he did. The bad news is I have no idea where he is or how to get in touch with him."

This brought a moment of silence.

"I understand how you must feel, Tandy," Jacob said finally. "First love is so powerful. So indelible. For me, it was a woman named Shira. She was a soldier and very brave. She died in a firefight. She was only twenty. We were only twenty."

If my math was accurate, Shira had died more than thirty years ago.

"Were you with her when she died?" I asked him.

He nodded. "I couldn't save her."

He was clearly still grieving after so many years. But before he could say more, there was a loud knock on the front door, and when the doorbell was pressed, the UFO chandelier in the foyer tootled the theme song from *Close*

Encounters of the Third Kind. It kind of killed the sharing vibe we had going.

Hugo ran to the foyer and, ignoring the peephole above his head, opened the door. A squad of Pest Control investigators poured in.

"I guess chat time is over," I said under my breath as Jacob stood up to greet them.

I bet we were the only family in America to have a serious heart-to-heart interrupted by a search for venomous spiders. The investigators spent the next three hours interrogating us and searching for spiders, finding nothing but the two flattened eight-legged corpses Jacob had laid out on a bath towel.

Much later, ensconced in soft bedding, I clutched my postcards from James and looked out at the moonlight caressing the treetops in the park.

I imagined I was holding hands with James, the two of us looking up at the moon together.

"Did you know there's a mineral named after the *Apollo 11* astronauts?" I asked James in my fantasy. "It's called armalcolite."

James laughed. "You are a *huge* geek."

I rolled over to face him. "Then you're in love with a huge geek."

He lifted his shoulders. "And I will readily admit it to anyone who asks."

Then I closed my eyes and let the imaginary James kiss me. I concentrated as hard as I could, until I could feel the smoothness of his lips against mine, and just like that, I wasn't entirely sure. I wasn't sure if I'd just made this moon-watching scene up, or if it was another memory, another real event, coming back to me.

This was what Fern Haven had done to me. I was never going to trust my memory again. But there is one thing I can tell you for absolute certain, my friend.

I'm more determined than ever to find James.

38

The next morning we arrived at the courthouse before the crowds and the press, all the Angel kids—at least the ones who were currently free—plus Jacob and C.P., who had gotten special permission from her parents to miss school. It was a show of unity and support for Matthew, but I felt better having them there, too.

We took our seats right behind the defense table, and I looked around at the carved mahogany panels I had thought so beautiful and awe-inspiring a few days before.

Now the height of the ceilings and the darkness of the wood, not to mention the carved creatures above the moldings, seemed sinister.

At five before nine, Phil entered through the side

entrance with Matty, who looked like he'd been living on the street. His dreadlocks were untied and untidy. Dark bags hung under his sharp blue eyes, and he was wearing a rumpled suit set off with shiny new handcuffs and leg chains. This could only mean that he'd done something menacing or crazy or both behind bars and couldn't be trusted to behave in court.

I saw the jury eyeing him with alarm. Disgust. Disdain.

Fan-freaking-tastic.

As the gallery filled, so did the business side of the courtroom. Lawyers, bailiffs, and the court reporter took their positions, as did the judge and jury.

Nadine Raphael stood, all goddesslike in her perfect black suit with her shiny coiffed hair, and called her first witness.

Barbara Tally wore a pencil skirt, a smart draped blouse, and stiletto heels. Her streaky blond curls were perfectly sleek.

"Ms. Tally, did you know Tamara Gee?" Ms. Raphael asked.

"Yes. Very well."

"And what was your relationship with the victim?"

"She was my cousin, and I also worked as her personal assistant," Barbara Tally answered.

"And were the two of you good friends?" Ms. Raphael asked.

"God, yes. We were like sisters. I knew all her business better than she did."

"I see. Now, do you know the defendant, Matthew Angel?" Ms. Raphael gestured at my brother.

"Yes. Very well."

"Do you like him?"

"Yes, actually, I did." Barbara Tally's gaze flicked toward Matthew. "At one time."

Ms. Raphael laced her fingers together at waist level. "Did Ms. Gee ever tell you how she felt about the defendant?"

The witness sighed. She paused long enough to look at her hands in her lap. "Tamara loved him."

"To the best of your knowledge, did Ms. Gee's feelings for the defendant change in the weeks leading up to her death?"

"When she got involved with Matthew's father, you mean?"

"That's right," said the prosecutor. "Can you talk about that?"

"Well, Tamara got pregnant, and after Malcolm Angel died, Tamara told a TV interviewer that the baby was Malcolm's," Barbara Tally said. "Matthew went crazy. I mean, completely nuts. So Tamara told Matty she was going to move out of their apartment."

"And, Ms. Tally, how did Matthew react when Tamara said she was leaving him?" asked Nadine Raphael.

"Well," said Barbara Tally, "he verbally abused her. He threatened her."

"Can you recount some of those threats, Ms. Tally?"

"Yes. One time, about two weeks before her death, I heard Matthew say, 'I could kill you. You whore.' And the day before she died, he said to her, 'If you think you're walking out on your own two feet, you're seriously deluded.'"

Ms. Raphael smiled thinly. She paused to let the witness's words resonate in the cavernous courtroom. I looked at Harry and Hugo. They were as pale as the white marble columns outside.

"Thank you, Ms. Tally," Nadine Raphael said in a satisfied tone. "Your witness, Mr. Montaigne."

39

Phil stood and walked across the well to the witness box. I hoped his cross-examination would defuse the power of Barbara Tally's words.

He put his hands in his pockets and said in a very non-threatening tone, "Ms. Tally, did you ever see any suspicious bruises on Tamara?"

"No."

"Did you ever see Matthew strike Tamara or in any other way physically hurt her?"

"No, I didn't."

"And did Tamara ever tell you that she was afraid of Matthew, that she was afraid for her safety?"

The witness was silent. It looked as though she was

organizing her thoughts or searching for the right answer. I held my breath. *Please, please don't say she was afraid of the loud, intimidating, physically superior man who was my brother.*

"Ms. Tally?" Phil prompted.

"No. She never actually said she was afraid of him, but she was leaving—"

"Thank you, Ms. Tally. I have no further questions."

The judge puffed out his cheeks, scribbled a note on his pad, then asked, "Redirect, Ms. Raphael?"

"Yes, Your Honor."

Ms. Raphael stood up and lifted her chin. "Ms. Tally, even if Tamara never told you she was afraid of Matthew, did you see or hear anything that led you to believe that she feared him?"

Phil jumped to his feet. "Objection, Your Honor. Calls for speculation."

The judge said, "Given that the victim cannot speak for herself, I'll allow it. Go ahead, Ms. Raphael."

Ms. Raphael repeated her question, and Barbara Tally said yes, she'd seen Matthew behave in a threatening manner.

"Please tell the court why you say that."

Tally's voice dropped, and she ducked her head as if to avoid Matthew's penetrating blue gaze.

She said, "Matthew has a bad temper. He yelled. He threw things. He made threats. I witnessed this myself. Even *I* was afraid of him. He could be a monster."

I closed my eyes and silently cursed my parents. Like father, like son.

"Thank you, Ms. Tally. I have no other questions."

40

Sitting in the courtroom isn't like watching a TV show, my friend. It's real. Barbara Tally was real. And she'd helped the jury see my brother with his face scrunched up in anger, fists balled up, threatening and swearing at his cheating girlfriend, who, for all he knew, had been impregnated by our father.

That had either been a mistake or Tamara had lied, but Matthew couldn't know that DNA testing would eventually prove that the baby was his. All he knew was that Tamara had said publicly she was pregnant by his father.

The motive would be fairly clear.

A moment after Barbara Tally skirted around Matthew on her way out of the courtroom, Ms. Raphael called her next witness, J.C. Webb. Almost everyone knew that J.C. was a defensive end for the New York Giants and one of my brother's best friends.

J.C. came through the doors like an explosion. He was huge, six-six, 290 pounds, so muscular that he was practically bulging out of his suit. His size 14 shoes thundered against the marble floor.

He crossed the courtroom, put his enormous hand on the Bible, and was sworn in. He nodded at Matthew as he took the stand.

"Why is J.C. a prosecution witness?" Harry whispered. "He's Matty's best friend."

"J.C. would never testify against Matty," Hugo said, clenching his fists on his legs.

I glanced at C.P., and she reached out to squeeze my hand.

Ms. Raphael began her direct examination by asking J.C. to state his full name and to say how long he'd known Matthew and what he thought of him.

"I love him, ma'am. Like a brother."

Harry and I sighed as one. This was going to be okay.

"Mr. Webb, did Matthew talk to you about his relationship with Tamara, specifically, in the weeks before she was killed?" Ms. Raphael asked.

"Yes."

"Could you characterize those conversations?"

"Uh…Tamara went on TV and said she got pregnant by Matty's father. He was all chewed up by that." J.C shook his head.

"Please go on," said the prosecutor.

"Matty loved her. He said whatever she did with his father was his father's fault," J.C. explained. "He said he wasn't going to leave her."

Ms. Raphael paused. She hadn't been expecting that answer. A little thrill went up my spine.

"Were you with Matthew on the night of Tamara's murder?" she asked finally.

J.C. nodded, and the judge asked him to answer yes or no.

"Yes," J.C. said. "I was with Matty."

I could see that J.C. didn't want to be on the witness stand. He looked at Matthew, and my brother held his gaze.

Ms. Raphael said, "Mr. Webb. Please tell the jury about that occasion."

J.C. spoke haltingly.

"We went out, played poker at some guy's house for a few hours. At one point between games, we went to the kitchen for some more beers, and Matty said Tammy was going to, uh, name the baby after his father. I said, like,

'You should quit on her, man. There's a lot of cute chicks out there that would fight for the chance to make you happy.' "

Someone, somewhere in the crowd, chuckled. Whoever it was, I wanted to smack them.

"And what did Matthew say to that?"

"He said, uh, 'I have to take care of this one chick first.' I'm sorry, man," J.C. said to Matthew. "I'm sorry."

So much for that thrill up my spine. Now I felt a hot rush of fury at my brother for talking about any woman like that.

Then I saw the tears of shame and regret in Matty's eyes. This was killing him.

"How long did Mr. Angel stay at the poker game after making this comment?" Ms. Raphael asked.

"Uh, not that long," J.C. answered. "Maybe fifteen minutes?"

"At what time did he leave?"

"It was right after midnight. I remember 'cause *Letterman* was on, and he was sitting down with Brett Favre, one of my heroes," J.C. replied with a smile.

"So the last time you saw the defendant was just after midnight," the prosecutor prompted.

I saw J.C.'s Adam's apple bob. His face fell as if he had just realized what that fact could mean for Matthew. "Yeah, but I—"

"And what frame of mind was he in when he left the poker game?" she asked.

"Objection!" Philippe yelled. "Calls for speculation."

"We've already established these two men are best friends, Your Honor," Ms. Raphael said confidently. "I believe Mr. Webb can attest to the mood of Mr. Angel."

"Overruled," the judge said.

J.C. hesitated.

"Mr. Webb?" Ms. Raphael said in a no-nonsense voice.

"He was pissed," J.C. said. "That's all I can say. He was definitely pissed."

"At Tamara Gee?"

"Objection!"

"Overruled."

Philippe sighed.

"Yeah," J.C. said quietly. "He was pissed at Tamara."

"I have no other questions," said Ms. Raphael. She barely hid her look of supreme satisfaction. "Thank you, Mr. Webb."

Philippe stood, a determined and disbelieving look on his face as he questioned Ms. Raphael's witness.

"Mr. Webb. Did Matthew tell you he had murdered Tamara?"

"No."

"Did you see him commit this crime?"

"No."

"So you have no actual evidence that Matthew lifted a hand to Tamara Gee, do you?"

"No," Webb said firmly.

"I have no further questions for this witness," Philippe said.

Like my brother, J.C. Webb was a football hero, and his testimony had seemed believable. But Matthew saying he had to "take care" of Tamara didn't mean he had. Had Philippe succeeded in pointing that out to the jury?

To be honest, I wasn't entirely sure he'd succeeded in convincing *me*.

41

Court adjourned for the lunch recess, during which time the Angel contingent grouped around vending machines and morosely ate cheese crackers and chocolate-chip cookies with very little conversation. Too soon, the doors of Judge Mudge's courtroom opened and the herd of interested parties stampeded back in.

Harry, Hugo, Jacob, C.P., and I slid into one of the pewlike benches near the front of the room, and within a few minutes, court reconvened.

Nadine Raphael called her next witness.

Troy Wagner was slim, red-haired, wiry, not much taller than me, and looked to be about twenty-five. He wore a very handsome sports jacket, well-creased pants, and good-quality rubber-soled shoes.

He took the stand, bounced a little as he got comfortable, and then made a tepee with his hands. I noticed that the pinkie and ring finger of his left hand were shorter than normal. In fact, they appeared to have been cut off on a straight line, as if he'd run his hand through a band saw or a food-slicing machine.

Wagner tapped his finger stumps and gave my brother a direct look that I thought might be support, or maybe admiration.

I hoped I was right. Nadine Raphael was overconfident, and she was winning. What we really needed right now was for this guy to throw her the proverbial curveball.

Ms. Raphael advanced on the witness stand and after some preliminary questions asked, "Mr. Wagner, where are you employed?"

"I manage the night shift at the Trattoria in the Village," he replied proudly.

"Is that the restaurant on the ground floor of the apartment building where Tamara Gee and Matthew Angel lived?"

"Right. The building used to be a hotel. The restaurant has been there since 1946." Wagner grinned. It seemed like he was enjoying the spotlight.

"Were you working on the night Ms. Gee was murdered?" Ms. Raphael asked.

"Yes," Wagner said with a nod. "I'm on the eight-PM-until-four-AM shift."

"Did Ms. Gee come to the restaurant that night?"

"She did. At just after eight," the witness replied. "She came to pick up baked ziti and a dinner salad."

Ms. Raphael cocked her head. "How would you characterize your relationship with Ms. Gee?"

"She was a customer, but she knew I was a Matthew Angel fan. So sometimes we talked about the game or what kind of season Matthew was having."

I saw a flicker of disapproval cross Ms. Raphael's face. She didn't like the fact that this guy was pro-Matty. Ha.

Ms. Raphael continued, "Mr. Wagner. On that last night of Tamara Gee's life, do you remember what the two of you talked about?"

"Well. She was mad at Mr. Angel, but that wasn't unusual," he said, shifting in his seat. "She said Matthew wasn't the man she thought he was. I said something like, 'Most men would be p.o.'d, you know, if their girl fooled around on them.' She said he was abusive and that's why she fell in love with another man."

"I see. And what else did you two discuss, Mr. Wagner?"

"I defended Mr. Angel. I don't remember exactly what I said. I didn't realize this was going to be important, but words to the effect that he was special, a tremendous athlete, and that this type of guy needs a woman to be very giving and very supportive."

"Please go on."

"I knew she didn't like what I said," Wagner continued. "She got very tight-lipped, because she was kind of a star herself and, hey, I was just the guy who worked in the restaurant downstairs.

"Anyway, she said she was moving out of the apartment as soon as possible—before Matthew killed her. Then she flipped me off. Last thing she said was 'Nice knowing you.' "

My heart sank.

"You're sure she said she was moving out *before Matthew killed her*," Ms. Raphael said, slowly enunciating the last four words.

"Yes. 'I'm moving out before Matthew kills me.' That part's a quote."

"Thank you, Mr. Wagner. No more questions."

Ms. Raphael turned around, but before she reached her desk, Troy stood up and shouted, "I should have believed her! I should have done something!" He jabbed his asymmetrical fingers toward Matthew and screamed, "He killed her, and she knew it was coming!"

42

Jacob, my brothers, and I walked in formation through the front gates of the Dakota, past the liveried doormen, and into the courtyard at the center of the building.

An easel had been set up with a sign reading:

EMERGENCY SHAREHOLDERS' MEETING TONIGHT AT 7 PM
NORTH COMMON ROOM
REGARDING POISONOUS ANIMALS IN THE BUILDING
     —THE BOARD OF DIRECTORS

Well. There was no way we were missing *that*. But first, we had something to do.

At six, we had an early mac-and-cheese dinner in the living room so that we could watch an unauthorized truTV special on Matthew Angel.

Hugo sat to my left on the sofa, Harry to my right with his hoodie pulled down to his eyes, and Jacob settled into the Pork Chair, which snuffled and squealed under his weight and then went silent as the title came up on the screen.

The Matthew Angel Story, in Progress.

The narrator was Jackie Kam, a young newscaster who had only been on TV for about a year but had covered pretty much every big crime story you could think of. She'd burst onto the scene as the first person to report the whole Whitney Houston thing, and a few months later she covered the Kinsey Killington kidnapping trial.

So of course she'd been right on top of the story when our parents were found dead and all the Angel kids were named as murder suspects. Unlike everyone else who had covered the Angel family saga, however, Kam had been kind. Shown restraint, even. While other people were pawing through our garbage, asking our classmates if they'd ever noticed erratic behavior, even interviewing the regular cabbies on our block to see if they'd ever taken us anywhere scandalous, Kam had stuck to the facts. I just hoped she'd do the same now, for Matthew.

The camera angle was in close on Kam's pretty face as

she told her audience that in part one of her story, she would interview the football hero who was charged with murdering his glamorous girlfriend and their unborn child.

"The last time Matthew Angel was accused of murder, the charges against him were dismissed," she said. "But this time, he is going to trial. And it's looking more and more like Matthew will be found guilty. Coming up, my exclusive interview with the New York Giants' Matthew Angel, a man accused of a double homicide."

Cut to: Baxter Street outside the Manhattan Criminal Courthouse, where Matthew's case was being heard. The narrow side street was lined with small Chinese shops and restaurants and brimming with reporters and interested bystanders.

Cut to: exterior shots of the courthouse; then the camera tracked Jackie Kam as she walked down a very familiar concrete hallway that dead-ended at a Plexiglas cell. Kam perched on the edge of the same folding chair I'd used, and Matthew was escorted into the transparent cage.

Cut to: Kam introducing herself to Matthew. And then the interview began. I held my breath. Everyone in the *room* held their breath.

"Matthew. What can you tell us about the last night of Tamara's life?"

Angle on Matthew: He looked as though he'd been

sleeping in a shopping cart on the street in the wind. His hair was a bird's nest and his eyes were red, with purple bags underneath.

"I don't know what happened that night," he said. "I was blind drunk when I got into bed. I don't see how I could have hurt her. I wouldn't have done it. I loved Tamara. I still do."

A second camera on Kam: "Let's say that you did attack Tamara in a drunken rage. What would you have done with the murder weapon, Matthew? How could you have made it disappear?"

On Matthew: "Good try, but I don't know anything about a murder weapon. Now please, leave me the hell alone."

On Kam: back in the studio telling us, the audience, "Matthew Angel's sunny disposition has clouded over. But it's understandable. He is in The Tombs, a very dark, dank, and hopeless place."

As Kam talked about what was coming up this week for Matthew, someone knocked on our door. The UFO chandelier sang its famous song as the bell was pushed. None of the Angel kids moved. I wasn't sure if I could have if I'd tried.

Jacob pushed himself up from the Pork Chair and went to the door. I heard a voice speaking from the hallway.

"Your presence is requested downstairs, sir. This meeting is mandatory. It's a matter of life and death."

43

The North Common Room was packed to the walls, and I'm not exaggerating. I knew from experience that the room was furnished with velvet chairs, usually grouped into conversational circles, and that there were tapestries and photos of old New York everywhere, but all you could see today were the tenants of the building standing shoulder to shoulder as Officer Frank from Pest Control stood at the front of the room. His expression was grave.

"This is the latest intruder," he said. "We're very fortunate that there have been no casualties."

He held up a creature by its tail, clearly dead. It was a huge orange-and-black-patterned lizard, around two feet long.

"Folks, this is a Gila monster," Officer Frank announced. "It is indigenous to the southwestern United States and northern Mexico. Its bite isn't lethal, but it's painful and would probably paralyze a person for a good long time."

He tossed the lizard into a cardboard box and went over to a blueprint of the Dakota that was set up on an easel.

"As you all know, this building has already been overrun by a swarm of venomous snakes and spiders, and now this lizard was found in the bathtub of apartment 2D. These creatures must be contained, and we need your help.

"Does anyone have any information that would help us figure out where these creatures are coming from? Have any strangers been inside the building? Are there rumors or stories anyone would like to share, either here or, perhaps, in private?"

Coughs cut through the dull hum as people talked to their neighbors. Officer Frank passed around a pad and pen, asking for the names and phone numbers of all those in attendance.

"If we can't find the source of this epidemic in the next few days," the man in green said loudly, "we'll have to take measures."

"What do you mean by measures?" our neighbor Mrs. Hauser shouted in her squeaky voice.

"We will have to evacuate the building, tent it, and fumigate it," he said. "Everyone and their pets and house-plants will have to leave for at least a week. Any other questions?"

There were.

"Are there poisonous swarms in any other buildings?"

"Not that we know about."

My hand shot up, and Frank pointed to me.

"Gila monsters live in burrows, underground. In the desert. I'm sure you've checked the basement, but I'm wondering if they could be coming up from the sewers."

"We've considered a sewer connection. We're still look-ing into that."

Hugo suddenly scrambled onto a folding chair. He stood up and cupped his hands around his mouth.

"Hugo? What are you doing?" Jacob said through his teeth. "Get down."

Hugo ignored him. He ignores lots of people. And warnings. And loud noises. And sometimes logic. "I have something to say."

There was a rumble of conversation that hushed as those assembled turned to look at my brother.

"This is my sister," he said, pointing to me. "She's a detective. Tandy Angel, apartment 9G. She'll help you, won't you, Tandy?"

Officer Frank looked unconvinced but said, "Ms. Angel, perhaps you'll consent to being our inside contact person?"

I shot Hugo a perturbed look. Like I needed more on my plate right now. Wasn't he the one telling me to focus on Matthew? But now he had me cornered and I couldn't exactly say no.

"Uh, sure."

There was a smattering of applause. Hugo jumped down, and as the meeting dispersed, the four of us walked out in a clump, surrounded by the rest of the tenants.

"Why'd you do that?" I growled at Hugo. "You should have volunteered yourself."

"You're the Mysteries Solved, Case Closed girl," he said. "I'm an author and the family agent."

I pinched him, hard, and he laughed as he squirmed away from me.

But I was already wondering: What if someone was trying to murder rich people by releasing venomous animals into our midst? As murder weapons went, they were pretty untraceable but not exactly efficient. You couldn't tell them which rich people to kill or when. You just had to hope they got the job done.

As we walked back into our apartment, my phone beeped. It was a text from C.P.

Meet me tmrw am at Brilling. Am working on something I think you'll like.

44

Even C.P. was getting mysterious these days. I sent a quick text back saying I'd be there, then went to my office. I stood in the open doorway and, freshly alarmed by the meeting downstairs, viewed the long, skinny room with suspicion. Slowly, carefully, I moved around the space, opening file cabinets with a twisted coat hanger and using a broom handle to open and shut cupboard doors.

Nothing crawled or slithered out of anywhere.

I gave the counters a good cleaning, straightened books and beakers, and when everything felt clean and clearly uninhabited by exotic guests, I finally relaxed. I took a bottle of water out of the fridge, slugged some down, and started up my computer.

Of all the madness bubbling inside my poor percolating mind—and there was a lot—the thoughts that kept rising to the top were about James Rampling.

Now that it seemed that James was alive and he had tried to contact me, I could hardly stop thinking about him. Could barely focus on anything else. I needed to find him. I needed to get back what had been stolen from us.

Nothing less was acceptable.

The postcards James had sent me had originated in several large and small European cities. I thought of the newspaper article I'd found in Maud's office in which Royal Rampling, Angel Family Enemy #1, had stated for the record that James was in school in Europe.

That could be true.

My e-mail to James's old address had come rocketing back to me, but that wasn't the end, not by far. I put "Ho Hey" on my iPod, and to the anthemic strains of The Lumineers, I typed *James Rampling* into my search engine. The top headlines:

JAMES RAMPLING MISSING

JAMES RAMPLING MISSING WITH WEALTHY ANGEL

JAMES IN EUROPE, SAYS RAMPLING SR

TANDOORI ANGEL AT CELEBRITY "RETREAT"

Ugh.

There was nothing specific about James's whereabouts in any of the articles. So I tried another approach.

I began a search of private schools in Europe, and within an hour, I'd assembled a list of excellent institutions of learning for filthy-rich teenagers. I starred the hundred schools that were within twenty-five miles of the cities pictured on the postcards. Then I composed an e-mail and addressed it to the headmasters of these schools. I quickly translated the note into French, Swedish, and German.

It read:

To the Headmaster:
I am a student at All Saints Academy in New York City, and I am urgently seeking a former classmate, Mr. James Rampling. I have an important communication for him regarding a dear mutual friend in New York, and I would appreciate your forwarding this e-mail to him.

With thanks,
Sincerely yours,
Ms. Tandoori Angel
New York, New York, USA

I thought of the Greek god Eros as I pressed the send button, and envisioned a thick flight of golden arrows arcing over the Atlantic Ocean. Cheesy, I know, but still.

I felt certain one of those arrows would find its way to James.

45

I met C.P. a few days later outside Brilling Day on Eighty-Third Street, where Marla Henderson attended classes before she was shot dead only days earlier on the Bow Bridge. Brilling is in an old brownstone residence, forty feet wide, just as deep, and four stories high. There are only one hundred and twenty students in all four grades, and it seemed like half of them were lined up at the coffee cart outside the building. Not that I was surprised. The espresso smelled like heaven.

"I've already interviewed a few of them," C.P. said, watching me eye the crowd.

"Without me?" I asked.

"I've always wanted to be a sidekick," she said wryly.

She showed me her iPad, five pages of notes from her

inquisition, all neatly organized with the students' names, ages, class affiliations, and e-mail addresses.

My eyebrows shot up. "You're hired."

C.P. smiled and did that little head-bobble thing she always did when she got happy news, like an A in chem or the announcement of some Hollywood hipster's unexpected pregnancy.

"Do you want a business card? Or a silver badge?" I teased.

Her whole face lit up. *"Yes."*

We both laughed and shook on it. C.P. brought up a new file on her tablet.

"I downloaded a complete dossier on Marla, everything I could find. Girl was *smart*. She had a three-point-nine average until the beginning of the second term, and then all of a sudden..." C.P. whistled like a bomb plummeting to earth, complete with accompanying hand-slice.

I winced. "Crash and burn? Any idea why?"

"Check out her Facebook page," C.P. said, opening the app. "Her father died of a heart attack at the beginning of the term."

"So you think she was too depressed to study?" I asked, intrigued.

"And considering that Adele was depressed because her brother had bailed on her for school—"

"We have a connection," I said, breathless. Finally.

C.P. grinned. "I love it when we complete each other's sentences."

I tried to smile back but found I couldn't. A cold wind blasted my hair off my face and I huddled deeper into my denim-and-wool jacket. A few of the kids in line were starting to give us the once-over. At a school so small that everyone probably knew everyone else's middle name, we were decidedly out of place.

"What? You think there's a serial killer out there hunting rich girls with weird families?" C.P. started to joke, cutting herself short of laughing when she saw my stony face. "What's the matter?" she asked, suddenly concerned.

"Nothing, I just—" I turned my back to one particularly intent lurker and lowered my voice. "If that's what this guy is doing, I'm surprised he didn't start with me."

"God, Tandy, morbid much?" C.P. asked, giving me a little shove. "Don't even say that."

She shuddered in her designer boots just as a gray sedan pulled up right in front of us, its brakes squealing two inches from the curb. Sergeant Capricorn Caputo unfolded his skeletal frame from the passenger seat as his partner, Detective Ryan Hayes, hoisted his pudgy self out from behind the wheel. Caputo's gaze was sharp and vaguely threatening. Like always.

"Hey there," I said casually.

"You thinking of transferring to Brilling, Pansy?" Caputo asked.

"I refuse to answer that on the grounds that you know full well I'm not transferring here."

"Who's your friend?" he asked, keeping his eyes on me but jerking his chin in C.P.'s direction.

"Claudia Portman," she replied, slapping her heels together army-style. "Sidekick to PI Tandoori Angel. And you are?"

"C.P., meet Capricorn Caputo, one of New York's Semi-Finest," I said.

C.P. laughed, and Caputo actually reddened around his collar.

Detective Hayes arrived at Caputo's side. "What's up?" he asked, hiking up his pants.

"What's up is now we've gotta deal with two of 'em," Caputo replied flatly.

"Wow. You didn't lie about this one," C.P. said, widening her eyes at me. Caputo ignored her.

"I'm going to take a wild guess that you two are here to 'investigate' Marla Henderson's murder," Caputo said, looking awkward as he tried to perform passable air quotes.

I smiled brightly. "That's why they call you Detective."

Caputo sniffed. "Both of you, buzz off. That's an order," he snarled. "Or I'll bring you into the station and we can talk about this in an official capacity, cop to nosy girls."

"You can't bring us in for standing on the sidewalk, Caputo," C.P. said, rising up on her toes and lifting her chin, like she was all badass. Unfortunately, she looked more like a ballerina trying to go *en pointe*. But I appreciated the effort.

"Yeah, and do you even have any suspects? Or do you just not want to solve this one?" I asked with a pointed look. "Do you not like teenage girls? Don't care if a half dozen more of us bite it?"

Caputo glowered. "Where do you get off—"

Hayes laid a warning hand on Caputo's chest. "Take it easy, Cappy."

"No. No. Not this time," Caputo said. "You know how many shootings we have on a given day in the Big Apple? So far any coincidence between these dead girls is looking like just that—coincidence. But speaking of murder, how's your big brother's case coming along?"

He might as well have punched me in the gut.

"Low blow, dude," C.P. said.

His eyes flicked over her, and for a split second he at least had the decency to look ashamed. I had thought

Caputo liked me, but I'd clearly deluded myself. Or maybe I'd used up all my goodwill with him when Jacob had called the police to search for us. I guess that apology note hadn't worked.

I cleared my throat. "Good-bye and good luck, Sergeant. You know how to reach me when you need me."

I threaded my arm through C.P.'s, and we strolled up the avenue while Capricorn Caputo laughed derisively behind us. Humiliation—another new emotion I wasn't loving—burned under my skin.

"Don't let him get to you, Tandy," C.P. said. "He's clearly an ass. And not even a hot one."

I snorted a laugh and held C.P. a little tighter to my side, making myself a silent promise: The next time I saw Caputo, I'd be the one laughing.

46

I was still burning from my encounter with Capricorn Caputo when my eyes flashed open the next morning.

I blinked in the shadowy morning light and took inventory of my caseload, quickly concluding that I was striking out on all fronts: the murdered private school girls, the poisonous critters, the identification of Tamara Gee's real killer, and—I checked before I wrote this, my friend—I had zero responses to my hundred e-mails seeking James Rampling.

But as much as I wanted to throw myself a first-class pity party, there was no time. We were going to court today, and it was the biggest day yet.

Of course, if I'd known what we were in for, I probably would have stayed in bed.

By the time the Angel contingent had emerged from the cab on Baxter Street, the press was waiting for us. Jacob took the lead. Harry and I held Hugo's hands, keeping him between us.

Hordes of so-called journalists shoved microphones and cameras into our faces, our names were shouted, and rude questions were fired at us from all sides.

"How does it feel to have a murderer for a brother, Tandy?"

I was torn between yelling "Go to hell!" and lowering my eyes. I chose the latter. For sure, anything I said or did would be shown on the six o' clock news, and it wouldn't help Matthew for another Angel to look like a lunatic. So the old Tandy won out this time: Show no emotion. Show no weakness.

The new Tandy wanted to rip the parasites to shreds, though.

Jacob was in a cold mood. He was on the job as our bodyguard, and totally on edge. I was relieved when we reached the courthouse, and he left his weapon with security.

I took a seat behind Matthew while Jacob sat on a

bench outside in the hallway with Harry and Hugo, per Phil's instructions.

Court convened, and not long after that, Nadine Raphael was continuing to build her case against our brother.

Her first witness of the day was Samantha Peck, a woman who had once felt like part of the family. She had been Maud's personal assistant and lived with us for several years. After we lost Katherine, Samantha tried to fill the role of an older sister for me. I loved her for it, but I'd always known she was loyal to my mother first.

When Maud died, Samantha left us and got another job. She and I had exchanged texts and e-mails, but I hadn't seen her until now. I twisted in my seat so that I could watch her come up the aisle.

Picture a thirty-year-old woman with creamy Scandinavian skin and blond hair. That would be Samantha. She glanced at Matthew and gave him an encouraging smile. Then she was sworn in and her attention was captured by the prosecutor.

Nadine Raphael led Samantha through her history with the Angel family and asked her if she had witnessed a fight between Matthew and Malcolm shortly before Malcolm's death.

"Yes, I did," Samantha said. She gripped a heart-shaped

locket, tugging it back and forth along a chain necklace. "I was working in the office next to the master suite. Malcolm was in the bedroom with Matthew, and Matthew was shouting. I couldn't avoid hearing them."

"What was this fight about, Ms. Peck?"

"Oh, Lord. Well, Matthew must have suspected that Malcolm was having an affair with Tamara Gee. This was before her public statement, mind you. I heard Malcolm say that he would stop seeing Tamara immediately."

Ms. Raphael asked, "What did the defendant say to that?"

"He said something like 'You have no idea how much I hate you, Dad. This is just the last blow. I'm going to'… uh…"

Samantha paused and dabbed at her eyes with a tissue.

After a few seconds, the prosecutor asked without a trace of compassion, "Can you continue, Ms. Peck?"

Samantha nodded. "Matthew shouted, 'You need to dic, Dad. You and Tamara both. And I'm the man for the job.'"

I couldn't help it. I gasped, and I saw Matthew's shoulders hunch at the sound.

"I see. And then what happened?" Nadine asked.

"Harry had been coming up the stairs when the shouting broke out. He burst into the room and got between his father and brother. He stopped an encounter that could have become very violent. Matthew left right after that."

My hands were shaking as Phil cross-examined Samantha. She loved us, but she had to report what she had overheard, and Phil couldn't budge the testimony of our old friend.

There was no question: Matthew had *not* killed Malcolm. But had he carried out his threat to kill Tamara? If *I* didn't know for sure, what would the jury think?

47

Samantha's testimony had hurt Matthew, but I was far more worried about what was coming next.

Samantha stepped down and walked quickly out of the courtroom without meeting my eyes. Once the doors at the back of the room had swung closed, Ms. Raphael said, "Will Harrison Angel please take the stand?"

The bailiff opened the front doors and said Harry's name, and my twin slouched into the courtroom. His hair was disheveled and his jaw set. He looked angry.

Harry didn't want to testify against Matthew, but there was nothing any of us could do about it. Even if we'd still had all the money in the world, there was no hiding from the justice system.

The bailiff asked Harry if he swore to tell the truth, and Harry said he did.

"Please state your name."

"Harrison Angel."

As Harry sat on the witness stand, Ms. Raphael asked, "Do you mind if I call you Harry?"

"Everyone else does."

Ms. Raphael sniffed a little at the slight, but she kept going.

"Harry, do you remember an incident in October when your father and your brother Matthew had an altercation in your parents' bedroom?"

"I can't say," Harry replied, glancing over at me. "I mean, Matty and Dad fought all the time."

"But do you remember a specific fight?" Ms. Raphael asked pointedly. "I must remind you, Harry, you're under oath."

Harry lifted his chin. "I don't really know what you're talking about. Only that you're talking down to me."

Ms. Raphael's big brown eyes narrowed. "Your Honor, please caution the witness," she said to the judge.

The judge spun in his chair and said nicely to Harry, "Young man, this is a murder trial. You are required to answer the prosecutor's questions. It's a law, and if you break it, there are penalties. Do you understand?"

Harry said, "Yes, sir. But what if I really don't remember?"

"Try harder," said the judge.

Ms. Raphael took a short walk back to her table, sipped from her water glass, then returned to Harry. I know that my brother can be passive. Sometimes he even seems weak. But when Harry digs in, he doesn't budge. Not for any reason.

"Harry. To repeat my question. Do you remember breaking up a fight between your father and Matthew in October of this past year?"

"No."

"Your Honor," said Ms. Raphael, exasperated. "Permission to treat the witness as hostile?"

The judge gave a curt nod. "Go ahead, Counselor."

Phil shot to his feet.

"I object, Your Honor. The prosecutor is badgering a young man who has clearly stated that he doesn't remember the alleged incident."

Ms. Raphael said, "I'd be happy to read from the transcript of his deposition."

"Go ahead, Ms. Raphael," the judge ordered.

"Thank you, Your Honor."

Philippe sat down again, hard. Ms. Raphael picked up a sheaf of papers and began to read.

"You said this for the record, Harry. 'My brother was

in a mad rage, and he threatened to kill my father and Tamara. He was taking drugs at the time, so I don't think he was in his right mind.' Do you remember saying that, Harry?"

"No," Harry said. "I'm drawing an absolute blank. But then, I was taking drugs as well."

Ms. Raphael threw up her hands.

"I have no further questions for this witness," she said.

After checking with Phil to see if he had any questions for Harry, the judge told Harry to step down.

Harry scrambled off the witness stand and shot me a triumphant look as he passed my seat on his way down the aisle. I gave him an affirmative nod, but my stomach was still twisted in knots.

Hugo was Ms. Raphael's next witness.

48

Hugo looked self-assured and collected in his dress pants, white shirt, and yellow tie, which he flapped a couple of times on his way to the witness stand. He put his hand on the Bible as the burly bailiff asked him if he swore to tell the truth, the whole truth, and nothing but the truth, so help him God.

Hugo said, "I do," and climbed up to the seat in the witness box. He squirmed a little to get comfortable, then slid forward so that he could lean on the edge in front of him.

The prosecutor came toward him, and Hugo fixed her with a steady, cheeky eye. He appeared completely confident, but it was all an act. A convincing one but an act. I twisted my hands in my lap because I knew the truth: My little brother was scared out of his mind.

Last night, Hugo had crawled into bed with me, crying. He was terrified of betraying Matthew and rambled on about running off to Brazil so he could hide in the jungle until Nadine Raphael forgot he ever existed. I'd calmed him down and told him he just had to tell the truth. That was the law. If he told the truth, everything would be fine.

I just hoped I was right.

I drew in deep, measured breaths as Ms. Raphael took Hugo through preliminary questions to establish his relationships and his whereabouts on the night in question. Then she was into the meat of her interrogation. Her demeanor was stiff, probably because after Harry's performance, she wasn't about to take any crap from Hugo. Good luck.

"Did Matthew ever show you a knife he owns?" Ms. Raphael asked, cocking her head in a quizzical way.

Hugo kicked at the half wall in front of the chair. "Uh-huh."

"You must answer either yes or no."

Hugo sniffed. "Okay. Yes."

Ms. Raphael walked a few paces away, then turned. "Could you describe the knife for the jury?"

"It's this big," Hugo said, holding his fingers six inches apart. "It's a switchblade."

"And what did Matthew tell you about this switchblade?"

Hugo's eyes flicked to Matthew, who was watching our little brother unflinchingly. "He said he didn't want to carry a gun, but he needed something to fight with."

"Anything else, Hugo?" Ms. Raphael asked.

I hoped he wouldn't give her whatever it was she was looking for. In fact, I willed him to stop talking. But Hugo and I weren't exactly psychic, and he didn't get the message.

"He said, 'People shouldn't screw with me,'" Hugo said, sitting up straight and proud. "And he said he wasn't taking shit from anyone."

Nervous laughter lapped the courtroom. Ms. Raphael didn't smile, but I could see in her eyes that she was pleased.

"Did he refer to anyone when he was telling you this?" she asked.

Hugo shrugged. "No."

Ms. Raphael's perfect eyebrows shot up. "Are you sure about that, Hugo? You've sworn to tell the truth."

"I'm sure." Hugo cleared his throat. "That's a pretty big stain on your blouse, Ms. Raphael. You should put something on that before it's too late."

"Thank you," said the prosecutor. She looked down at her blouse, then hooked her hair behind her ears and said to Hugo, "Do you remember my question?"

"Who was he talking about when he said he didn't take shit from anyone?" Hugo repeated.

"That's right, Hugo. Do you remember when you had this conversation about the knife with Matthew? Was it after you saw an interview show on television?"

Hugo trained pleading eyes on me. My heart felt heavy, but there was nothing I could do. I nodded, hoping he'd get my message.

"Objection! Leading the witness," Phil called out.

The judge hesitated a beat. "Overruled."

Hugo tore his gaze from me and focused on Ms. Raphael. "Okay, yeah. Now I remember," he said. "Matthew showed me his knife right after Tamara told that TV lady she was having a baby with Dad."

"I see. And when Matthew said he wasn't taking any 'shit' from anyone, did you get the feeling he was referring to someone in particular?"

"Uh-huh. I mean, yes." Hugo averted his eyes from me, from Matthew, from the prosecutor. "He was mad at Tamara."

"Thank you, Hugo. Your witness," Ms. Raphael said to Philippe.

49

"*Hugo, how are you doing?*" Phil asked my little brother.

Hugo stared at a random spot on the floor. "I've been better."

"I think everyone here understands that," Phil said. "You love Matthew very much, don't you?"

"Like, more than anyone," Hugo said. "Sorry, Tandy."

More laughter, some of it sympathetic this time. I couldn't help smiling. The courtroom liked Hugo.

"I have only a few questions for you, young man," Phil said. "Did Matthew ever tell you he killed Tamara?"

I held my breath, suddenly realizing I had no idea what Hugo might say.

"Nope," Hugo said. "I mean, no," he added, pointedly

staring at Ms. Raphael. "He never told me he killed Tamara."

Nice.

"Thank you for your truthful testimony, Hugo."

"But I don't think he would tell me if he did it," Hugo added.

It was all I could do not to cover my face with my hands. Of all the amazing traits Hugo had been born with, brevity couldn't have been one of them?

Phil paused, probably considering whether there was anything he could say to nullify Hugo's afterthought. Then the moment passed.

"Thank you, Hugo," he said. "You may step down."

I almost collapsed in relief when Hugo climbed down out of the witness stand without saying another word and walked across the courtroom floor.

But before he went through the gate, Hugo veered off, ran to Matthew, and threw himself on top of him. Matthew held him as best he could with his cuffed wrists, and both of them cried—Matthew silently, Hugo like a calf being led to the slaughterhouse.

"I'm sorry, Matthew! I just want you to come home!" Hugo cried. "Are they gonna let you come home?" All around the gallery, people gasped and *tsk*ed.

I jumped up, but the judge slammed down the gavel

and the bailiff yanked Hugo off Matthew. He held Hugo firmly by the arm and marched him out of the courtroom.

That, my friend, is what I call a really bad day.

And it wasn't over yet.

50

Hugo was still crying his great big heart out when we got to the street. He turned his face up to me and wailed, "I'm such a traitor! I hate myself!"

"You're not a traitor," I told him. "You did what you had to do. You swore to tell the truth and you did it."

Jacob hailed a taxi, and when reporters began to stampede toward us, I fended them off with a stony "No comment."

I must have looked fierce. Or insane. Either way, it worked.

Harry got into the cab first, then Hugo, then me, while Jacob held the door and stared down the press. Jacob took the front seat next to the driver, and the cab shot away from the curb, headed uptown. I put my arms around Hugo, and he buried his face in my coat. Harry sat with his forehead pressed up against the grimy window, deflated. I knew the feeling. I was so grateful that I hadn't known about Matthew's knife or threats against Tamara. I was so glad I hadn't had to take the stand like my poor brothers.

We were on the move, but as we left Lower Manhattan, reporters who'd been rebuffed on Centre Street put out the word that we were heading north so that by the time we got to the Dakota, there was a mob waiting for us.

Jacob spoke to the cabdriver in Arabic, and the cabbie drove us around to the back entrance. My doorman friend, Sal, opened the back door and locked it behind us. He tousled Hugo's hair as we huddled inside the hallway. Hugo cracked a half smile, which made me feel a million times better.

Once inside our apartment, we peered out the windows at the shifting crowd on Seventy-Second Street. Soon whooping sirens came from two directions and cops piled out and dispersed the throng.

Relief at last.

Harry turned on the lights in the apartment and took Hugo to their rooms to get ready for dinner while Jacob and I went to the kitchen. Jacob had thrown something into the slow cooker before we left for court that morning, and he stirred our hot dinner as I set the table. Jacob poured a glass of wine for himself, then poured a smaller glass for me.

"To surviving the day," I said.

"*L'chaim,*" he said. "Do you know what that means?"

I rolled my eyes. "Of course. It's Hebrew for 'to life.'"

My brothers appeared wearing pajamas and white terry-cloth robes, their faces pink from hot showers.

Fittingly, they looked like angels.

My eyes welled with tears as I sat with our stripped-down little family. Our mother, father, and big sister were in the ground, our big brother was locked up, our uncle was God knows where. But we were in the capable charge of a mysterious man we'd met less than a week ago.

Jacob had made a tasty pot of chicken, rice, and beans, and soon we started to loosen up and chat—not about Matthew, but about easy things, like school, and movies, and Harry's next concert. Jacob's meal was exactly what we needed—comfort food.

I thought he might just be the best friend we'd ever had.

51

As *we cleared the table,* Harry signaled that he wanted a private word with me. We went around to the alcove where the absolutely lifelike, museum-quality sculpture known as Robert sat in his recliner, watching the staticky TV, beer can in hand. I tasted bile in the back of my throat, remembering that awful woman Uncle Pig had brought in here to put a price on Robert's head, like she had a right to all our stuff.

"What's up?" I asked Harry.

"I want to give this to Hugo."

Harry held a small statue in his hand: a crystal seal perched on a marble stand, clapping its front flippers. The Seal of Approval had been awarded to Harry by my parents for a piano recital in which he'd performed best in class. I knew it was one of his most prized possessions—one of the few signs of their approval Malcolm and Maud had ever shown him—and it meant a lot for him to give it up.

"Wow, Harry," I said, squeezing his shoulder. "Excellent idea."

We returned to the table as Jacob dished up ice cream in huge, deep bowls.

"Let's have a family meeting," he suggested.

We took our dessert into the living room, and when we were all comfortable, Jacob said, "I'm so proud of the three of you. And you know what? Your gram Hilda would be proud of you, too.

"I knew her, you know, and I know people who knew her. Let me tell you about your grandmother."

Hugo, Harry, and I exchanged an intrigued look. Jacob had actually known the grande dame of our psychotic little family? This was exactly what we needed. We kicked back with our ice cream, our feet up on the coffee table.

"Ready!" Hugo announced, shoveling a huge spoonful of chocolate-chip ice cream into his mouth.

"She was quite a character," Jacob told us. "She was sparkling and witty and, as you kids would say, fierce. Hilda dressed beautifully and journeyed far and wide, by herself, long before it was considered proper for women to travel alone.

"I heard once that she had been imprisoned in Egypt. She was found guilty of some infraction. Perhaps she'd had the audacity to smoke a cigarette, who knows? That part of the story has been lost.

"At any rate, the family legend is that when her jailer came to bring her something to eat, she advanced on him and hit him with her shoe. And he was so taken aback—or *afraid*—that he just let her out."

"Nice," I said with a laugh.

"Go, Gram!" Hugo said, impressed.

"She had what some would call a secret life," Jacob continued. "For instance, although she lived in New York, she had a house in Paris, and she used to go there in the spring without telling anyone when or how long she'd be away. She was a very romantic woman, and she didn't talk about her time abroad. At the same time, she had high ideals. I know your gram Hilda would be very proud of every one of you."

I could see my grandmother in my mind, her hair upswept, wearing pearls and a long pale dress with a tiny belted waist. She was going up a stone walk. In my imagination, she looked determined and joyful, elegant and strong.

"Really?" Hugo said hopefully. "Even after today?"

"Especially after today," Jacob said.

Hugo smiled and sat back with his ice cream while Harry ruffled his hair.

"Hugo, Tandy and I want to give you something," Harry said. "Something we both think you deserve to have."

Harry took the glass-and-marble statue out of his pocket and handed it to Hugo.

"I won this when I was your age," he said with a smile.

"The Seal of Approval? For me?" Hugo said, sitting up so fast his ice cream bowl almost slid off his lap. Luckily, Harry caught it just in time.

Hugo turned the little trophy in his hands and looked at it reverently from all angles. Then, holding it tightly, he said to us, "Thank you. This is awesome. I swear I'll keep it safe."

Hugo beamed, and the rest of us beamed right back. Earlier today I'd been worried that he might go into a depression or something, like Matthew used to, but I could tell he was feeling better now, and I felt a lot lighter, just knowing he'd be okay.

Whatever was waiting on the other side of this moment—and I stopped myself from enumerating the dozen bad things that could be lining up right outside our door—I knew I would never forget this precious evening at home, the four of us, together.

I held on to that thought as I put Hugo to bed, pried the trophy out of his hands, and turned off his light. That was when my mind lurched and I thought of Matthew.

How could I even consider being happy when my brother was in lockup, facing a lifetime in prison?

52

The following evening, Hugo was running a cutting-edge train simulator on his computer, showing Jacob how fast he could go in the system he'd designed, while I watched over their shoulders. On the screen, the virtual locomotive barreled through tunnels and towns, and suddenly I was shocked by a powerful memory. So shocked that I turned around and sat down on Hugo's mattress on the floor, my head in my hands.

Luckily, neither Hugo nor Jacob noticed. If they had, they might have rushed me right to a hospital, because suddenly I was shaking and sweating, and I was sure my skin had gone waxy pale.

My memory had been coming back in fits and starts

since I'd gone off the drugs, but this was different. This was like a crack had opened up inside my mind out of nowhere and real memories, sharp and true and pure, were spilling out everywhere.

Take *that*, Dr. Keyes.

I remembered walking out of school one sunny afternoon; I saw my favorite brown brogues against the stone steps as I jogged toward the sidewalk. My phone beeped, and I pulled it from my jacket pocket. My heart leapt. It was a text from James.

Corner of 74th and West End. Meet me!

I grinned, biting down on my bottom lip to keep from being too obvious. James and I had only been hanging out for about a month and were determined to keep our relationship private from the gossip girls at my school.

I found James staring out at traffic, hands in his pockets, looking gorgeous in a Yankees T-shirt, denim jacket, and jeans. Everything bluer than blue, including his eyes.

I was wearing a short, flippy brown skirt, a white cotton pullover, and a cut-velvet scarf. I'd used a new shampoo that morning, and my hair smelled like coconuts and rain.

The memory was so vivid I could practically smell it, even sitting there in Hugo's messy, sweat-sock-scented bedroom.

I called out to James, and he spun around. He grinned when he saw me, and my heart began to beat against my rib cage like a spoon on a steel drum. I wanted to run, but I held myself to a cooler pace and walked casually across the street. He stretched his slim but strong arm around me and pulled me close.

I swear every girl in a five-block radius turned green.

"How was your day? Hope you didn't daydream about me *too* much," he said, giving me a quick kiss. "Actually, I take that back. I hope you did."

"You're lucky I'm such a great multitasker. I can daydream about us together in Paris someday *and* take excellent notes," I replied lightly. "So? What're we doing?"

"Wanna go for a walk?" he suggested.

He glanced around us, as if checking to see whether anyone was watching. I realized for the first time that he was tense. His jaw was set, his eyes narrowed, and as I studied him, his cheek twitched.

"Is everything okay?" I asked him tentatively.

"Yeah. I just want to get moving," he said, clasping my hand firmly. "Let's go."

He tugged me across Seventy-Fourth Street, swinging our hands between us, but there was something forced about it. Rehearsed.

And I started to feel—not scared exactly, because back then I didn't feel fear—but curious. Concerned.

I hoped he wasn't doubting the concept of us. Because he was the best thing in my life by far. Maybe *ever*.

As we hit the sidewalk on the opposite side of the street, I swallowed back my own potentially dangerous secret. I had made a mistake. A big one. The day before, I had told Maud about James—how amazing he was, how perfect we were together, and that I'd never been as blissfully happy as I was when I was with him.

I'd even gone so far as to hope that my mother would be happy for me—excited that her only living daughter had fallen in love.

But as it turned out, when I'm wrong, I'm really, really wrong.

53

My mother was in bed that Sunday morning, propped up against silk pillows reading the *Times*, when I slipped into the room.

"Mom, there's something I have to tell you," I said, standing at the foot of the huge bed she shared with my father.

She lowered the paper and folded her hands atop the pages. "You have my full attention."

"I've met someone," I told her. "His name's James Rampling and I think...actually, I *know*. I'm in love with him."

I pictured her beautiful face lighting up. Imagined her opening her arms for a huge hug. Conjured up what it might feel like to hug her back. To close my eyes and feel connected to her in a real way. In a mother-daughter way.

But no.

Instead, she stared at me with her lips pursed.

"How?" she snapped. "How did this happen?"

Then, while my mouth was still hanging open in disappointment, she got up, waving a hand at me not to answer, and left the room in her poppy-covered pajamas. Two minutes later, she and my father came back upstairs. My dad was already dressed in a cashmere sweater, the collar of a button-down shirt sticking out the top, and pressed pants. His standard Sunday attire.

"Tandy, sit," my father said, like he was talking to a dog. He pointed at the child-sized slipper chair near the fireplace. I did as I was told.

"This is not love," he began. "It's infatuation. You are far too young to be in love."

"No, I'm not," I argued. "Plenty of people fall in love in high school. Some people for life."

"You are not 'some people.' You're an Angel," my mother interjected. "We expect you to focus on your studies, and you can't do that if this...person...is absorbing your attention and monopolizing your time."

"But I—"

"And *James Rampling*!" my mother cried, throwing up

her hands and looking at my father. "James Rampling? Of all people!"

"But what do *you* know about—"

"Don't argue with your parents!" my father thundered. "We know what's best for you."

I felt like I was on the verge of earning myself a Big Chop, so I bit down on my tongue. Screw my parents. If they didn't want me to see James, fine. I'd already been doing it for a month without them knowing. I could just keep doing it.

"And don't even think about sneaking around behind our backs," my father said. Again my jaw dropped. He shook his head. "Tandy, I'm sorry to have to tell you this, but there's a good chance that Royal Rampling set this whole thing up—that he's using his son to get to us. He could be trying to get close to you so that he can undermine the family business, the business that will be yours one day."

"Dad. Come on. Not everything is about the family business," I said. "James and I are—"

"This is not up for negotiation, Tandoori," he snapped. "You will e-mail James and tell him that we forbid you to see him. You will not take his calls, you will not answer his texts. And if you see him on the street, you are to walk the other way. Do you understand?"

End of discussion.

I looked up into my parents' eyes, and I knew for sure. If I didn't comply, there was a Big Chop looming, and the last few Big Chops had been creative and brutal. Like Hugo's punishing summer job in agricultural boot camp, for example. I knew they were already devising what they'd do to me if I disobeyed. So I sat up straight and stared straight ahead.

"I understand," I said.

But that didn't mean I was going to follow their orders.

Which takes me back to the most crucial turning point in my life so far. James and me, walking down West End Avenue, hands clasped between us.

"My father overheard me talking to you on the phone," James said. "He kind of freaked out when I told him about you."

"Shocker," I said quietly.

"He started going off about how your parents are criminals and he won't let them get their hooks into me," James continued, looking ahead toward the next traffic light.

"Criminals?" I repeated.

James nodded, squeezing my hand. "He warned me that if I keep seeing you, he'll cut me off. Trust fund. College fund. Everything. And that if I disobey him, I'll be very sorry. I know him, Tandy. He's ruthless. But I'm not giving in to him. There's no way I'm giving you up."

The way James looked at me, I knew he meant it. I paused at the next corner.

"My parents threatened me, too. They said I had to cut off all contact with you," I told him.

He lifted our hands and kissed the back of mine. "How's that working out for you?"

I smirked but then rolled my eyes. "It's like we're living in a police state."

"We are," he replied, his blue eyes going serious. "We've always been prisoners. All that matters to them is *them*. They couldn't care less about what we think or feel."

"Well, that's stating the obvious," I said with a wry smile.

He took a deep breath, still solemn. "What if we escaped?"

"What do you mean, escaped?" I asked, intrigued.

"You know." He leaned toward me, his eyebrows arching. "Ran away."

Run away? I imagined what that might be like, and a tingle shivered through me: Being truly alone with James. Spending the night. Waking up in bed beside him. Making a real life for ourselves. Free from our parents' cages.

But then I saw Malcolm and Maud bursting into whatever room we were staying in and dragging me away.

"We'll get caught," I said.

"Maybe. And maybe we'll outwit, outlast, and outplay them," he said, the sunlight dancing in his eyes. "On our terms."

Our terms. I liked the sound of that.

"I'm in." I smiled. "Take me with you."

54

James and I walked south, surrounded on all sides by speed-walking streams of office workers surging along the sidewalk toward the subway. The avenue was jammed with honking vehicles that shot ahead, then squealed to a stop at the next red light. Horns and sirens blared.

I was quiet, clutching James's hand, as my mind ranged over the undefined, wide-open possibilities. *Running away.* It sounded as impossible as *eloping*—like a thing from a storybook or a bygone era. But this was real. We were making it happen. Together. Right *now.*

I'd never disobeyed my parents on this kind of scale. This wasn't like wearing my mother's tank top or sneaking a slug of vodka. This was huge.

I was exhilarated. And I was scared.

"We should text them," James suggested as we turned to walk east along Sixty-Fourth Street. "Tell them we're going over to friends' to study or something. Then we'll take the batteries out of our phones so they can't track us. That will buy us some time."

"Sounds like a plan," I said.

Except I didn't really have any friends to speak of, so a text like that would instantly raise suspicions. Instead, I told Malcolm and Maud I'd been forced into a study group and was meeting the group at the library. Then we disabled our phones and kept walking until we got to Penn Station, the overcrowded, labyrinthine station that services three major rail lines. From there we could go to Chicago or Miami or Montreal—and connect in those cities to anywhere in the world.

We descended by escalator two stories underground, and James led me to the Long Island Rail Road portion of the station, where thousands of people crisscrossed the gray granite floors to ticket booths and platforms, pulling luggage, carrying children, taking pictures.

James told me to look down so our faces wouldn't be caught on cameras of any kind. He bought tickets, and we boarded our train.

55

The train was a perfectly romantic getaway transport, with its sleek styling and luxurious bilevel interior. I felt like I was stepping into some classic black-and-white film as James and I settled into our double seat on the top deck. The conductor punched our tickets to East Hampton and hovered longer than necessary.

"Weekend getaway?" he asked.

"Something like that," I said.

He smirked like he knew what I was thinking. I looked away because I didn't even want to *know* what he thought I was thinking.

"I'd like to be either one of you for a day," he said, smiling as he moved on.

"Personally, I think he'd rather be me," James said with a grin. He leaned in and kissed me, pressing me back against the leather seat, until I was so flushed I could hardly think straight.

And then my stomach growled. James broke off the kiss and we both laughed. "I think your stomach is trying to tell me something."

He reached into his bag and pulled out a gourmet picnic—provolone and prosciutto sandwiches from Zabar's, with a side of olives and little squares of mozzarella, plus two cold bottles of springwater. We tore into the food as if it was our last meal. At one point I dropped half a slice of prosciutto into my lap and James scooped it right into his mouth and we both laughed. I thought of all those girls at school who ate nothing but greens when their "better halves" were around, not wanting to look like pigs in front of them, and it was one of those moments when I was glad to be with someone who let me be myself.

"Do you think our parents are freaking out yet?" James asked as the train slid out of the station.

I cuddled back into the crook of his arm and sighed. "I know mine are."

But I didn't care. We were going to spend the night together. Maybe more than that. Maybe, just maybe, I'd never go back.

"Do you love me?" James asked suddenly.

"Yes. I do." I didn't even have to think about it. It was so freeing.

"I love you, too," he replied. "I've never said that to anyone before."

It was so hard to believe. "Really?"

He grinned and gazed out the window. "Well, except my first motorcycle, Ramona. But she was a Ducati, so you can't blame me. In fact, I think I might have loved her more than I love you."

I punched James in the spot between his chest and shoulder. Not as hard as I could have, of course. Just a love tap. He winced and laughed.

"Kidding! You know I'm kidding."

"Yes. I know you're kidding," I replied. "I just thought you should know I can punch."

"Duly noted," James replied. He rolled his shoulder back, winced again, then pulled me back into his arms. I rested my head against his chest and felt myself start to drift off slowly, lulled by the even tempo of his breathing and the rhythmic rattle of the train.

I dreamed a dream that was soft and happy, peaceful and safe. A dream that was entirely un-*me*. Way too soon, I was gently shaken awake.

"Tandy, wake up," James said, his voice soft in my ear. "We're here."

56

The sky was dark with low-hanging clouds as we climbed down off the train and onto the platform of the elegant white station. A sea-scented wind quickly reminded me that I was still wearing the tissue-thin clothes I'd worn to school that day, and I shivered. James put his arm around me and we walked out to the taxi queue.

I leaned into him and we smiled and I knew he was feeling exactly what I was feeling: free.

A cabdriver—short and spry, wearing a ball cap low over his eyes—picked us out of the throng. He bounded over to the passenger-side door and opened it for us.

"Got bags?" he asked.

"We're traveling light," James said.

He gave the driver an address and we slid into the back-seat. I nestled into James's arms and watched the lights flash by outside the windows until the cab turned into a long pebble driveway. The black car behind us zoomed past, its engine revving, and I turned to see it careening off into the night.

The cab pulled up in front of a magnificent estate, all white stucco and arched doorways and tiled peaks. The windows seemed three stories high, and the wide porch stretched across its many wings.

James paid the cabbie and held my hand as we got out. "Nice, huh?"

I stared up at the second-floor terraces, the wrought-iron railings, the bursting flower boxes.

"Oooh..." I searched for the right word. "It's *very* nice."

"*Just* nice?" James asked, pretending to be shocked at my lack of praise.

"Yes. The house is nice," I said, smiling. "But honestly, I wouldn't care if it was a shack with an outhouse. Being here with you is what's incredible."

He grinned. "Come on. I'll show you around."

Instead of heading inside, James led me across the landscaped grounds and around the side of the mansion, between walls of evergreen shrubs. When we got to the back lawn, I saw an Olympic-sized pool and heard the muted roar of the ocean close by. And there, right in front of us and centered behind the pool, was a small shingled house with a little porch and quite a few doors and French windows.

James lifted a flowerpot from the front step and showed me the key. He fitted it into the lock and threw open the door.

"After you," he said with a cocky little bow.

"Wellll, I do declare," I joked, putting on a southern accent.

I stepped into the sweet, sparsely decorated pool house. The living room had timbered ceilings, pale blue walls, and painted furniture clustered around a blue enamel woodstove. Two easy chairs faced it, and there were two more chairs at a small dining table near the alcove kitchen.

It was a cottage made for two.

"My friend's parents will be away until Christmas," James said, sliding his arms around my waist from behind. "We can stay as long as we like."

"How about forever?" I said.

"Works for me," James said.

We both knew we were living in a dream world, but for the moment, I chose to set that aside. I was having way too much fun to care.

I crossed the living room and stepped into the small bedroom. The queen-sized bed practically filled the space and was covered with a downy white spread and a dozen pillows. In the petite armoire hung basic clothes of various sizes, stocked for unexpected visitors.

James walked up behind me, took my hand, and tugged me toward the bed. We fell on top of the soft comforter together, and he pulled me against him without a word, kissing me like he'd been waiting all day, all week, his whole life just for this. Our legs entwined, and I ran my hands up his torso, clutching the fabric of his T-shirt against his back.

James's hands were everywhere, and my breath caught each time he found a new spot to explore. My hips, my chest, my legs, my neck, the small of my arched back.

I'd never been touched like this. Not even close.

And I wanted more. More of James, more of his body, more of his kiss.

More, more, more.

Then, suddenly, James held me away from him. I searched his beautiful blue eyes.

"James? What's wrong?"

"Maybe we should slow down," he said.

"What? Why?"

"Because, I just...I think we need to make sure nothing goes wrong," he told me, fiddling with the hem of my shirt, which was halfway up my chest by now. "We need to consider our next move. If we keep going right now... all thinking will go out the window."

He leaned in and kissed me again, deeply, searchingly, and I couldn't believe that, on any level, he actually wanted to stop. But when he broke away again, I sighed.

"Okay. You're right. We have all night for...this," I said. "Why don't we take a walk?"

James's eyes traveled over my body covetously. "Good idea."

Still, it took a gargantuan effort for us to get off that bed, a huge amount of self-control.

I grabbed a cozy cardigan from the armoire and pulled it on over my clothes.

James took a blanket from the bed. "Maybe we'll sleep on the beach."

I smiled. "I like that idea."

The beach. The beach would be the perfect setting for my first time. We'd go for a walk, talk things out, and then we could finish what we'd started. I couldn't wait. I couldn't wait to show James exactly how much I loved him. I couldn't wait to feel what it was like to be completely loved.

As we slipped out of the pool house into the night, I didn't think the wait would be long.

57

No exaggeration, the moment our feet hit the sand was the happiest I'd ever been in my life. It was like stepping out of the densest fog imaginable and finding myself in the rainbow world of Munchkinland. No parents and no pills could suppress what I was feeling. I was overjoyed. I was *alive.*

James and I were walking, hands clasped, hip to hip, at the lacy fringe of the ocean. The night was utterly black—no moon, no stars. Suddenly I realized I didn't want to think about our next move. I didn't want to think about anything. I just wanted to be with James. I wanted to live in that moment with the sand between my toes and the breeze whipping my hair around my face.

I paused and James looked down at me. His breath was short, and I touched his chest. We were idiots to think that just getting out of the house would take our minds off each other.

He dropped the blanket in the sand and pulled me to him. I threw my arms around his neck and we kissed. Passionately, desperately, fiercely...

I was just tugging up his shirt when engines roared out of the black void and headlights pinned us to the beach.

"What the *hell*?" James said, breaking away.

Loud voices cracked like gunfire.

"Don't move!"

"Hit the ground! Hands where we can see them!"

I dropped to my knees and shielded my eyes, blinking against the blinding lights. Rough hands grabbed me from behind and wrenched my arms behind my back. Sand blew up, pelting my eyes and lips.

I screamed over and over, and I heard James calling my name, but I couldn't see him. I couldn't see anything but blinding white light.

Then a bag came down over my head.

I didn't know what was happening, only that I had to fight. I strained against the plastic strap binding my wrists, but it held tight. When I tried to stand, I fell forward into the sand and was then yanked to my feet.

"James!" I shouted as loudly as I could.

"Tandy!"

I lunged forward, and a needle jammed into my thigh. It took two seconds for everything to go black.

58

The sting of a needle going into my hip snapped me awake. I was on the hard floor of a vehicle, hands still cuffed, a black bag over my head.

"Where am I? What the hell are you—"

The vehicle braked hard, and I was thrown forward, my head slamming into the back of a seat. The cuffs and hood were removed. I tried to get my bearings, but the sunlight nearly blinded me. I must have been out for a while. A pair of grubby hands grabbed me by the arms, the doors opened, and two husky men hustled me out of a white van. I went boneless, trying to make it harder on my captors, but they just dragged me across the asphalt.

"Let go of me!" I shouted. "Do you have any idea who I am?"

Someone stifled a laugh. As my eyes adjusted to the light, I could just make out mown grass fronting wide steps up to a Greek-style portico. The building was white stone and fairly grand. I'd never seen it before.

My mind spun as the two thugs hauled me up the steps. Who were they? Why had they grabbed me? Was James okay? How had they found us?

And then the flashes started. James glancing around nervously on Seventy-Fourth Street, like he was afraid he was being followed. The overly familiar train conductor. The cabdriver who hailed *us*. The black car trailing behind the cab from the East Hampton station to a narrow, unlit road.

Someone had followed us all the way from the city. Someone had kidnapped us, two of the wealthiest kids in New York City, and were probably planning on holding us for ransom.

But where were we? And where the hell was James?

A man with thin black hair and a mustache walked over to where I was struggling in the clutches of the thugs. "I'm Tandoori Angel," I told him, resisting the urge to spit on his polished shoes. "My parents are powerful people, and they're not going to pay you off. They're going to call the head of the FBI. They'll call the president, and he'll take their call. If you don't take me home right now, you're going to go to prison. For life. Nod your head if you understand."

Wispy Hair Man smiled and said, "Now, now. You're upset. But trust me, Tandoori. Your parents know quite well where you are, and they are quite happy about it. Mission accomplished."

My vision went hazy. My parents had *arranged* this? "Where is James?"

He cocked his head. "I don't know who you mean."

I screamed as loudly as I could and tried to pull away from the thumbheads who were gripping my arms. One of them had close-cropped white hair and a flattened nose. He smiled as I thrashed and struggled and used language that I'd never used before. F-bombs fell thickly on the driveway and also on deaf ears.

Nothing worked.

When I was bruised and scraped and heaving with exhaustion, the man with the mustache leaned down to look me in the eye.

"I'm Dr. Narmond. Welcome to Fern Haven, Tandoori," he said. "I hope you enjoy your stay."

59

I was taken into an office, strapped to a chair, and force-fed bitter, horrid-tasting medicine. When I spat it out, my head was tipped back and the medication was poured directly down my throat while I gagged and choked. After that, I got a shot in the arm and passed out.

Later, the weaselly Dr. Narmond sat in a chair across a desk from me. I can't recall what the office looked like. Not even part of it. I was fixated on Dr. Narmond—his tiny eyes, his stringy hair and mustache, his long-fingered white hands tapping the desk like he was playing piano scales.

Then the interrogation began. And as soon as I heard myself answering his questions, I knew I'd been doped with sodium thiopental, also called truth serum. It's an evil drug used on prisoners of war so the interrogators can get information. It's also used in psychiatric hospitals, to help doctors do exactly the same thing: gather information against their patients' wills. Bottom line, if you're on a hypnotic like sodium thiopental, you tell the truth and are perfectly primed to be indoctrinated.

Think of me, dear friend, strapped into a chair, the conscious part of my brain reduced to a perfectly malleable chunk of organic tissue. The real me—feisty, nerdy, analytical, bossy, intellectual, sarcastic—had been smothered. Canceled out. And I didn't even own enough of my mind to care.

I answered the doctor's prying questions until he was satisfied.

"Your mind is quite responsive, Tandoori," he said finally, sounding impressed and a tad gleeful. "I believe you will do well with us and will be much better equipped to be a proper citizen than before your visit."

I didn't have enough will to protest, but I had enough in me to hate myself for it.

In the following days, I saw only my keepers. No unkempt insane people, no muttering wanderers or crazed addicts looking to score. There were no gross smells, unless you count the eye-watering aroma of chlorine disinfectant. I didn't hear screams. It was a very quiet place, this home for the insane elite. An exclusive and restful stop for the seriously nutty one percent.

I was dressed in white cotton pajamas and white socks and given a slim little room with a slim little bed and an overhead light that was always left on. My cell had barred windows and a locked door with a spy hole. I stayed in my bright box most of the time, forced into a heavy, drugged sleep. It was as if I'd been wrapped in a cocoon of white light and was waiting to be reborn as something less than myself.

At random intervals, probably deliberately random intervals, I was taken out to a little table near a window with a view of a forest glade. I was given a bib and bland white food that could be eaten with a plastic spoon.

My "therapy sessions" with Dr. Narmond were conducted in a medical examination room. He sat on a wheeled stool and rolled around me as he questioned me and flashed lights in my eyes. I sat in a high-backed chair, and a helmet was brought down over my head. I'm fairly certain that the helmet was wired with supersensitive electrodes.

I don't believe that the point of the therapy was behavior modification. I think the point was information collection. My parents wanted to know everything I knew about James.

Dr. Narmond asked intrusive personal questions that I was compelled by the drugs to answer. I was defenseless. When I was asked about James, I'm certain that somewhere outside the exam room a neuroimaging machine mapped my brain.

And then there was "treatment."

I never knew when I would be awakened, or told to put down my spoon, or interrupted as I gazed out at the fern-floored forest. The element of surprise, keeping me in an anxious state of high alert, was part of the treatment.

They kept me scared. And that made me compliant.

"Ready, Tandy?" was the signal that got my blood pumping, my nerves sizzling. And then, ready or not, I was walked between two orderlies to a darkened room. I was placed on a slab. Headphones were clamped over my ears and restraints were tightened across my thighs and chest and forehead.

"Ready, Tandoori? Good girl."

The slab slid into a short tunnel. A metallic sound bonged, and Dr. Narmond's amplified voice boomed through headphones, vibrating the bones of my skull. There, in the dark tunnel, those parts of my brain that lit up when I had seditious thoughts were zapped.

I heard tiny *zzzt* sounds as my thoughts about James, my memories of him, every second we'd spent together, were systematically deleted.

Systematic destruction.

I imagine Fern Haven was famous for that.

CONFESSION

It's so hard for me to talk about the time I spent at Fern Haven, my friend. But being able to share my greatest fears with someone has helped me already, so I have another confession to make.

While I was there, everything passed in a series of light and dark moments that didn't belong to me. There was dreamless sleep like a white death. I never wanted to wake up, but it didn't matter. I was always awakened by a shot of adrenaline in my hip.

Then came my morning bowl of white food and a view of the ferny glade, followed by talk-talk-talk and static. Next there was being strapped to the slab and a short slide into the tunnel, where my fragile, precious memories of first love were erased.

Then the showers. Well, the showers were two high-powered hoses held on me while I screamed. I never even saw the people who held them.

Finally, another injection, and I was dropped into dreamless sleep.

And that's not even the worst part. Are you ready for the real confession? After days of this dehumanizing routine, I gave up. I gave in.

Does that surprise you? It surprises and embarrasses me. But as soon as I submitted to Dr. Narmond and cooperated with the treatment, my days at Fern Haven got easier. Bruises healed. My mind calmed. And finally, I was released by Dr. Narmond, who pronounced me *well*.

"You're going to be much happier now, Tandoori. If you ever feel anxious, think of the cool green glade at Fern Haven."

Right.

When I returned home, I was basically a zombie. And I had no memory of James or of why I'd really been sent to Fern Haven. I hadn't a single clue as to what had happened to me. So my parents came up with a story.

Malcolm and Maud sat me down and told me that I'd been stressed out, actually on the verge of a breakdown, but it had been forestalled, thank God, because they'd rescued me in time.

Then Dr. Keyes was brought in to reinforce my treatment.

"FOF, Tandy. Focus on the facts."

I went back to school and told the story I now believed. I'd been to a health spa for a couple of weeks. I'd needed the rest. I picked up right where I'd left off, before James, because I didn't remember that James existed.

I got As in school, and since I really had no friends, there weren't too many people clamoring to ask me questions. My daily coaching sessions with Dr. Keyes were going well, at least according to my parents, and I continued to take my special concoction of "vitamins" every morning. Vitamins that I now know had been altered while I was away to help keep any residual memories tamped down—to help keep me under Dr. Keyes's and Malcolm's and Maud's control.

But now my parents were gone, and with them, their special drugs. And now I remembered all of it. Officially and completely. But there were still some things I didn't know. Like when I was dragged off to Fern Haven, what the hell did they do to James?

I stood up from Hugo's bed and stared through the windows at the city lights flecking the cobalt sky. Hugo and Jacob were still immersed in the train game, and I could hear Harry practicing at the white-winged Pegasus grand piano down the hall. No one noticed when I went to my room and closed the door.

I got the postcards out of my biometric-protected desk and took them to bed.

I sat down and read:

Dear Tandy, I swear I can't take it anymore. Not knowing where you are, what you're thinking. Wishing we'd never left that stupid pool house. That we'd finished what we'd started so I'd at least have that to hold on to. This quote is by William S. Burroughs.

"If I had my way we'd sleep every night all wrapped around each other like hibernating rattlesnakes."

That's what we should have done.

I love you. James

I gathered the five cards and put them in an envelope, then placed it carefully under my pillow. I laid my head down and clutched the corner of the pillow near my cheek.

I'm going to find you, James. We'll be together again. I promise. Just don't give up. Please, don't give up.

60

There is truth in dreams, but especially in nightmares. That night I dreamed of the snakes Burroughs had written about. They were sleeping together, entwined as James and I had been on that bed in East Hampton. But as I watched, the snakes shook off their hibernation and rose up. They swelled larger and larger and unfurled their hoods, and just when I was about to scream, I felt the room around me moving, slithering, slipping.

Snakes crawled through cracks, slid along baseboards, dripped from light fixtures. They were all around me. Everywhere. And they were closing in.

I shot straight up and threw on the lamp beside my bed. My eyes searched the room, but I saw nothing moving, or dripping, or slithering, and felt nothing under the blankets. I jumped and tossed my bedding to the floor anyway.

I stood in the corner of the room and watched for any sign of an animal of any kind, hand to my chest, gasping for air.

At last I was satisfied that I was alone.

So what was the truth in the nightmare?

Was there a truth about James that I was hiding from myself? Was there anything snakelike about him, as my parents had suggested?

As much as I resented the implication, I allowed the thought to have its way, let it circle my mind for a few charged minutes, but it didn't ping on a truth.

So I took my mind for another spin, let it roam around the list of things I was worrying about, trying to figure out what the snakes meant. The murdered private school girls; Matthew, who was penned in only a few city miles from my room. Then I thought about the obvious—the snakes loose in the Dakota. And suddenly it hit me.

Snakes in the Dakota.

The Dakota.

I remembered the blueprint that had been set up on an easel at the shareholders' meeting. Something I'd seen there now struck me as wrong. An anomaly.

There was a flaw in the floor plan.

61

I *dressed quickly* and tiptoed through our dark apartment until I got to the kitchen. Inside the freezer, I dug around until I found the last unopened pint of Graeter's chocolate-chocolate-chip ice cream, a family favorite. And I just happened to know someone who was highly vulnerable to full-fat ice cream of this type and at this hour.

I grabbed the frosty pint in my sweaty hands, snatched a spoon from the drying rack, and ran downstairs.

Virgil was sitting behind the front desk in the lobby talking with Oscar, the night porter. Virgil was big, with a glittering diamond in one ear. He had been our personal driver until bad times descended on the Angel family.

Luckily, there'd been an opening for a night doorman at the Dakota, and Virgil had snagged the job.

"I've got something to trade," I said, sauntering over to him.

His eyes sparkled when he saw me. "What's that, Tandy?"

I pulled the ice cream out from behind my back, and the sparkle grew. "A little tub of something delicious," I said.

"Uh-huh." He crossed his arms over his chest, trying to play it cool. "And you're trading it for what?"

I leaned in and told him. He almost fell off his stool.

"You trying to get me fired?" he asked.

"Virgil. I'm Captain of Snake Patrol and Venomous Animal Security at the Dakota," I said, lowering my chin. "I'm pretty sure I outrank you."

"You're funny," he said, laughing. "Oscar, can you take the desk for about ten minutes while Ms. Angel here puts my job at risk?"

"I gotcher back, boss," Oscar answered.

Virgil slid off his stool. "Give me that ice cream."

I handed it over, and we went to the elevator together. Virgil pried the top off the tub and began to eat.

"Oh. My. God. Totally worth it," he said with a sigh.

As the elevator lifted the two of us skyward, I thought through the layout of the apartments on the ninth floor.

Some of them, like our apartment, are duplexes. Our front door is on the ninth floor. Malcolm and Maud's suite can only be reached by our interior circular staircase, which goes up one flight.

But other duplex apartments on the ninth floor have been split up over the decades and are no longer attached to the suites on the tenth floor. Those smaller tenth-floor apartments are directly under the roof, with steeply sloping ceilings and smaller windows.

When our neighbor Mr. Borofsky moved out of 9F months ago, he split his duplex and sold the ninth-floor unit—but the tenth-floor suite was never sold.

What I'd realized earlier was that the blueprint displayed for the Pest Control meeting in the common room showed 9F as a duplex. So it was possible that the upstairs suite had not been searched.

When the elevator finally came to a stop on the tenth floor, Virgil and I walked to the vacant apartment known as 10F. Virgil knocked on the door. When no one answered, I held out my hand for the keys.

"I'm not allowed to go in there without express permission from the tenant," Virgil told me.

"There is no tenant," I reminded him. "At least, not one that we know of."

Virgil narrowed his eyes. He handed me his flashlight along with the keys. "Be careful, Tandy. And return the keys when you're done here," he said. "In, say, fifteen minutes?"

"No problem," I said.

Wrong again.

62

Virgil walked off with his ice cream, and I waited for the elevator doors to slide closed behind him. Then I stood outside apartment 10F, thinking. *I am out of control. Who sneaks out in the middle of the night to go investigating deserted apartments in a building known for murder and scandal?*

But if it was an empty apartment, it was harmless. Right?

My hands shook as I tried to shove a key into the lock. I dropped the flashlight on my toe and cursed under my breath. When I bent to pick up the flashlight, I dropped the keys.

Honestly, I was a hot mess. Fear, as has been previously

established, sucks, especially for someone not used to feeling it.

Finally, I fitted a key into the lock, wiggled it, and turned the knob, but the fireproof door wouldn't budge. So I stuck the second key into the top lock and gave it a half turn. The bolt slid back, and this time when I turned the knob, the door opened.

I held my breath and peeked around the door. Inside the room was another room, this one made of glass. It was like a large terrarium with sliding doors facing me.

What the hell?

I shone the flashlight beam on the door handle and slid the doors open.

I was immediately hit with a tsunami of stink, a smell so overpowering and nauseating, it could only be rotten meat. Imagine if you were to dump a pile of garbage in the middle of the kitchen, then turn off the air-conditioning and leave the house for two weeks in the dead of summer.

This was ten times worse than that.

Bile rose up in the back of my throat and I swallowed it down, trying not to heave on my shoes. Still, my inquiring mind was running over the options.

What had happened here? When Mr. Borofsky supposedly checked out of the Dakota, had he left food and garbage in the upstairs apartment?

If so, he was disgusting.

Gagging, I gripped the flashlight on a level with and perpendicular to my right ear, like it was a spear. Then I forced myself to enter the glass-lined inner room.

I expected to see trash.

Instead I saw a horror movie unfolding before my eyes. The room was crawling with reptiles and spiders. They slithered over and around one another, crawling and sliding and squirming in undulating piles. Terror glued my feet to the floor. If I moved, something could strike. If I moved, I could die.

I stared along the flashlight beam at overturned aquariums and terrariums, shards of broken glass, glowing fluorescent lights that had crashed to the floor. In the center of it all was a heap that looked like a filthy sack of clothes. But on second glance I saw fingers blooming out of the sleeves of a shirt. And then a naked foot.

"Oh my God," I said aloud, my hand fluttering up to cover my mouth.

I had just registered the fact that the pile of clothing was, in fact, a decomposing body when the body started to move. The scream that came out of my mouth filled the entire room. My mind went weightless, and I clung to consciousness as hard as I could, knowing that if I passed out in here, I was a goner. I inhaled to scream again and saw that the body wasn't moving after all. It was the snakes writhing over the body, playing with my mind.

Move, Tandy. You have to move.

Slowly I backed out of the glass enclosure and felt for the front door with my left hand, holding the flashlight with my right. I was afraid to make any sudden movements. My shoes crunched as I went along, and I didn't even want to know what I was stepping on. Finally, the edge of the door hit me in the middle of my back.

I squirmed backward through the doorway and slammed the door behind me as hard as I could. I felt something crawling on my neck and slapped at it, but nothing was there. There was a skitter on my leg. Another slap. Nothing.

Phantom spiders. I was sure I'd be feeling them for days. Shaking from head to toe, I made my way toward the elevator, trying as hard as I could not to heave, not to cry, not to scream.

Focus, Tandy. Focus on the facts. That was what Dr. Keyes used to say.

It had to be Mr. Borofsky in there. What if he hadn't checked out of the Dakota? What if he'd paid the monthly maintenance bill in advance and moved upstairs to the sealed-off suite without telling the board? I could see him stowing away in the building with his venomous zoo, maybe sneaking out the service entrance occasionally to get food.

Maybe he hadn't meant to squat permanently but just needed a while to smuggle his collection out of the Dakota a few beasts at a time.

God. Who kept a collection like that? Especially under the same roof with other people? Unsuspecting people. It was totally insane and definitely against code. Suddenly, I kind of couldn't stand Mr. Borofsky.

But I suppose he'd paid for what he'd done. One of his pets had probably bitten or stung him, and then he'd fallen over, taking some of his tanks with him, and died all alone. And pretty unpleasantly. Then, over the course of time, creatures had found ways out of the apartment, through spaces and holes in the walls.

I glanced at the apartment door, shivered, and jabbed the call button again, but the elevator was way downstairs and seemed to be sleeping there. Forget this. I didn't want to stay in this hallway another minute. So for the first time in a long time, I took the stairs, racing downward on shivery legs, trying to call Jacob the whole way.

63

I was so happy to see the front door of our apartment open and Jacob coming toward me that I practically flung myself at him.

"What, Tandy? What's happened?" he asked, putting his arms around me.

"Upstairs," I said, gasping for breath. "Snakes. And spiders. And dead...dead..."

Jacob held me at arm's length now, his eyes wide.

"Tandy, have you been bitten?" he demanded.

I shook my head.

"Where are the snakes?" he asked.

"Upstairs, Jacob! Millions of them. In Mr. Borofsky's apartment, 10F. At the other end of the hall. They're all over the place and there are spiders and I don't know what else." I took a breath. "And I think Mr. Borofsky is dead on the floor."

I leaned forward to brace my hands over my knees and realized I was still holding Virgil's keys and flashlight. I'd need to get them back to him at some point.

"Come inside," Jacob said, putting his hand on my back. "Let's get help."

Six minutes later, an ambulance tore through the front gates, and while it left its engine running, waiting to receive the decaying corpse of Ernest Borofsky, a platoon of green-uniformed men and women piled out of their official SUVs and surged up the fire stairs to the tenth floor.

I didn't follow them up. I was pretty sure I was never going to the tenth floor again. Soon we could hear banging and scraping overhead, plus a few shouted curses and one unpleasant scream. I guessed the uniforms were caging and bagging critters, tearing off moldings and dismantling cabinetry to find hiding places, and sealing up any egress points to prevent further snake and spider leakage.

Thank God.

Not long after that, the doorbell rang and the chandelier bonged. Jacob opened the door for the investigator from the New York City Department of Health, plus two uniformed cops.

The investigator said his name was Captain Kaplan and gave Jacob his card. The cops introduced themselves, and we all gathered in the living room and were questioned. Even though Harry, Hugo, and Jacob were there, most of the questions were directed at me.

"Did you know Mr. Borofsky?"

"Only slightly," I answered. "Like, hello in the elevator. That kind of thing."

"Did you know about the snakes and other animals in his apartment?"

"Are you *high*?" Hugo asked Captain Kaplan.

He was answered with a serious death glare.

"No," I said. "Never."

"Could he have had any accomplices?" one of the cops asked, directing a pointed look at Hugo.

"Me?" Hugo grinned. "You think I was an accomplice?"

Clearly, Hugo liked that idea.

"Seriously?" I said. "What do you mean?"

"Was anyone helping him subsist illegally in his upstairs apartment?" the officer clarified.

"We didn't know him," said Harry. "He was just

the grumpy old dude who lived at the end of the hall. That's all."

"Any ideas? Anyone?" the cop asked.

"I've got nothing," I said. "But obsessive collectors can be psychologically unbalanced. Or so they say."

"Tandy. What you did took guts," Captain Kaplan said. "You ever want a reference from the New York City health department, you call me. Your neighbors owe you, big-time. You may have saved lives here, and you certainly made it possible for us to wrap up this whole deal to everyone's satisfaction. So thank you."

I smiled. "You're welcome."

Kaplan stood, walked over to the Pork Chair, and shook my hand. Then Jacob escorted them all to the door.

"I don't think I can take being woken up in the middle of the night like this anymore," Harry said, scratching at the back of his head as he rose from the sofa. "Seriously, Tandy. Could you just stay asleep?"

"I kinda like it," Hugo said, bouncing on his toes. "It's like living in a movie."

"To bed. Both of you," Jacob said, returning from the door.

The boys scattered, leaving Jacob and me alone.

"That was sincere praise from the captain," Jacob said.

"I know," I replied, knocking my fists together. "I'm actually kind of proud of myself."

I felt an itch on my cheek and slapped at it. Jacob's brow knit.

"You okay?" he asked.

"Sure." My leg squirmed as a phantom snake slid over my toes. "Fine."

He narrowed his eyes but didn't press it.

"You were reckless, Tandy. But you were selfless," he said. "I'd say that's a pretty good definition of heroism. I don't have a Seal of Approval for you, but I want you to have this as a token of your bravery."

He pulled a key ring out of his pocket and detached his keys. The key fob was a silver coin.

"This is a French five-franc piece, quite an old one," he told me, letting the coin dangle between us. "It belonged to your grandfather Max. He died before you were born, of course, but I think he would have liked you to have this, to keep it with you."

I took the coin almost reverently. "Thank you so much, Jacob," I said, running my thumb over the coin's rough surface. "How did you know my grandparents?"

"I'll tell you some other time. It's a good story, but a long one."

"Promise?" I asked.

He smiled. "Promise."

I hugged him and went to my room clutching my grandfather's coin. This had been one of the weirdest nights of my life—ranking up there with the horrific night my parents were found dead. I would never have thought that this one would end with me being really proud of myself.

But not so fast, Tandy. The night wasn't over yet.

64

Sleep was impossible.

I lay in bed staring at my plain plastered ceiling and imagined making banana bread from scratch, hoping that going through the steps one by one would lull me to sleep. It didn't.

Because banana bread was one of my favorite treats, but the person who really loved it was Matthew. Subconsciously, I was always thinking about him.

"Matthew, even if you *are* a murderer, you're still my brother," I said aloud. "And I still love you."

I should have said that to his face when I had the chance. Now I just sighed. Since I was already talking to people who weren't there, my next imaginary conversation was with my dead classmate, Adele Church.

Adele wore a peach-colored strapless Hunter Dixon minidress, and she told me that, yes, she had been very sad lately because she missed her sister, but that she had been taking medication for depression.

"Who killed you, Adele?" I asked.

She shrugged. "I didn't notice."

Then a gunshot split the air. My eyes flew open and I sighed, loud and long.

"Chill, Tandy. Just calm down and go to sleep."

I closed my eyes again and started to doze off, but suddenly my subconscious flooded with writhing snakes and skittering spiders.

Yep. Still awake.

After half an hour of flopping around in bed, trying to shut off my brain, I finally threw off my covers and went to my desk. I turned on my computer, thinking I would answer some mail, maybe do a Google search to see if there had been any new developments on the schoolgirl shootings. But the second my e-mail screen came up, I saw a name that obliterated every other thought in my mind. For a split second, I swear my vision went black, but when I came to, the name was still there.

An e-mail message from Royal.Rampling@gmail.com. And the subject line read: *Tandy, I regret to inform you.*

Nothing could be more ominous. Telegrams from

commanding officers to dead soldiers' next of kin began that way.

I regret to inform you.

My hands started to shake.

Please, God. Please don't let James be dead.

THE STORM AFTER THE CALM

65

I was fixated on my computer screen. On the name Royal Rampling. At that moment, there could have been a thousand snakes slithering down the walls, a serial killer breaking into the apartment to take out his next depressed private school girl, and a stealthy reporter sneaking up behind me to ask whether I thought Matthew had really killed Tamara Gee, and I wouldn't have seen, heard, or sensed any of them.

I stared at my in-box; then, with a trembling hand, I clicked on Royal Rampling's message.

The e-mail from James's father filled my screen.

Tandy,

It has come to my attention that you are searching for James all over Europe. You will never find my son. And if you persist in this juvenile and deluded quest, I will unleash cease and desist orders and a few European legal remedies that you can be sure will be unpleasant.

My eyesight blurred. Rampling's threats bounced off me like Ping-Pong balls. Because beneath them, he'd revealed the only fact that mattered.

James was alive.

I took a breath and blew it out, tears of relief filling my eyes. Then I got up and walked slowly to the bathroom, where I splashed water on my face again and again until I was sure I wasn't dreaming.

Only when my hands had stopped shaking did I sit down again in front of my computer and continue reading the e-mail where I'd left off.

Here's a little incentive, Tandy. If you stop this delusional hunt for my son, I may leave you and your brothers a small sum from your wretched parents' estate. If you continue on your mad quest, I won't leave you a dime.

By the way, Tandy, I regret to inform you that James doesn't know that you're alive. Actually, he doesn't remember you at all. The memory of your ill-conceived adventure has been deleted from his mind. He wouldn't know you if he was sitting right there with you now. But don't worry. His incredibly attractive, highly sophisticated girlfriend, Natasha, makes him very happy.

Take this word to the wise.

I mean it.

Sincerely,
Royal Rampling

66

One thing was clear. Royal Rampling had no respect for James, for me, or for my family. I saved his e-mail, thinking that his threats might be grounds for a lawsuit, but even as I stewed and seethed and wrote furious replies in my mind, I knew that a sixteen-year-old girl taking legal action against an international mega-tycoon's legion of high-powered lawyers and winning would be impossible. The idea was hilarious, actually. I let out one short private laugh.

And then the pain flooded in.

James was out there somewhere, but Royal Rampling was determined to keep us apart. He'd hit on the one thing that could have trumped my overwhelming need to see

James again—the safety, security, and financial stability of my family. If there was any chance that Rampling would leave me and my brothers something to live on, I had to do what I could to ensure that it happened. I wouldn't have Harry and Hugo thrown out on the street for anything. Nothing.

Not even a reunion with the only person I'd ever loved. The only person who might ever understand me and my insane family enough to love me back.

I flopped face-first onto my rumpled bed and just let myself cry. And then, when I got sick of feeling sorry for myself, I reached under my pillow for James's postcards.

He had written two of them in small writing unlike his usual tall scrawl. The back of the one I picked up now was so cramped that my name and address were almost pushed onto the picture side.

Dear Tandy,
I read this last night in Les Misérables *by Victor Hugo.*

"Separated lovers cheat absence by a thousand fancies which have their own reality. They are prevented from seeing one another and they cannot write; nevertheless they find countless mysterious ways of corresponding, by sending each other

the song of birds, the scent of flowers, the laughter of children, the light of the sun, the sighing of the wind, and the gleam of the stars—all the beauties of creation."

> *I haven't forgotten you. I never will.*
>
> *James*

Was that still true? Or had Royal Rampling done the same thing to him that my parents had done to me? Had I really been deleted from his mind? Had a girl named Natasha filled my empty place? I imagined James holding some exotic, dark-haired beauty in his arms, walking with her along a beach on the other side of the Atlantic. Imagined him lifting her face to be kissed...it was too much.

"Enough, Tandy," I said to myself, shaking my head to clear the images.

I knew what my mother would say if she knew what I was doing right now. This was not productive, this pining over what might never be. And when it came down to it, aside from saving the Dakota from infestation, I hadn't done anything productive since being flooded with these new memories of James. I hadn't completed any of my schoolwork. I hadn't done a thing to help Matthew. I hadn't avenged Adele Church or even worked on finding her killer.

I stood up, walked to the nearest mirror, and stared myself in the eye.

"You *have* to stop obsessing about James," I told myself firmly. "It'll be better for everyone."

Of course, the second I made this declaration to myself, my mind was filled with *him*.

Dropping onto my back on my bed, I pulled the covers up under my chin, plugged in my earbuds, and cued up a recording of Harry playing the solo part from one of Bach's concertos. It would have been a perfect sound track for my dreams of James.

But I couldn't let myself go there anymore.

Instead, I concentrated on the ebb and flow of the music until finally, mercifully, I drifted into sleep.

67

Something was tickling my feet. I woke up with a start, already screaming, and kicked my legs like crazy. My heel hit C.P. right in the forehead and sent her sprawling.

"Oh my God! C.P.! Are you okay?" I demanded, scrambling to the edge of my bed.

"Damn, girl. You should go out for Team USA soccer. What the hell was that?" she asked, rubbing her head.

"Sorry. Today is not the day to wake me up by tickling," I told her, shivering. "I saw a lot of spiders last night. A *lot* a lot."

C.P. winced and sat up. She was wearing a green jacket over a white T-shirt and rolled-up jeans with flats. "Yeah, Harry told me. I guess I should've thought of that."

I yawned and looked around at my bright, sunlit bedroom. "What time is it?"

"Twelve thirty," she replied, standing up and dusting off the back of her jeans. "Harry and I have been up for hours."

"You're kidding! I slept all morning?" I asked, shoving myself out of bed. "Why didn't anyone get me up?"

She shrugged. "It's Saturday. They figured you had a long night."

I glanced at my computer screen, remembering the evil e-mail from Royal Rampling. They had no idea.

"Anyway, the men have gone downtown to see Matthew, and we have work to do." She picked up a sweater from my window seat and tossed it at me. "So get dressed. I'll meet you in the kitchen. We got bagels."

I groaned but pulled on the long striped sweater and dug some leggings out of a drawer. As I shoved my feet into my favorite suede booties, I twisted my hair into a low ponytail. Satisfied that I didn't look like I'd been up half the night crying—not to mention battling poisonous creatures—I joined C.P. in the kitchen.

"Here. Cinnamon raisin," she said, handing me a plate with a bagel slathered in butter.

As I munched on my food, I wanted to tell her about the late-night bombshell courtesy of Gmail, but it meant I'd have to catch her up on the entire story of James, which I'd actually never told her. How could I? Until very recently my memory bank of him had been shot full of holes.

"Coffee to go?" C.P. asked, handing me a full paper cup as I got up from the kitchen island.

"How do I love thee? Let me count the ways," I said, taking a sip.

C.P. grinned. "That seems to be the consensus around here lately."

It took a few seconds for her words to sink in. We were already in the elevator when it hit me. I narrowed my eyes and looked at C.P. as she rocked back and forth from her toes to her heels, watching the lights flash as we headed toward the lobby.

"What did you mean before when you said, 'Harry and I have been up for hours'?" I asked.

"Did I say that?" she asked, blushing.

She was saved from further interrogation when the elevator came to a stop on the main floor and the doors clanked open. Standing there, waiting for the elevator, were a half dozen tenants, all of whom thanked me for putting a stop to the Attack of the Exotic Creatures.

"No problem," I said with a modest laugh. "Apparently, whenever anything weird happens, you should just call me."

C.P. darted through the lobby and out the door. I excused myself from my new fan club and chased after her.

"You didn't say 'Everyone has been up.' You said 'Harry and I,'" I reminded her when we reached the sidewalk. "Start talking, Claudia Portman."

"Okay, okay!" she said, grinning from ear to ear. "I like Harry. A lot. And oddly enough, he likes me back."

"Are you kidding me?" I brought my free hand to my forehead. "Oh my God. Were you here last night? When the...with the..."

Her face said it all.

"I hid in Harry's bedroom. He was afraid Jacob might kill us both if he found me," she said. "This morning I snuck out and then rang the doorbell like I was just showing up."

"Oh, God! Have you two...?" I closed my eyes and shook my head. "I can't even think about saying it."

C.P. nodded, then covered her face with both hands.

"I'm seriously going to be sick, C.P.," I said, and turned away. "Hey, serial killer dude!" I called toward the street. "You can come get me now! I can't live with the image that is now burned on my brain."

"Tandy! Take that back!" C.P. said.

"Okay, fine. I take back the part about wanting the serial killer to come get me," I told her. "But the rest?

This is insane. I can't believe it. You and my *twin brother.* Freaksome."

C.P. rolled her eyes and hooked her arm through mine. "Come on, Tandy Angel, PI. We have an appointment to get to."

"Are you going to tell me where we're going?" I asked.

"You'll find out soon enough."

On our way down the avenue, C.P. told me all about how she and Harry had started out—taking the odd lunch together, him teaching her piano basics, her "updating his look," as she put it.

"Just swear you will never, ever share with me any intimate details of your sex life," I said as we crossed Sixty-Second Street. "I think my brain would completely implode."

C.P. laughed. "I solemnly swear."

She stopped in front of an upscale Art Deco apartment building called the Century, four times larger than the Dakota. It was also less fancy, less spooky, and somewhat less stuck-up, but still on prime Central Park West real estate facing the park.

In fact, the building had a view of the Bow Bridge, where Marla Henderson had been shot to death.

"This is it!" C.P. announced.

"This is what?" I asked, looking up toward the tip-top of the building.

"Our appointment."

C.P. led me inside and over to the doorman behind the desk.

"We're here to see Mrs. Henderson," C.P. said with authority. "She's expecting us."

68

"*Mrs. Henderson?*" I hissed as we stepped into the elevator. "Are you serious?"

"Why not go straight to the source?" C.P. replied.

As we crawled skyward, my stomach lurched and clenched. I wasn't sure if this was a fantastic idea or a terrible one. Mrs. Henderson had endured the death of her husband and the murder of her daughter and had probably been grilled by the police several times over. And now she was about to get a visit from Tandoori Angel, girl detective, and her trusty sidekick, C.P., brother dater? I'd be surprised if she didn't toss us out of her apartment in less than two and a half seconds.

The apartment door opened, and a red-haired woman

of about forty smiled weakly at us. She wore a black dress and a silver cross on a long velvet cord.

"Tandy? C.P.? Come in. I'm Marla's mom. Please call me Valerie."

We stepped over the threshold, and Valerie clasped my hands and gave C.P. an impulsive hug.

"I can't tell you how good it is to have visitors who want to talk about Marla," she said, leading us into the airy cream-colored living room. "Most people are afraid they'll make me cry. It doesn't take much to make me cry these days."

C.P. said, "We're so sorry about what happened to Marla."

"Thank you."

Valerie sat on a sofa in front of a marble fireplace and nodded at us to sit. C.P. and I chose a pair of soft love seats across from her.

"We're here because we want to do something to help find whoever did this to Marla," I began, speaking quietly. "We've been interviewing people she knew—kids from her class, really—but we were wondering if you could answer a few questions, too."

Marla's mother shrugged. "If you think it might help."

As C.P. asked Valerie some preliminary questions, my eyes naturally traveled the room. There were dozens of family photos grouped on the table behind the couch. I saw family snapshots taken in the Caribbean, as well as more recent pictures of Marla playing soccer, accepting an award at Brilling Day, and sitting atop a horse in full riding gear.

But the picture that kept pulling me in was an oil painting over the mantel. It depicted a young Marla blowing out seven birthday candles. Her parents were behind her, bent close as if they could help make Marla's wish come true, their faces lit with candlelight.

The painting was draped with swags of black crepe.

Valerie saw me staring. "Larry and Marla were so close. My daughter was absolutely devastated when he died. He had a heart attack, completely unexpected."

I cleared my throat. I knew something about unexpected deaths. I decided it was time to focus before my head and heart went off the rails.

"Mrs. Henderson, C.P. and I go to All Saints," I told her. "A friend of ours was recently murdered."

"Adele Church?" Mrs. Henderson said. "I read about her."

"Yes. Adele. She was shot just two days before Marla died, and we think there may be a connection," I said. "When we started looking into Adele's case, we found out two other girls who went to private schools on the Upper

West Side had died recently as well, also by gunshot. Lena Watkins and Stacey Blackburn. Did Marla know any of them?"

"Not that I know of," Mrs. Henderson said. "Most of her friends were from Brilling, and she would have told me if she'd met anyone new."

"Did Marla have any enemies? A stalker, maybe? Or a jealous friend?" I asked.

"I really don't think so," Valerie said, sounding tired. "If you check out her Facebook page, you'll see. She had so many friends."

"Valerie, if it's okay, may we see Marla's room?" I asked.

She nodded. "Sure. It's just the way she left it."

Then she put her face in her hands and started to cry.

69

Marla's room was painted in tangy tangerine, with smart white molding and white furniture. I saw a pair of short brown leather boots, similar to the ones I was wearing, lying by the side of the bed as though Marla had just tugged them off and dropped them there. The bed was unmade.

C.P. went to the closet and, after riffling through Marla's wardrobe, pronounced, "You know what? Marla had style."

Photos were stuck in the frame of Marla's vanity mirror: snapshots of sports events, a class play, and three separate pictures of Marla with boys our age, their arms around her shoulders.

There were also pictures of Marla and her father at a varsity basketball game, and one of Larry Henderson dancing with Marla at someone's wedding.

My thoughts veered to my own family, and I know this is awful, but I felt a twinge of jealousy. I didn't have family photos like these. Marla's parents loved her and participated in the things she liked. My parents demanded excellence and forced us to do what they wanted us to do. What I wouldn't give for just *one photo* of me and my now-dead dad looking casual, happy, and unstressed. Really *alive*.

"You okay, Tandy?" C.P. asked, coming up behind me. "You went all radio silent all of a sudden."

"I'm fine," I told her, dragging my brain back to the task at hand. Over her shoulder, I spotted the open bathroom door. "Why don't you get on the computer while I check out the bathroom?"

"You got it, boss," C.P. joked.

She tapped into Marla's computer with the password Valerie had given her, and I made a beeline for the medicine cabinet. The tiny shelves were packed with zit cream and nail polish and contact lens solution. On the bottom shelf was an amber-colored plastic bottle with a label from Giuseppe's Pharmacy, only five blocks away.

Paxil. An antidepressant. I shook the bottle. It was almost full.

Valerie poked her head into the bedroom. "Girls, come have some tea and biscuits."

"We'll be right there, Mrs. Henderson," I called out, pocketing the bottle and quietly closing the cabinet door. I rejoined C.P. in the bedroom. "Anything?"

She lifted her shoulders. "Other than the fact that she'd written like four dozen short stories about horses? Nope."

"Girls! The tea is getting cold!" Mrs. Henderson called. I think she really missed having teen girls around.

Together we walked to the kitchen. Valerie had brewed a fragrant pot of tea and arranged a plate of scrumptious-looking cookies on a crystal platter. As she poured the tea, C.P. settled in and looked around.

"This kitchen is huge," she said. "Is that a pizza oven?"

"My husband loved to make pizza," Valerie replied.

"So cool," C.P. said. I smirked as I munched on a butter cookie. When C.P. got excited she sometimes reminded me of Hugo, like a ball of childlike energy. "What's that little door over in the corner?"

"Oh, that? That's a dumbwaiter," Valerie replied, sipping her tea. "It's like a little elevator. It's not in use anymore, but it used to be for bringing up food from the kitchen downstairs."

"I need one of those in my room," C.P. joked.

I'd seen dumbwaiters before. The Dakota once had

an enormous common kitchen in the basement, where servants worked on meals together and sent the steaming dishes up to their employers' dining tables. The old out-of-service dumbwaiter in our apartment had long been walled up behind plasterboard, but in some of the other apartments, they were still exposed.

My mind flashed to Matthew's apartment and I almost dropped my teacup.

"Oh my God," I gasped.

"Tandy? What's wrong?" C.P. asked.

I got up, putting my cup down with a clatter. "I've gotta go."

"Is everything okay?" Valerie asked, alarmed. "Sweetie, you look pale."

"No. I just...there's someplace I have to be." I grabbed C.P.'s arm, my mind crackling with excitement. "It's about Matthew," I whispered.

"Oh my God. Well, then, go," C.P. whispered back. "I can finish up here."

"Thank you!" I hugged C.P. quickly, waved good-bye to Valerie Henderson, and bolted for the door.

I was about to blow this case wide open.

70

I hadn't forgotten what it was like to see Matthew behind that horrid Plexiglas. Hadn't forgotten what he'd said, what he believed he might have done. Every time I thought about it, my jaw clenched and I felt like I wanted to hit someone. Mostly because I felt like there was nothing I could do to help him.

But now I knew otherwise. Matty had said that if he could go back to his apartment and look around, maybe he'd remember something about Tamara's death. Well, he couldn't go there, but I could.

I got off the subway at Christopher Street and walked quickly to West, where Matthew had lived with Tamara. The streets of the Village were humming with neighborhood denizens: blue-collar workers; smartly dressed, highly paid professionals; artists; and kids who lived with their families in the dozens of former commercial lofts, now reconfigured as roomy apartments. More movie and rock stars live in the Village than anywhere else in New York.

But at that moment, I wouldn't have noticed if I'd careened face-first into the entire cast of *The Walking Dead*, because all I was focused on was the building where Matthew had lived. It was the former home of the Merchant Seaman Society, with a blinking red neon sign over the door of the Italian restaurant on the ground floor.

Matty's doorman was leaning near a discarded armchair at the curb, watching pedestrian traffic while he enjoyed a smoke. He jumped up when he saw me.

"Tandy, how you doing? How's Matthew?"

"Hi, Paulie. It's a slow news day," I told him. "I have to go into Matty's place to check on something."

Paulie's eyebrows rose. "I believe that place is still considered a crime scene."

"Didn't you hear about how I beat the NYPD at their own game after my parents died? Come on. I know you did." Paulie looked dubious and hesitant. "I'm family, Paulie." I jangled Matty's spare keys in front of him. "You can trust me."

He sighed. "Go on, Tandy. But make it snappy. And I want to warn you. It's not pretty."

I took the elevator to the third floor and paused. It was the first time I'd been there without Matty waiting for me in his open doorway. Trying not to dwell, I took a right turn and went down the carpeted hallway until I reached 3F. I stood in front of my brother's apartment door gripping his keys in my hand.

Just last night I'd stuck keys into a lock and opened a door to hell. What was I going to find behind door number two? I took a deep breath, then worked the keys into the locks and opened the door.

71

The locks on Matthew's apartment door were working, and I saw no sign that they'd been forced, just like the cops had claimed. The living room looked just the way it had when I'd seen it last—a huge white space with high ceilings, black leather seating, and six flat-screens grouped on the longest wall so that Matthew could watch several football games at once.

I had the briefest flash, maybe it was even a hallucination, of Matty sprawling on the leather sofa with the TV clicker in his hand. He turned and said, "Hey, sis."

My eyes filled with tears. God, I wanted him out of that hellhole. No matter how twisted and complicated he was, I loved Matty. I just wanted him back.

I knew I had to go into his bedroom. I had to see where Tamara had been killed. I could hardly think of anything I wanted to see less, but I put one foot in front of the other and walked along the hallway. The walls were lined with glamour photos of Tamara, action photos of Matty, and photos of them together, in love and clinging to each other, not so long ago.

It was unbelievable, how quickly and completely everything could change.

When there was no way to go but forward, I made the turn into the bedroom and was faced with a crime scene that had been frozen in time. It was like a museum exhibit of a terrible slaughter.

I'd seen the gory photo Nadine Raphael had held up for the jury, but standing in this room was far more immediate, more real, and more horrifying than any photo. There were bloodstains on the walls and spatter on the floor. The bed had been stripped by the cops, no doubt, but the mattress still showed the crusty brown remains of Tamara Gee's life draining out of her veins.

So much blood.

I could almost see Tamara fighting to survive this attack and to save her baby. Had my brother really killed her, here in this bed? How could he have done it?

The Angels were crazy, but could any of us be *that* crazy? How could anyone not remember this?

I thought of Fern Haven, of Dr. Narmond and Dr. Keyes, and of James, and snapped myself out of my daze. There was work to do.

I searched for anything the police might have overlooked, perhaps the murder weapon. But judging by the clouds of fingerprint powder on the walls and the markers still in place beside the constellations of splattered blood, it seemed that the crime-scene unit had done a thorough job.

I peeked under the dressers and the bed for good measure, and then I went to the spot I'd been intending to visit all along. Like the Century and the Dakota, the Merchant Seaman Society building had once had a large commercial kitchen on the ground floor.

I left the bedroom behind and retraced my steps. When I got to the living room, I hooked a left turn to Matthew and Tamara's kitchen. It was glittering and modern, with glass-tile counters, hardwood floors, high-tech stainless steel fixtures, and copper-bottomed pots hanging from ceiling racks.

There were no knives, of course. I was sure that anything that could slice, dice, or puncture had gone along with the sheets to the forensics lab. But I wasn't looking for a weapon here. I was searching for access to this apartment, a secret entrance that the cops hadn't even known to look for.

I went over every surface, looked inside every cabinet, then did it all again.

Nothing. My heart sank to my toes. It had only been a theory, but I'd been so sure.

I glanced around the kitchen one more time and spotted the broom closet. Saying a silent prayer, I approached. The door had a spring catch, so I poked it with the heel of my hand and it jumped open.

Inside the door was an attached rack of hanging brooms and mops. Two slop buckets, some cleaning supplies, and a vacuum occupied the floor. I found a light switch on the wall and a dim bulb flickered to life.

My breath caught. There, on the back wall, was an old elevator call button. I blinked to make sure I wasn't hallucinating, and yes, it was still there. The call button was to the left of a dark metal frame, about four feet high by two feet wide, surrounding a pair of guillotine-style double-hung doors.

It was a dumbwaiter, and not a small one.

I held my breath and pulled up on the door handle. The double-hung doors split, the top one sliding up, the lower one sliding down.

Behind the sliding doors was the mini elevator shaft, complete with cables running from top to bottom to carry the elevator car from floor to floor. But that wasn't all.

Inside the dumbwaiter, I saw proof that Matthew hadn't killed Tamara.

Not only that, I knew for a fact who had.

72

I stood like a block of stone in Matthew's kitchen, staring into the broom closet at the evidence Tamara's killer had left behind. I double-checked and triple-checked what my eyes were telling me, and I was sure.

I saw what I saw, and I knew what it meant.

Shaking from head to toe, I phoned Sergeant Capricorn Caputo and got the operator at the Twentieth Precinct, who insisted that I leave a message for the sergeant.

"Sarge is so busy, he hasn't seen the sun all day. Spell your name for me, miss, and I'll be sure to get him the message."

"This is Tandoori Angel. A-N-G-E-L!" I shouted, my

voice quavering. "I have evidence of a murder. Put Caputo on the phone."

"Please hold."

Many long seconds later, Caputo picked up.

"Hey, Pandora—"

"I know who killed Tamara Gee," I said through gritted teeth. "I've got proof. And just FYI, it wasn't Matthew."

I told him what I'd discovered and instructed him to get to Matthew's apartment. Caputo said that even if he put the sirens on, it would take him twenty minutes to get there.

"Then jack up the sirens and step on it!" I shouted.

I hit the off button and paced. Would Caputo take me seriously? Would he hurry? And what the hell was I supposed to do in Bloodbath Central for twenty freaking minutes?

I sat down on Matthew's couch and called Philippe. He didn't answer, so I texted him and then C.P. and then Harry. None of them replied.

What the hell were C.P. and Harry doing that they wouldn't answer a text announcing that Matthew was innocent?

Oh. Right. Ew. I didn't want to go there. I tried calling Philippe again. Still no answer.

Finally, I couldn't take the waiting anymore. I grabbed my stuff and went downstairs to wait for Caputo.

You understand that I was manic, right? I could not sit still. My mind was churning with anxiety, hope doing battle with despair.

Would this unbelievably solid clue give Phil the slam dunk he needed to get Matthew out of jail? Or would the new evidence be inadmissible because I'd walked around in the former crime scene? Would Matty go free? Or would he come *this close* to exoneration before being locked up for life?

I breezed past Paulie on my way out the door and was about to call Caputo again when I heard the sirens.

Thank God.

The unmarked car squealed to a stop four feet from the stoop I was standing on.

Caputo got out and buttoned his black jacket. "I put a hot murder investigation on ice, Tweedledee. You'd better not be wasting my time."

"Don't worry. I'm not," I said, nodding hello to Detective Hayes as he joined us on the sidewalk.

I took my heirloom key ring out of my bag and led the cops into the apartment building, past a stunned Paulie. No one spoke in the elevator, and we remained silent until we were inside Matthew's apartment.

I took the detectives to the kitchen, opened the broom closet, and showed them my big find.

Caputo stared, his jaw hanging open ever so slightly. He blinked a few times, then turned to me.

"So what do you think this means?" he asked.

I told him in one long unpunctuated sentence.

His face registered surprise but, to my total elation, not doubt.

"I owe you an apology, Tandy," he said. "You've got something here. And now I'm calling the Sixth Precinct. They're gonna reopen this crime scene, and you have to skedaddle. Pronto."

73

I was shocked.

Number one, Caputo had *apologized* to me. That was a first.

Number two, he'd called me by my actual name.

Number three, he'd told me to leave my brother's apartment after I had just done his job for him.

"I'm not leaving, Caputo. I'll stand off to the side and I won't say a word, but I think I've earned—"

"You can't stay here, Tandy. Not if you want this evidence to count for something," Caputo said gruffly. "I'm going to downplay your presence here for your brother's sake. Okay? And still, I'm making you no promises."

"Fine. If it's for Matthew." I took out my phone and snapped a few shots of the dumbwaiter for Philippe.

"Keep me posted."

I reluctantly walked out onto the street, where I found Paulie in the wing chair, watching girls, smoking.

"Can I get a drag?" I said, gesturing at his cigarette. I didn't smoke, but it seemed like an appropriate moment to start.

He handed it over.

I puffed, then coughed. For the millionth time I wondered at the mystique of smoking tobacco. Tastes nasty and ruins your health. I just didn't get it. I spat a flake of tobacco off my tongue and handed the cigarette back to Paulie.

He said, "Everything okay, Tandy?"

"Absolutely," I said. "Never better."

"What the hell is going on up there?" he asked, glancing toward the third floor.

"Only good things," I told him. "At least, I hope."

He nodded, as if he understood my cryptic words. "Tell Matthew I said to hang tough. I'm rooting for him."

"Will do."

I had a MetroCard and about eight dollars in singles, so I joined the herd jogging down the steps to the Christopher

Street subway platform and caught the 1 train. I found a seat near the conductor's door and suddenly wondered if my silver franc was safe. Had I mistakenly handed it to Caputo? I dug around in my bag, kind of panicked until I touched the coin. Yes, it was there.

As I was retracting my hand, I brushed the pill bottle I'd taken from Marla Henderson's medicine cabinet.

While the subway car rattled and rolled, I studied the small amber bottle. According to the label from Giuseppe's Pharmacy, Marla was on her first month of the prescription antidepressant, with one refill left to go.

I wondered if Adele Church had also been on antidepressants and, if so, whether she'd gotten her prescription filled at Giuseppe's. Granted, there wasn't much chance I could ferret out this information, and if I could, what would it mean?

Giuseppe's Pharmacy was on my way home. I could stop there and still be home before curfew. And besides, after finding Mr. Borofsky last night and the evidence in the dumbwaiter today, I was kind of on a roll.

Might as well see where it would take me. Right?

74

Giuseppe's Pharmacy is on Sixty-Eighth and Columbus, only four short blocks and an avenue over from the Dakota, set back and nestled between two high-rise apartment buildings. It's small and old-fashioned, way different from the big chain drugstores. I'd passed it many times, but I'd never been inside.

I'll admit I didn't have a plan. You could almost call my stop at Giuseppe's a distraction from thinking about the cops going through Matthew's apartment and having to trust them with evidence that might be Matthew's last lifeline.

I got out of the subway at the Lincoln Center stop and walked quickly to Giuseppe's. Out front, a gangly boy, about nineteen or so, was sweeping the sidewalk.

He had bad skin, a straggly soul patch, and running shoes that he'd worn to death, but he had a nice smile and held the door for me.

"We're closing in about ten minutes," he said. "Better hurry up."

I thanked him and walked through the center aisle of the store, past shampoos and skin-care products, and arrived at the back, where the pharmacist was working behind his high counter.

He had white hair and a matching jacket with his name stitched in blue over the pocket: ALAN. The man looked up, pushed his glasses to the top of his head, and said, "I can't fill a prescription for you tonight, you understand. You'll have to pick it up tomorrow."

I held up the pill bottle in my hand, shook it, and said, "A friend of mine takes this. Paxil."

"And?"

"Well, I'm pretty jittery, and Marla told me it really helps her focus. And I was wondering—"

I paused as the scraggly helper guy came to the back of the store and said to the pharmacist, "I put the newspapers away and I'm done sweeping the walk, Alan. I can lock up when you're ready."

"Thanks, Gary," Alan said with a nod. "You were saying, young lady?"

"Marla likes Paxil, and I have another friend Adele. I think she gets her Paxil here, too," I said, fishing for a connection, just casting my line. "I was wondering if you know Marla and Adele," I rambled on, following a hunch, "and if you can tell me if they, or really anyone, had any side effects from this. Before I ask my doctor for a prescription."

Alan narrowed his eyes and gave me a curious look. Granted, it was kind of a strange set of questions. "May I see that bottle?" he asked.

I handed it over, and he snatched it, put it in his drawer, and slammed the drawer shut.

"I'm sure you know it's dangerous to take someone else's prescription drugs, miss. Now off you go. We're closing up."

Great. I was being booted out. Again.

I didn't say a word. Just spun on my little boot heels and strode out of Giuseppe's. Outside, I took a deep breath and sighed. It'd been a long shot, anyway.

I glanced at my watch and my eyes widened. How had it gotten so late? If I wasn't home in a minute, I was going to be in serious trouble.

75

The traffic light was against me on Sixty-Ninth, so I crossed over to the park side of CPW and kept up my pace, stepping around a dog walker coming toward me with a yappy pack on twisted leashes.

It was after I was clear of the dogs that I thought I felt someone behind me. I turned my head casually and saw a man maybe fifteen feet back and holding steady. This was a public sidewalk, of course, and a fellow traveler on the dark side of the street was not exactly weird. But still, I felt uncomfortable.

There's a low stone wall that runs between Central Park and the sidewalk. At Sixty-Ninth Street, there's a break in the wall for a pedestrian walkway that leads straight into the park. I took this detour, hoping the guy would just keep walking straight.

Guess what? He turned into the park, closing the distance between us. Was I paranoid, or was I in trouble?

I walked up a little rise and veered to the left onto a path I'd walked many times before. But this was different. It was getting dark, and I was nervous.

The walkway was descending now to where it intersects with a bridle path. Just beyond the path is a two-lane road that loops around the park. There was a steady stream of cars on the road, their headlights cutting through the deepening dusk.

I kept walking, faster now, heading north toward home. I looked both ways and behind me. I didn't see the man anymore, or anything else suspicious, but still, as I crossed the road, I grabbed at my shoulder bag, feeling for the outside pocket where I kept my phone.

I whipped it out and, still walking, sent a text.

Ahead of me was an outcropping of batholithic rock, overgrown in some places with grass, within view of a statue called *The Falconer*.

Harry and I sometimes went there to sunbathe.

I climbed this knoll because it was a pretty good lookout. If anyone was coming for me, I'd see them. I was surrounded by a stand of six trees ahead of me and six behind me. Through the trees, I could see the Dakota only a few short blocks away across the avenue. I could actually pick out the lights in our apartment.

I took a few moments to catch my breath and was gathering myself to run home when I felt a stunning crack at the back of my head, followed by radiating pain.

I grabbed air, then went down and rolled to the foot of the slope. I covered my head as I grappled with the inescapable fact that my attacker was right behind me.

And then he was standing right over me.

I peered through my fingers and saw his face. I was seeing double, but I recognized him. It was the guy from the pharmacy, the scraggly teen who had opened the door for me.

Gary.

He'd had a nice smile then, but now his smile was cruel and cold and his eyes totally black, as if his sockets were empty.

I was terrified, but I refused to whimper or scream or beg. Cowering encourages tormenters and makes them even more aggressive. I couldn't show fear.

"I heard you asking Alan about those dead girls," he said with a sneer. "Your parents should have taught you to not be so inquisitive."

He could have been right. After all, this wasn't the first

time I'd been harshly punished for being inquisitive. *Especially* by my parents.

"You're about to take your last breath," Gary said. "Sound like a plan?"

"Not a very good one. We can do better," I told him, my heart pounding in my temples. "Help me up. If we put our heads together, I'm sure we can come up with something."

"You're not funny."

"So I've heard."

He leaned down, and for a brief, surreal moment, I actually thought he was going to reach out his hand and help me up. Then I saw the gun.

76

As my gaze fixed on the black eye of the gun barrel, time stretched so that each second broke into a hundred little fragments, each one amazingly sharp and clear.

I saw Gary's finger on the trigger and I knew that this was the man who had murdered at least four girls like me, in places not far from where I lay in leaf mold and lichen at the foot of an outcropping.

I was sure he had followed them from the pharmacy, tracked them through the trees, and waited for an opportunity. I visualized each of the dead girls' faces: Stacey, Lena, Adele, and Marla, and knew I was the next in line. That this was the last moment of my life.

Still, I had questions: Why hadn't Gary just shot me from behind?

Why didn't he pull the trigger now?

Maybe he wanted to draw out the moment because he was having a good time. Maybe he got off on watching my terror.

My fractured thoughts shot out to Harry and Matthew and Hugo and C.P. and Jacob. And I thought of James. I thought about my life ending, here and now, before I'd had a chance to really live, to find out who I was going to be.

That was too unfair. I couldn't die now.

Something inside me snapped and instinct took over.

"Please don't hurt me," I said. "I have a family who needs me. I swear I won't tell anyone what I know."

"What you *think* you know," Gary spat.

"Exactly! I actually know nothing!" I rambled, my eyes wider. "Nothing about anything at all."

Gary tightened his grip on the gun, and my mind just went blank. I tried to scream, but my throat was rigid and gagged by fear.

"*Noooo*," I croaked.

He laughed. "Well, if that's all you have to say, time's up—"

And then my throat unlocked. I let loose a loud, shrill banshee shriek that could have been heard over the traffic on the road. Suddenly the gun and Gary's looming face jerked violently back, as if I'd blown him away with the force of my scream.

I sat up and saw that a second figure had joined us in the little copse of trees. A man had Gary on the ground and was sitting astride him, hitting him again and again with his fists. Gary screamed as I had done, and I saw him try to protect his face from the storm of blows.

With a brilliant shock of relief, I recognized his attacker.

It was Jacob.

He had gotten my text.

Come quick. I'm on the rock near the Falconer.

And now Jacob was on his feet, kicking Gary again and again and again. In the fight between a nineteen-year-old loser and a highly trained military commando, the loser had no chance.

Gary groaned and foamed and pleaded with Jacob to stop. And finally, Jacob did. He twisted the killer's arm around, pulled it up high on his back, and sat on him hard.

I stared through the gloom, utterly transfixed, until Jacob called out to me, "Tandy? Tandy, would you mind calling the police?"

77

The name of the boy who had just tried to kill me was Gary Semel. Because of the beating he'd taken from Jacob, he had broken ribs and a busted nose and probably internal injuries.

I hoped Gary was in serious pain and suffering a lot.

Caputo bent down to where I sat on the ground. "Christ, Tandy. Look at you."

"What're you doing here?" I demanded, wincing as I turned my head. "Shouldn't you be at—"

"I left the other crime scene in the capable hands of the Sixth Precinct," Caputo said. He put a calming hand on my shoulder. I stared at it, surprised that he was capable of being that gentle. "Not that I don't enjoy having you wrap up my cases and making me look bad, but if you get injured or, God forbid, killed, I'll never forgive myself," he said. "That's the truth, by the way. So take care of yourself, Tandy. Please."

Detectives Caputo and Hayes took possession of Gary's gun and arrested him for assault with a deadly weapon. Then they cuffed him and stuffed him into the first of the two ambulances idling nearby, got in after him, and raced toward Roosevelt Hospital.

"Can we go home now?" I asked Jacob, wincing as a fresh stab of pain slammed through my skull.

"We have to get you to a hospital to be checked out," Jacob replied.

"You've been pistol-whipped, miss," one of the EMTs told me. "That's no joke. You don't want to take chances with a blow to the head."

So I was placed on a gurney and loaded into the second ambulance. Jacob climbed up, took a seat on the bench beside me, and held my hand.

I don't love clichés, but there are times when the only way to say something is the way it's been said hundreds of times before.

"You saved my life, Jacob," I said. "I don't know how to thank you."

There were tears in Jacob's eyes. "Just doing my job," he replied.

"Your job? You're supposed to be our babysitter, but you keep risking your life for us. It's insane. Uncle Peter can't be paying you enough."

He smiled, then bent over and kissed my forehead.

"Who said I'm being paid?"

I blinked. "What?"

"Close your eyes, will you? Focus on your breathing. Try to calm yourself."

Believe it or not, I did as I was told. I chilled for the next two minutes, but my eyes snapped open as I was being jostled, unloaded, and then rolled through the ambulance bay and into the emergency room.

Jacob kept his hand on the rail of my gurney as he gave the nurse my information. I was rolled into a curtained stall, where another nurse undressed me and helped me into a paper robe.

I flashed on Fern Haven, of course. How could I not? Here I was, in a small enclosure, all white, with overhead lights and a narrow bed. I yelled for Jacob, and he parted the curtain.

"I'm here. I'm right here."

A young Dr. Magnifico asked me questions, and I

admitted I had suffered double vision for a minute. I confessed to brief paralysis. I said my head still hurt. The doctor put his moving finger in front of my face and asked me to follow it with my eyes. I tried to do it.

"Let's not take any chances," he said.

Panic flared as I was strapped onto another gurney and wheeled down a corridor, then lifted onto a slab at the mouth of a high-tech machine. I was given a dye injection, and then a nurse came toward me with headphones. I jerked away as if she was holding a flamethrower. Or a snake.

"You need to wear these so we can talk to you, Tandy, during the CT scan."

"No! I don't want this!" I shouted, my head pounding. "I won't do it!"

The nurse looked at Jacob.

"Just give us a minute," he said to her. "Please."

78

I couldn't breathe. Sweat poured from my hairline down my temples and pooled in my ears. In my mind, I was back with Dr. Narmond in the CT scan room. I could hear those piercing buzzes that were zapping and burning my memories away.

"Don't let them," I wheezed to Jacob.

"This isn't Fern Haven, Tandy. This is just a hospital. You do have a hard head. We all know that. But if that guy clocked you with enough force—"

"It's just a headache," I pleaded. "Give me some Tylenol and let's get out of here."

"I'm going to be right here."

Jacob wheeled over a stool and sat down next to me. When I turned my head, his eyes were on a level with mine.

"I wanted to take care of you and your brothers," he said, gripping my hand. "We're the same flesh and blood, Tandy. You and your brothers and Peter and your father and I. We're family."

"What?" I asked.

He smiled and touched my forehead, his skin cool against my burning, panicked flesh.

"Jacob, what the hell are you saying?"

Jacob laughed. In fact, he suddenly couldn't stop laughing.

"Stop it!" I barked. "Stop laughing and talk!"

He almost got the laugh under control, but not quite. He took a deep breath. "I'm sorry. I'm just so glad you're okay. You really are a remarkable girl, Tandy."

"Thanks," I said. "Now start talking."

"What I was awkwardly trying to say is that I'm your uncle."

"No," I replied. "No, you're not."

His eyes glittered with amusement. "Actually, yes. Yes, I am."

I stared at Jacob, the CT forgotten, my mouth agape.

"How, exactly?" I asked shrilly.

"Your gram Hilda was my mother. I have a different

father than Malcolm and Peter, so they're my half brothers," he explained. "That's the short version."

I must have blinked two hundred times just trying to process this information. My father had another brother and had never told us? How was that possible? How many other long-lost relatives slash Israeli commandos did we have walking around? "I don't want the short version. I want the long one. The supersized one. The IMAX, 3-D, cross-your-eyes version."

"We really should get started," the nurse said, stepping back into the room.

"Five minutes," he told her. "We just need five minutes." She slipped away quietly, and Jacob told his story.

"When your grandmother was seventeen, just a little older than you are now, she went to a farm commune in what is now Israel, known as a kibbutz. It was quite the vacation for Hilda. She fell in love, got pregnant, and gave birth to a baby boy. A very cute one, if you ask me. Named him Jacob."

"Cute? Yeah, right. I bet all the other babies were terrified of you."

Jacob laughed, then continued. "Well, when Hilda had to go back to New York, there was a lot of talking about what to do with the awkward situation known as *me*, but in the end, it was decided that I would stay on the kibbutz with my father, Ezra Perlman, and the rest of my family.

"Hilda left, and a few years later, she married Max Angel, and they had your father and uncle, but she stayed in constant touch with the Israeli branch of the family. And when she died, my story was passed along to my brothers. When your parents died, Peter contacted me, and I made plans to come to New York."

"You dropped everything and came here for us?" I asked. "Why?"

"Because you're my family. And that means something to me," he said. "I had to make sure you were all going to be okay."

I felt a pang in my heart and tears filled my eyes. Someone who actually cared about family, no matter what? How could this guy share any DNA with my father? "Why didn't you tell us from the beginning?"

"I should have, Tandy," he said with a sigh. "But I really didn't know your father or Peter. And what I did know of them made me think that you kids would probably be... a lot like them. I didn't think we would get along, and I didn't know if I'd be staying beyond helping you all get settled in your new lives. I thought it might be easier on all of us if we kept our distance."

Distance. Spoken like a true Angel.

"But, Tandy," Jacob added, "please believe me when I

say that now that I know you guys, I love you all more than I could ever have imagined. You've enriched my life."

My tears spilled over then, and I sucked in a deep, broken breath. "We love you, too." I laughed and sobbed at the same time. "Oh my God, the boys are gonna freak."

Jacob smiled and squeezed my hand again, and when the nurse came back in, I realized I felt safe. I stayed perfectly still during the entire scan because I knew that my uncle Jacob was behind a wall, watching me through a window and that he was waiting to take me home.

79

The courtroom was packed tight, wall to wall, standing room only. Everyone with a connection to the court, anyone with a press pass, anybody with an interest in Matthew Angel or murder trials had lined up early, eager to hear the closing arguments in the case against my brother.

Matty's family fan club was there, too, and we took up the entire row behind the defense table—me, Hugo, Harry, Jacob, and C.P., plus Virgil. Mrs. Hauser from the eighth floor was stationed behind us next to Paulie, who had finagled a day off so that he could attend.

Across the aisle, behind the prosecution table, sat the Tamara Gee contingent: her family and fans, who believed she'd been coldly and brutally slashed and stabbed to death by her boyfriend.

Closing arguments were to begin in just a few minutes. Nadine Raphael would tell the jurors why my brother was guilty of killing Tamara Gee and their unborn child, guilty beyond a reasonable doubt. Then Philippe Montaigne would say that Matthew was innocent and that the prosecution hadn't proved its case.

This was to be the climax of the last two weeks of Matthew's stomach-churning murder trial, but I was pretty sure it wasn't going to be the climax that the prosecution was expecting.

At least, I hoped it wasn't.

The buzz in the courtroom hushed as the judge came in through the back door and ascended to the bench. Normally, at this point in the proceedings, Judge Mudge would review his notes, speak with the bailiff about court business, and make sure all the key parties were present. When administrative court duties were squared away, the bailiff would bring in the jury and court would be convened.

Today was entirely different.

The judge came in. Phil got to his feet, handsome as ever but with a different look in his eye than I'd seen since the trial began. Today he was confident.

"Your Honor," Phil said. "Permission to approach the bench."

"Okay, but keep it simple, Counselor. We've got a full day ahead of us. Ms. Raphael, please join us."

Nadine Raphael didn't look pleased, but I'd only ever seen her happy when she had her foot on Matthew's throat. She was salivating to put him away—and annoyed that her euphoria was being postponed.

I grasped Harry's hand as Ms. Raphael and Phil walked over to the bench and Phil began to whisper to the judge. When the judge's face registered surprise, my heart leapt. Nadine Raphael's body went rigid. Suddenly, their voices rose as the defense and the prosecution talked over each other. A few snippets were heard clearly by everyone in the crowd.

"This is an act of sheer desperation, Your Honor," said Ms. Raphael.

Then Phil said something that included the phrase *offer of proof.*

I glanced at Hugo. His chin was tipped up as he tried to see the judge's face, and he looked about to burst out of his suit. There was more back-and-forth between the lawyers and the judge, who finally had enough. His voice carried when he said, "I'll see counsel and the parties in chambers."

Then he looked directly at me.

"You, too, young lady. Now."

80

Judge Mudge's office was arranged around a modern desk made of twisting wood and glass. Two ergonomic chairs faced it, and photographic studies of natural objects like leaves and vegetables blown up almost beyond recognition, adorned the walls.

Sergeant Caputo held the door open for me, and we were followed in by Phil and Ms. Raphael. The judge took his chair behind the desk. Everyone else stood.

I was glancing around, wondering what was going on, when the bailiff brought Matthew into the office. My heart did a happy dance at the sight of him, even though he looked as tired and haggard as usual. He shot me a curious glance, and I signaled him to just wait.

This was going to be *amazing*.

"Defense counsel has asked to present new witnesses, and at this point in the proceedings, I can't let him introduce new testimony to the jury without my hearing it first," the judge began. "Now, Sergeant Caputo, put your hand on my Bible. Do you swear to tell the truth, the whole truth, and nothing but the truth, so help you God?"

Caputo did. Then the judge asked Caputo, "Sergeant, did you go to Matthew Angel's apartment this past Saturday?"

"Yes, I did."

"And why did you do that?"

"Ms. Angel, the defendant's sister, went there to check for any personal items the defendant might want," Caputo explained, glancing over at me. "The apartment is no longer a crime scene and Ms. Angel has keys."

"Go on."

"She called me from the apartment, saying she had found evidence that pointed to Tamara Gee's killer. Evidence that would exonerate her brother."

Matthew's head rose. Just an inch, but it rose.

"So you went to the apartment," the judge prompted.

"Yes, Your Honor. I have experience with this kid and she's not a liar. My partner and I went and found interior access to the apartment that no one had noticed before. A dumbwaiter inside a utility closet comes up from the restaurant downstairs and was never put out of service from the old days."

"A dumbwaiter? For food transport? And it was large enough for a person?" the judge asked.

"Yes, sir. It's big enough for a person of small stature."

Using his hands and, at one point, a pad and pencil, Caputo described the dumbwaiter with its double-hung guillotine doors. He explained that the elevator call buttons and door handles were outside the dumbwaiter and that if a "passenger" was squatting on the platform inside, he'd have to reach outside the dumbwaiter to operate the lift. He'd not only have to press the call button to send the elevator to a different floor, he'd also have to grasp the upper door with his hand and pull it closed.

"Here, on the outside of the dumbwaiter door," Caputo said, stabbing his drawing on the pad. "That's where we found the bloody handprints."

"But you didn't find any other prints in the apartment?" the judge asked.

"No, Your Honor. The killer wore thick rubber kitchen gloves. The yellow kind. They kept his prints out of the scene, but they weren't tight. They were awkward. Once he was inside the dumbwaiter and in a rush to escape, he took them off to get a better grip on the door.

While he was maneuvering around in that small space, he cut the palm of his hand with his own knife. Big mistake. He bled profusely."

"And the print was clear?" the judge asked Caputo.

"Yes, Your Honor. It's pretty much a unique handprint with only two full-sized fingers and the thumb. And there were two prints from half fingers—stump prints, I'd call them—from when the perpetrator accidentally sliced off some finger joints a few years ago."

Now Matthew stood up straight. His eyes were huge and elated and angry all at once.

"Hunh," the judge grunted. "And you're telling me this man is willing to admit to the killing?"

"We said we'd help him if he helped us. Also, Your Honor, he has his reasons."

Then the judge drilled me, confirming my involvement and the observations that Caputo had just recounted. The judge grunted again and turned to the prosecutor. "Ms. Raphael, are you satisfied with Sergeant Caputo's sworn testimony?"

Nadine Raphael's sculptural face was tight with scorn.

"How very convenient, Your Honor. We've wrapped our case, about to tie it up with a big bow, and just before the jury goes out, we have this. Forgive me if I don't accept the sergeant's testimony as proof that Matthew

Angel is not guilty. The jurors should make their own determination."

The judge scrubbed at his scalp with both hands, swiveled in his chair, and even looked out the window.

Then he turned to Phil and said, "Tee up your confessed killer, Mr. Montaigne. Let's see if the jury buys what he's selling."

81

There was an unbearably long recess as Troy Wagner was brought from The Tombs, cleaned up, and prepped for his appearance in Judge Bradley Mudge's court.

By the time we were corralled into the courtroom and took our seats, my residual headache from the attack had bloomed into something that was almost tangible. Dr. Magnifico had said that I didn't have a concussion, but my skull still hurt like hell.

Matthew, sitting at the defense table with Phil, turned and smiled at me. He mouthed, *Love you.*

Despite my fear and tension and pain, I felt a thick but invisible cord connecting me to my brother.

"Love you back," I whispered.

How would the next few hours play out?

Would Troy, the night-shift manager from the restaurant in Matthew's building, convince the jury that he'd killed Tamara? Would the prosecution's case disintegrate?

Harry put his hand on my leg to stop me from jiggling it. "I know how you feel, T. But please chill."

Right. No problem.

Eventually, court convened. The jurors filed in, and Judge Mudge explained to them what had caused the delay.

"The defense has a new witness. Actually, Mr. Wagner was on the stand last week when he testified for the prosecution that he was the last person to see Tamara Gee alive.

"He will expand his testimony in this regard."

The jurors had questions, and the judge said he would address them again before they were asked to deliberate.

Troy Wagner was called. He came up the aisle, was sworn in, and took his seat in the witness stand.

He sported the same look he'd worn when he'd last sat in that chair and told the court that Tamara Gee had told him she was moving out of their apartment before Matthew killed her.

You can't imagine how much I hated this man. For what he'd put my brother through, for what he'd put my family through, but most of all, for what he'd done to Tamara and the baby who would have been my first nephew. My fingers balled into fists in my lap, and Harry put his hand over mine.

As before, the short, wiry man with the coarse red hair made a steeple with his hands, highlighting for me and everyone close enough to see him that the pinkie and ring finger of his left hand were shorter than the others.

I hoped and prayed that the print from this self-inflicted deformity would free my brother and indict Troy Wagner.

It would, if Troy told the truth.

82

Philippe approached the witness and, after coolly reestablishing Wagner's previous testimony, asked, "What was your opinion of Tamara Gee?"

"I thought she was evil and had too much power."

Dead silence in the courtroom. This was a new side of Troy Wagner.

"What kind of power did she have, Mr. Wagner?"

"Isn't it obvious? She was a succubus," he said, shifting in his seat. "She had the power to ruin men's lives."

My palms grew sweaty as my heart pounded. This guy was crazy. Like, certifiably crazy. This was going to work. *Please, please, let it work.*

"Mr. Wagner, do you remember your thoughts when

Ms. Gee came to pick up her dinner order on the last night of her life?"

"Yeah. Per usual, she dissed Matthew. She clearly didn't understand the kind of person Matthew Angel is, what he means to people, what kind of athlete he is. He's one of the greatest football players of all time. He's going into the history books, or was. But Tamara's loose ways, her disrespect, her downtown diva bitching, that was ruining his game. I thought it was time to take her out."

There was a loud rumble in the gallery. The jurors gasped and covered their mouths and turned to one another. As I glanced around, I saw nothing but shocked faces, abject confusion, and reporters furiously scribbling in notebooks.

It was pretty clear that no one had even guessed at the reason for this witness to reappear, but it was hitting them now. Wagner saw himself as Matthew's avenging angel.

I turned my palm up and clasped hands with Harry.

"To be clear," Phil said, "do you mean it was time to kill Tamara?"

"That's right. I couldn't stand what she was doing to Matthew," Wagner replied. "I'd thought for a long time how to do it, and now she was giving me a time frame. She was going to move out, and she was home alone. It was that night or never."

More gasps and chatter from the gallery. So much that

the judge had to bang his gavel a few times to shut everyone up.

"What happened after that?" Phil asked.

"Well. Like I said, I had thought about this for a while. I had the perfect setup. My shift is from eight until midnight. I sent the dishwasher home and locked up the restaurant. I watched to see if Matthew came home, and when he didn't, I got it done."

Phil froze in anticipation. I could hardly breathe. Harry's tight grip on my hand was about the only thing keeping me from passing out.

"Could you be more specific, Mr. Wagner?" Phil asked.

"How specific? Oh, what I did? I am one of the few people who knew our old dumbwaiter still worked. I had a knife. Well, I had my choice. I chose a paring knife. I put on rubber gloves and an apron. I climbed into the dumbwaiter, pressed the button, and took it to the third floor. Is this what you are asking me?"

I glanced at Nadine Raphael. She had a death grip on a pencil and was staring straight ahead.

"Yes, it is, Mr. Wagner," Philippe said. "Please go on."

"Okay. So the elevator opens inside a closet inside Tamara's kitchen. I went into the bedroom and Tamara was asleep, so I killed her."

He said it so casually, it was like he was reading today's

specials off the board. The courtroom was practically sucked into oblivion by one group gasp. Then Tamara's mother cried out, someone shouted, and chatter filled the room.

"Order!" the judge yelled, banging his gavel. "I will have order in my courtroom!"

Eventually everyone calmed down. Mrs. Gee was quietly crying against her husband's chest. I couldn't see Matthew's face. He was looking down at his hands, still as stone.

"Please continue, Mr. Wagner," Philippe said. "What did you do next?"

"I left the way I came in. I took off my gloves so I could get a grip on the door, and when I got down to the restaurant, I washed the knife, bagged the gloves and apron, and changed my clothes. Then I took all of it to Greenpoint, where I live, and threw it in a Dumpster. That's it."

Oddly, silence reigned throughout the large vaulted courtroom once the story was finished. Apparently a cold-blooded confession was a lot to process.

Phil turned the witness over to the prosecution, and Nadine Raphael slowly rose from her chair. I saw that a few hairs had slipped free of her bun. Otherwise, she looked perfectly calm and composed.

"Were you offered a deal to make this confession, Troy?" she asked.

"Unofficially. Cop said if I confessed, he'd try to get

me a lighter sentence. Look, they had my handprint. The DNA will convict me, so I took my best shot. I've fully cooperated. Right, Your Honor?"

The judge was so stunned he looked like he was about to keel over. "Uh, yes. Right."

"I have no further questions," Ms. Raphael said.

"Hey, Matthew," Wagner called out, leaning toward where my brother was sitting. "You're free now, buddy. I've saved your life. I hope you appreciate all I've done for you."

Matthew rose up like a grizzly bear, knocking his chair to the floor. His fists clenched and he looked like Goliath in chains. In other words, the Matthew I knew and loved was back.

"You killed Tamara, you sick son of a bitch!" he bellowed. "You killed my son!"

Matthew took one step forward, and that was all that was needed. Chaos erupted. Guards lunged for Matty. The audience rose to their feet for a better view as first two, then three burly men wrestled my brother back into his seat. The jurors were almost falling out of the jury box.

The judge pounded his gavel until the plate he was pounding it on shot off the bench. Then he pounded the bench itself until he got a semblance of silence.

"Bailiff!" he thundered. "Clear the courtroom! Do it now!"

83

Matthew was escorted out of the courtroom, having just shown the jury what he looks like when he's angry. It was a pretty unfortunate last image, considering he was still technically on trial, and I hoped it didn't make the jury second-guess everything they'd just heard.

The courtroom finally came to order.

Phil put Caputo on the stand, and after the cop testified about the physical evidence on the dumbwaiter, the defense rested its case.

Nadine Raphael made her closing argument to the jury, saying in summation, "In the months since Tamara Gee was murdered, the apartment where she died was left unattended. How can we know if the evidence was genuine, or if it was tricked up? You cannot believe Troy Wagner, a narcissist who testified so that he could be a hero to his hero and bask in his fifteen minutes of fame. This is not Troy Wagner's trial. It's Matthew Angel's trial, and we've proved to you that he's the man who killed Tamara Gee."

Phil's summation was equally simple and brief. He said, "Matthew Angel is innocent. The prosecution has not proved him guilty beyond reasonable doubt, or guilty at all. The prosecutors had a circumstantial case that was destroyed when Troy Wagner, one of their key witnesses, told you he killed Tamara Gee. Wagner didn't just make a confession. He left pristine, irrefutable evidence at the murder scene that backs up his confession. Troy Wagner killed Tamara Gee by stabbing her fifteen times with a paring knife and in so doing, also killed Trevor, her unborn child.

"You must do the right thing, ladies and gentlemen. You must find Matthew Angel not guilty, so he is free to pick up what remains of his unjustly shattered life."

I looked at Harry and Hugo. They were both beaming with hope. Philippe had done a good job. Now all we could do was wait.

The judge told the jury that their decision was very important and it had to be deliberated based on the facts brought to them during the trial. The twelve shell-shocked men and women filed out, and court was adjourned.

"I don't get it," Hugo said. "That guy just confessed. Why don't they just say Matty's innocent so we can get him the heck out of here?"

"Doesn't work that way, bud," Harry said, ruffling Hugo's hair. "But hopefully it won't take the jury too long to state the obvious. It doesn't look like we'll hear anything today though."

We all stood there for a moment: C.P. holding Harry's hand, Hugo leaning against my side, my hand clasped around his shoulder. I was exhausted, but I had no idea where to go or what to do.

"Come on, you guys," Jacob said, slinging his arm around my back. "Let's go home."

84

An hour later I slipped into baby-blue fleece pajamas and lay back on my bed. Dr. Magnifico had prescribed lots of rest, so when we'd returned to the Dakota, Jacob had ordered me straight to my room, which was fine by me. I'd never been so exhausted in my entire sixteen years. I cued up Debussy's *La Mer* on my iPod and pressed the buds into my ears.

It was still light outside my windows, but with the blinds drawn, my room was dark. Still, I slept fitfully, my dreams peppered with images of guns and knives, of Gary, of James, of Adele, of Matthew and my parents, and of snakes and Mr. Borofsky. I kept waking up with a start, but every time I did, I found someone sitting in a chair near my bed. Harry. Hugo. Jacob.

"Has the jury come back yet?" I'd ask, clutching my sheets.

And each time the answer would be "Not yet. Try to sleep."

The last time I dozed off, it was finally dark outside and Jacob was watching over me. I finally sank into a deep, dark sleep.

"Where is she?" a voice growled.

I blinked my dry eyes and sat straight up in bed. Hugo was curled next to me like a giant jungle cat.

"What the hell was that?" I gasped.

Hugo rubbed his eyes. "What?"

Suddenly, a huge shape filled my doorway.

"Matthew!" Hugo and I screeched.

My big brother barreled into the room as I got to my knees, and hugged me so tightly I could hardly breathe. I saw Philippe over his shoulder, hovering in the hall, grinning from ear to ear.

"How can I ever thank you, Tandy?" Matthew said. "You saved me. Do you know that? You saved your big brother."

"All in a day's work," I said with a shrug, but my huge grin betrayed my indifference.

"I can't believe you're back!" Hugo shouted, jumping on Matty's back. He locked his arms around Matthew's neck and held on for dear life. Matthew reached around and pulled him off with a laugh, tossing him back onto my bed like a rag doll. Hugo was so happy he was practically hysterical.

"Dude. You're *back*?" Harry said, stepping into the room in a daze.

Matty clasped hands with Harry, then drew him into a tight one-armed hug. My emo twin's eyes were quickly oozing tears. Jacob joined Philippe in the doorway, and it was all I could do to keep from choking out a happy sob myself.

My family was together again. It was a perfect moment.

Matthew looked around at all of us, his eyes shining, and put it more aptly than I ever could have.

"Damn, it's good to be home."

85

Hugo shouted, "Farty time!"

He let one loose and laughed. Gotta love little brothers.

"No, Hugo," I said, waving my hands in front of my face. "Just no."

"Sorry. I meant *party* time!"

There was a one hundred percent consensus that we were in desperate need of a big blowout family celebration. Jacob huddled with Harry and Hugo, money was distributed, and I was elected to stay home with Matty while the men went out in search of exoneration-worthy food.

"So? What do you want to do?" I asked Matthew.

"I want to take a shower," he replied with a sigh. "A nice long hot shower."

So he did. And he was still in there twenty-five minutes later when the guys returned with bulging bags of assorted booty and unpacked it on the kitchen island.

Jacob had bought wine with low—almost negative— alcohol content and had gotten something totally booze- free and fizzy for Hugo. Harry and Hugo had gone to the store and loaded up on chips and guacamole, then hit our favorite local pizza place. They'd bought two extra-large pies. Extra everything. Especially artichokes, which were Matty's favorite.

"Is he ever coming out of there?" Hugo asked, hovering near the bathroom door.

"Give the guy a break. He hasn't had a real shower in weeks," Harry said.

"Why don't you set the table?" I suggested, kneading Hugo's big shoulders. "By the time you're done I'm sure he'll be out."

Hugo was just placing the last napkin as Matthew emerged from the bathroom in comfy sweats, his skin ruddy from the hot water. He paused at the entrance to the kitchen, whipped the towel off his head, and spread his arms wide.

"Meet the new Matty Angel!"

"Oh. My. God," I said, my mouth hanging open.

Matthew's dreads had been completely sheared off. His

dark hair was about a half inch long all the way around. He rubbed his head and grinned.

"What do you think?"

"You look like an alien," Hugo commented.

Matty whipped the towel at him.

"Actually, you look like you've lost twenty pounds," I said. "How do you feel?"

"Clean," said Matty. "I can't say enough about being clean. I'm never taking a hot shower for granted again."

Harry loaded up his favorite old bands—the Stones, the Who, the Velvet Underground—into a playlist, plugged his iPod into the stereo, and dialed up the volume while Jacob laid out the food. As soon as everything was set, we attacked. The five of us ate and laughed and then ate some more. By the time it was over, I felt like I was about to burst.

At this point, some city kids our age would have gone clubbing and gotten seriously, unattractively drunk. But this was us, and we had Hugo. When the food was gone, we whipped out some games we hadn't played in ages.

We played Apples to Apples. We played Bananagrams. We played Trivial Pursuit and The Settlers of Catan and Never Have I Ever. We cracked one another up until we were spraying fizzy apple juice across the table.

We were high on life. Matty was home, there were no

snakes, Jacob had saved me from certain death, and a serial killer was headed to Rikers Island, thanks to us.

Honestly, if Santa Claus and the Easter Bunny had walked through the door right then, it wouldn't have been that big of a deal.

Jacob sipped his wine and basked in the kid stuff, laughing out loud, fending off the calls from the lobby about the noise. I watched as he and Matty chatted, getting to know each other for the first time. It seemed like they liked each other, and I was glad. Because I knew Jacob wasn't going anywhere anytime soon.

At midnight, Harry said good night and headed off to bed. Matthew was next, carrying Hugo over his shoulder. He paused halfway down the hall and looked back at me.

"Home sweet home," he said with a contented sigh. "Thanks again, Tandy. I owe it all to you."

"Anytime," I replied, my heart brimming.

A moment later, Hugo's door closed, and then everyone in the building probably heard Hugo screaming and screeching and laughing as Matty tickled him half to death. The two of them would be bunking together until Matty figured out his next move, and I had a feeling that in the meantime, there would be no peace.

Not that I minded. Not one bit.

I cleared the table and tried to help with the dishes, but Jacob waved me off.

"Go to bed, Tandy. Doctor's orders, remember?"

"Right," I said, letting out a breath. I realized for the first time that there was a dull, persistent throb at the base of my skull. It had probably been there all night, but I'd been too happy and distracted to notice. "It's been a long few days, huh?"

"That is an understatement," Jacob replied with a smile. He gave me a long hug. "Good night, Tandy."

"Night, Jacob."

I turned and padded down the hall to my pale blue sanctuary. I didn't plan on going directly to bed, though. There was something I had to do, but I'd been avoiding it.

The time had finally arrived.

86

I sat on the edge of my bed and took the postcards from James out of the drawer in my bedside table. The card on top of the stack had the newest date, the fifth in the series of five.

The front of the card was a cityscape shot from the window of an airplane. The clouds were fluffy and pink from the waning sun in the foreground. The plane was heading into the night sky in the distance.

I turned the card over and read what James had written:

Tandy, Tolstoy wrote this in War and Peace, *and I swear it's almost as if he leapt into the future and wrote it for me.*

"The whole world is divided for me into two parts: one is she, and there is all happiness, hope, light; the other is where she is not, and there everything is dejection and darkness..."

Tears came into my eyes. James really had loved me. But so much time had passed. He was with another girl now, and my fantasies about finding him and getting back to the way we'd been were not just futile, they were messing with my brain, with my life. And if Royal Rampling was on the up-and-up, they could even mess with my family's future.

I took a deep breath and walked over to the shredder next to my desk. I ran the postcards, one at a time, through the metal teeth. I only hesitated once. I read the last note again; then I pressed on. When the cards had all been chewed to shreds, I took the basket out to the hallway and dumped the contents down the chute into the incinerator.

I know what you're thinking, friend: *Are you kidding me?*

But no, in fact, I'm not.

Don't get me wrong. It wasn't easy. In fact, it felt like someone was slowly tearing a jagged slit through my pericardium—that's the membrane that surrounds the heart—and then hacking away at its center.

Paints a pretty picture, doesn't it?

So yeah, it was painful beyond belief. But I had to do it. I had to acknowledge that my fantasy of living happily ever after with James Rampling was over.

And now it was time to move on.

THE
GRANDEST
GONGO
OF THEM ALL

4

87

I awoke to find Jacob shaking my arm. Again.

"Tandy, this is your second and last wake-up call. You have to get up."

"Why?" I moaned. "Why, why, *why?*"

I cracked my eyes open and saw tension in my uncle's face. What had happened now? More snakes? Had Matthew gone AWOL? Was Hugo hanging from the ceiling beams again?

I sat up straight. "What's wrong?"

"Nothing, for once," he said, almost disbelieving. "You need to pack. Take enough clothing for at least three weeks. Bring casual clothes, rubber-soled shoes, and also nice things for dinner at, say, very good restaurants."

I watched with narrowed eyes as he walked toward my bedroom door. I was waiting for the punch line. "Did you finish off that bottle of Mogen David all on your own?" I asked.

Jacob laughed. "I'm not drunk, and this isn't a joke. It's a *surprise*, Tandy. So let's go. That's an order."

"When did I join the Israeli army?" I groused, throwing the covers off my legs.

"Oh, and please make coffee after you pack. I've got to drag the others out of bed."

I stared at my now-empty doorway, trying to piece this together. What kind of surprise required clothes for three weeks?

I heard Jacob next door in Harry's room, giving him the same pitch he'd given me. Good luck. Harry practically lived to sleep. I pulled a suitcase down from the top shelf of my closet, bunched up half my clothes into it, tossed in some shoes, and zipped it up. I was officially packed.

A half hour later, my brothers and I were on the street, shooting dazed looks at one another. Each of us had asked where we were going and Hugo had even threatened to fart some more if Jacob didn't talk, but Jacob's only response was "It's a surprise."

He was putting name tags on the luggage, which was lined up at the curb, and making sure the bags were all securely closed. About half a dozen horns honked, and I looked up to find C.P. coming toward us, crossing against the light.

"Hey, C.P.!" I said happily. "Come to—"

But she breezed right past me and basically flung herself into Harry's open arms. They hugged for a second, then walked away from us, their heads bent close together.

"Wow, T. You got dissed," Matty said joyfully. I shoved him as hard as I could. He didn't flinch. I scowled over at Harry and C.P. They were hugging again and she was crying.

"Enough already!" I resisted the temptation to roll my eyes.

A livery cab pulled up at the curb—a big black SUV. "Harry! Let's go!" our uncle shouted, getting into the front seat with the driver. Matty and Hugo climbed into the third row and I slid across the second.

Harry kissed C.P. good-bye—briefly, thank God—and got into the backseat next to me.

"Red Hook, Brooklyn," Jacob told the driver.

Brooklyn? Not JFK or LaGuardia? Not Newark?

"Yes, sir," the driver said.

Harry said, "Hang on a minute."

Then he jumped out, exchanged a few words with C.P., and gave her a back-bending, tongue-twisting, totally disgusting kiss that lasted at least thirty seconds.

"Gross," Hugo said, scrunching his face.

"Took the words right outta my mouth, Hugo," I said, giving him a fist bump.

Matty laughed and slid his sunglasses on. "When are you two going to grow up?"

"But what about the germs, Matty?" Hugo wailed. "The germs!"

Even I had to laugh at that one.

Finally, Harry got back in the cab and slammed the door. He was grinning like an idiot. "Okay. Let's go."

Rolling my eyes, I Googled Red Hook, Brooklyn, on my phone, opened the link, and showed it around to the boys. "Red Hook is famous for two things. Unless we're moving into public housing, I guess we're going on a cruise."

"Come on," Harry said.

"What else could it be?"

"For three weeks?" Harry said. "Where the hell are we going? It only takes like six or seven days to get to Europe."

"Maybe we're going to Australia!" Hugo said, bouncing in his seat.

"Or Antarctica," Matty said. "That'd be cool. At least there are no reporters there."

Jacob said nothing.

"Come on, Jacob. Don't you think you should at least give us a clue?" I hated being out of the loop.

He crossed his arms over his chest and looked me in the eye. "All right. Here's your hint. If you want to know how the court ruled in the case of your parents' estate, I suggest you come on this trip."

88

Once we figured out where we were going to be for the next several weeks, Hugo and I decided to explore the *Queen Mary 2* to pass the time until the ship cast off.

"Lookit that, Tandy!" he gasped, pointing toward a top deck. "Lookit that!"

There was a shopping area the size of a land-bound mall, a three-story, red-carpeted spiral staircase leading to the Grand Lobby, a huge theater as big as Radio City Music Hall, and a restaurant designed to look like an English garden. A deck circumnavigated the ship, as wide as a boardwalk, lined with lounge chairs and so high above the waterline, we were on the same level with the seabirds in flight.

After an hour or two of wide-eyed wandering, Hugo and I found Harry in the piano lounge. He was playing a jazz medley, drawing in people who stood in the entrance. After a stellar rendition of "Piano Man," we grabbed Harry and dragged him with us to the main deck as the ship prepared to leave her mooring. Tugboats that seemed as small as toy cars had lines attached to our ship and began their work of heavy tugging as the ship's horns sounded.

Hugo covered his ears, grinning the whole time.

And then we were being guided through the harbor toward open waters. The movement of the ship was powerful, graceful, monumental. For a while, anyway, I stopped wondering where and why and turned myself over to what could be the thrill of a lifetime. Like it or not, we were on this seagoing luxury hotel for an entire week.

I supposed it wouldn't hurt to enjoy it.

After admiring the dramatic open ocean awhile longer, we met Jacob for dinner in the Queens Grill, where the menu featured tandoori-baked prawns—which Harry immediately renamed Shrimp Tandy.

Then we followed Jacob up and down stairs and along carpeted hallways to his suite on the ninth deck. Jacob's room was pretty luxurious. He had a flat-screen TV, creamy bedding on his king-sized bed, a wonderful abstract oil painting, and a wide balcony overlooking the foam-flecked ocean nine stories below.

"Geez," Hugo said. "Your room is much nicer than ours."

"Of course. I'm wealthier than any of you. At least for the moment."

He was wealthy? And had he just said we were about to become even wealthier?

How could that even be true? We had been on rock-bottom austerity measures since he'd come to live with us. As far as I knew, we were being sued by Royal Rampling, who had promised to make us destitute.

Jacob definitely had our attention.

He opened a chilled bottle of apple cider and poured glasses for us all. Matty was leaning up against a wall, enjoying himself. I had the distinct feeling that he and Jacob had done some male bonding and that our uncle had clued my big brother in on this new development.

Jacob sat in a round leather swivel chair with his back to the sea and sky.

"I've got good news and bad news," he began. "What do you want first? Show of hands on bad news first."

We all raised our hands high.

"Don't drag this out, Jacob," I snapped.

"Patience, Tandy. Okay. The bad news is that the court

ruled in favor of Royal Rampling, who is your parents' principal creditor. He was awarded the co-op, of course, and the furnishings, and whatever equities and bonds were in Malcolm and Maud's possession at the time of their deaths."

"What about the Pork Chair?" Hugo asked. "Can we keep that?"

"The Pork Chair is worth tens of thousands, Hugo," Jacob said gently. "So are Mercurio and the Pegasus piano, and all the other artwork your parents owned, including Maud's emerald ring. Unfortunately, it's all gone."

"That's so unfair," Harry said. "The piano was mine. It's like a part of me."

"I understand and I'm sorry, Harry," Jacob said. "But it wasn't in your name. Angel Pharmaceuticals is being taken over by Rampling Limited, and even Peter's shares are worthless. He will be filing for bankruptcy."

Uncle Peter had a huge co-op on the West Side and an elaborate social life. I felt a little sorry for him. Uncle Peter without money was going to be pathetic. I didn't think I'd be able to call him Uncle Pig anymore.

"Did Rampling leave us anything?" I asked, seeing his e-mail to me in my mind's eye. His offer to leave us something if I stayed out of James's life. "Anything at all?"

"The clothes on your backs, the clothes in your closets,

and whatever personal items in your bedrooms, Royal Rampling can't sell. As we speak, a moving company is boxing up your possessions and putting them in storage."

My fingers curled into fists. I wanted to kill someone. Not be arrested erroneously for killing someone, but actually kill someone this time.

And that someone was Royal Rampling.

"That bastard," I said under my breath.

"I'm very sorry, kids. This is pretty terrible and none of you deserve it," Jacob told us. "But as I said, there is good news, too."

I held my breath.

"Who's paying for this trip?" Harry blurted. "And why is Matthew grinning like that?"

"Well, that would lead us to the good news," said our uncle Jacob. He was smiling now, too. Like he just couldn't wait to spill whatever he called good news.

"Here we go," I said quietly to my twin. "More surprises."

89

Jacob opened his briefcase and removed a worn leather wallet about eight inches long and four inches wide, with a buckled leather strap going all around it. It looked like an envelope for military communiqués, something I'd seen in a movie once.

I held my breath as Jacob unbuckled the strap, opened the wallet, and took out what looked to be a letter, written by hand on yellowed paper.

Just then, the loudspeaker came on, and the captain welcomed us aboard the *Queen Mary 2*. He told us endless details about the air temperature, ocean conditions, and distances in both English and metric formats. Then the entertainment director started rambling on about the highlights of the upcoming trip. I heard none of it as my mind riffled through all the possibilities of what we were about to hear from Jacob.

"Okay, is she ever gonna stop talking?" Harry asked.

The second she did, there was a knock at the door—Jacob's butler inquiring whether he required turndown service. Jacob thanked the young man but sent him away.

"Sorry about all that," Jacob said. "Kind of spoiled the moment."

"Can we get on with it already?" I asked.

"As you wish." Jacob unfolded the letter and said, "This is from your gram Hilda."

"But she's dead," Hugo said.

"Yes, she passed away twenty-five years ago, before Matthew was even born, but even though she didn't know any of you, she expected that her children would have their own children, and she wanted to make sure that her grandchildren were...well, I'll let her tell you herself."

He picked up the letter and began to read.

90

"'*My darling son,*'" Jacob read. "'I am still laughing at your delight in French pastries and small, silly dogs. My pampered life must seem so frivolous to you, and yet you seem to enjoy it. I must thank you again for the wonderful photos of you and your dear family. You have much to be proud of: a promotion and so many accomplishments at such a young age, and for being such a good son, brother, and soldier. I love you, Jacob, and could not be happier for you.

"'Obviously, I'm writing to you to formalize our discussion of yesterday regarding my bequests to my heirs.'"

Jacob stopped reading and said, "If I may summarize here, your parents received the infamous one hundred dollars, Peter got his inheritance in advance to start Angel Pharmaceuticals, and Hilda put my inheritance in a bank in Zurich. And now she goes on to speak of future grandchildren."

"'As we discussed, I cannot spend all that my dear Max left to me, if I live for a hundred years. Given my condition, the general unpredictability of life, and the likelihood of Maud bearing children, I have set up a trust fund.

"'I'm appointing you executor of this fund, Jacob, because I trust you and because you already have the wisdom of a man twice your age.

"'I am leaving my beloved town house in Paris to my grandchildren, with one condition. They must visit the house and decide whether they wish to keep it or sell it. Their decision must be unanimous.

"'The trust fund to be divided by my grandchildren will mature twenty-five years after my death. The legal documents and account number are in your safe-deposit vault.

"'Jacob, dear, I have few regrets in this world, but one of them is that I wasn't with you for all your special childhood moments. But then, we have had our unforgettable, even luminous summers, a priceless treasure. Even though you only left yesterday, my house feels empty because you are gone.

"'My love, as always, goes with you.

"'Your mother, Hilda.'"

Jacob carefully returned the letter to the leather envelope. Then he looked at us.

"That day she speaks of. Well, it was a marvelous day," he said, his voice cracking. "Not just the poodles and the éclairs, but we walked around the streets of Paris and laughed and reminisced about many things. It was the last time I saw her.

"She died a few months later of a heart attack at the age of seventy. That was twenty-five years ago today. The four of you are her only grandchildren. And, Tandy, now I can tell you why we're on this ship and where we're going.

"We're going to see your grandmother's house in Paris. It's on the Right Bank in the Sixteenth Arrondissement. I would say that this area is comparable to the Upper East Side, but with wide boulevards and beautiful gardens and not far from the Arc de Triomphe. You could not pick a better home in Paris."

I stared at Jacob, stunned. No one moved. No one spoke. No one breathed.

And then, all at once, everyone started talking.

"We're moving to Paris?"

"How much money are we talking about here?"

"What about C.P.?"

"How much money, Uncle Jacob?" Hugo shouted.

Silence reigned. Jacob smirked.

"We'll let the bankers and accountants work that out, okay, young man?" he said. "But it will be a lot. It will be quite a lot."

Talk about surprises. Talk about one door closing with the force of a sonic boom and another opening as wide and as welcoming as angels' wings. Screw Royal Rampling and his threats, his broken promises. The Angel family was going to be just fine.

That night we all trooped to the stern of the imposing *Queen Mary 2*. I unhooked the keys to apartment 9G in the Dakota from my grandfather's key chain, and my siblings took their keys in hand.

With the wind whipping our hair into our eyes, we tossed our keys into the churning wake and said good-bye to the only home most of us had ever known.

91

Beautiful morning light streamed through the glass doors of my room. I was enjoying the distant hum of the engines, thinking about my gram Hilda, formerly characterized as fierce and mean but now clearly our savior, when there was a knock on my door.

I called out, "Who is it?"

"It's Jacob."

I put on some sweats and went to the door. Jacob said, "Is this a bad time? I can come back."

"No, no, please come in."

I sat cross-legged on my bed as Jacob dragged over a desk chair.

"I want to talk to you privately," he said.

He had another envelope in his hand, this one plain paper with the *QM2* logo in the corner.

"Another surprise?" I asked.

"Tandy, transatlantic crossings used to be called passages, and I think that, more than for your brothers, this trip can be a life-changing passage for you," he said.

I drew my legs in closer, keeping an eye on the envelope. "I'm intrigued."

"Three days ago, you were almost killed. You rescued your brother from a very probable life sentence, and you found a decomposing body in the Dakota, along with innumerable poisonous creatures. The months before I arrived were apparently rife with death and betrayal, and I'm pretty sure your first fifteen years weren't exactly merry."

"Merry?" I said with a laugh. "What does that word even mean?"

Jacob nodded, then went on.

"This ocean voyage is an opportunity for you to relax. I hope you will rest and heal, and that you will take pleasure in spending time with your brothers. You may never have an opportunity like this one again."

I felt tears pooling in my eyes. I never in my life had heard my parents use the words *relax* or *heal*.

"Go to the spa every day. Get your hair done, have massages. Swim. Go dancing. Savor your meals. And sleep, Tandy. Sleep a lot. If anyone is found dead on this ship…"

I started to laugh. For a couple of minutes, I couldn't stop.

"Here's my advice, girl detective," said my good uncle, his eyes twinkling. "If someone dies on this ship, don't interfere. Stay out of it. Do you understand me?"

"Yes, Uncle Jacob," I said. "I understand."

"Good." He grinned. "Now I have something for you." He tapped the envelope against his knee. "It's an e-mail from someone you want to hear from, or at least, you did. Now it's up to you."

He handed me the envelope, and I tore clumsily at the flap until I'd ripped it open. I took out a sheet of paper, a printout of an e-mail, and saw Jacob's name at the top.

Just below that, I saw the subject line: *For Tandoori Angel, Suite #9,023.*

My eyes dropped to the signature.

My heart started slamming against my rib cage before my brain even recognized his name. But I knew.

I knew I was holding a letter from James.

92

Uncle Jacob rose to his feet. I dragged my eyes away from the paper in my hands.

"How did you get this?"

"I have connections, Tandy. And I used them." He smiled. "I'll leave you to your letter."

"Wait." I jumped up and hugged Jacob with all my might. "Thank you."

"You're welcome." Then he kissed the top of my head, and as I turned, I heard the door close. I sat down on the bed again and read the message from James.

Dear Tandy,
I can hardly believe I'm writing to you with the

confidence that you will actually receive this. For the last six months I've been at the Collège Belvédère du Pic, a boarding school in the Swiss Alps. When I say "in" the Alps, I mean at the pinnacle of the Alps, and although it's the most expensive boarding school in all of Europe, it's more like a prison. Leaving has always been out of the question, and there's no way to communicate with the outside world without going through the headmaster.

Two months ago, I escaped and found out fast that I didn't have the skills or the gear to survive the climb down this mountain. I was captured within hours, in a whiteout that should have buried me alive. I didn't even manage to clear the shadow of the school, that's how ill equipped I was to escape.

When my saintly father found out what I'd done, he threatened to have me charged with kidnapping you to East Hampton last year. He said he would testify against me.

He wasn't kidding.

I'm going to spare you the rest of his threats, but let's just say I knew I had to give up. So I've just been trapped in this mountain jail, worrying about what happened to you, wondering if you're all right, and wishing I could talk to you, see you, hold you again.

Then, two days ago, I was driven to the Swiss border and released without explanation. The driver just handed me a letter and left me there. The letter was from Jacob Perlman, and there was a wad of cash inside.

He told me some of what was done to you, and I'm so sorry, Tandy. If I'd known what would happen, I would have found a way to protect you. We knew our parents wouldn't like it, but I honestly had no idea what kind of torture they were capable of.

I'm writing this from the only Internet café for eighty miles in any direction, including up and down. I'll make my way to Paris, by train, by thumb, by foot, and I'll wait for you to arrive no matter how long it takes.

I want you to know that I love you as much as I did the last time I saw you. I'll meet you at the Carrousel du Louvre near La Pyramide Inversée in Paris on Saturday. At 12 noon, if that works for you. God, I just can't wait to see you again.

All my love, James

I read the letter again, then a third time, then a fourth. This couldn't be real. In a few short days, I was going to see James? Actually see him, touch him, kiss him?

Yes.

I fell back onto my bed, clutching the letter, and wondered if the sheer brute force of anticipation had ever actually *killed* anyone.

Because it felt just possible that I might die from the excitement that overwhelmed me right then.

CONFESSION

Here's a little something you may have observed over the past couple hundred pages of my story, friend: I don't know how to relax.

My tiger parents went to the most extreme lengths to promote hard work and brilliance, even though it meant using me, using all of us, as guinea pigs. I was taught to achieve great things, to overachieve, to recognize excellence and go after it.

I wanted to take Jacob's advice. I wanted to kick back and enjoy myself and just let this tremendous feat of human engineering squire me directly to the guy I loved, and I tried. I did. I went to the spa and got a massage but was so fidgety I only lasted ten minutes before I got up, scaring the hell out of the masseuse, and walked out. I tried to float in the pool, but my brain was too crowded with what-ifs.

What if James had changed?

What if my memories of him had been tainted and twisted by Dr. Narmond's mind-altering machine and he wasn't at all as I remembered him?

Or, worst of all, what if I had changed so much that James didn't like me? The real me? The me I was now, off the drugs?

I ended up falling off the float and nearly drowning myself. Then, after a healthy salad lunch with my brothers, I got so obsessive I threw up over the railing.

Lovely, I know.

But it all begged the question: How the hell was I going to survive an entire week of this? Would I even make it to Paris, or would they have to sedate me and fit me for a straitjacket before I ever got there?

93

Exercise. Exercise turned out to be my savior. It expelled all my nervous energy, got my blood pumping in a positive way, and cleared my mind. I was jogging around deck seven that afternoon when it finally got through to me, what Jacob had said about being with my brothers, really being with them.

I didn't even know where we would be living next week, or on what continent. Now was the moment for quality time.

So I joined in on Matthew's exercise routine, morning and late afternoon. Working out with him finally relaxed me enough to do all the other things Jacob had suggested. I went to the Canyon Ranch Spa with Harry. We had massages and mud baths (separately, of course) and I indulged in all manners of facials and nail treatments. I had my hair cut a couple of inches while I was at it, and added a blond streak to the front.

I also swam with Hugo. My little brother was like a fish. He loved being in the water. We did laps, we played ball, we made up stories and laughed and made friends with some other kids on the cruise.

Harry and I stretched out on lounge chairs and just talked. He told me that C.P. really listened to him and he'd been missing that in his life. I realized she'd done the same for me. I guess lately Harry and I hadn't been quite as tight as we'd been right after our parents' deaths.

"I know you listen to me, too, Tandy," Harry said. "But you've been so...unstoppable lately, you know? C.P. just chills out and lets me talk."

"I get it," I told him. "But when we get home, wherever that turns out to be, I promise I'll try to be there for you more."

Harry smiled. "Right back at ya."

I went to the dance club with Jacob, and it turned out that, for an old guy, he could really dance. We held a contest to see who could spin the longest without hitting the deck, and when Jacob took out a table full of party girls, I laughed so hard I almost hyperventilated.

Once Jacob was able to see straight again, he grasped my arm and smiled.

"It's great to hear you really laugh, Tandy," he told me. "I didn't know you had it in you."

I took my grandfather Max's five-franc piece to the jewelry store, and they put a gold band around the perimeter and added a loop and a gold chain. I was wearing it now, and I didn't think I would ever take it off.

I sat in the Golden Lion pub with Matthew.

The lounge is in the bow of the ship, on the second level, so we were really close to the waves breaking around the prow. Matthew told me about Tamara and his grief at the loss of her and their unborn child, and how betrayed he still felt by our parents in every way.

"I'm not going to take my share of the inheritance, Tandy. I'm going to go back to the team next season, and I make enough on my own," he told me. "You guys keep the money, and if you ever need more, just let me know. In fact, let me know if you need anything. Blood, internal organs…"

I laughed and shoved his arm. "Gross!"

Matthew smirked and tipped his head toward the sun. He was looking healthier every day, morphing back into confident Matthew Angel, football star. I even caught a couple of girls eyeing him as they walked by.

Hugo made friends with the sailors. He learned knots. He learned celestial navigation. He lifted huge metal parts and humped them around the deck, showing off, making people's jaws drop. He lifted a two-hundred-pound man in a lounge chair. And then he lifted the man's even bigger wife.

Hugo was so in his element, I wouldn't have been surprised if he'd eventually decided to make his living on a cruise ship. But it was Harry who landed an actual gig—in the piano bar.

He played old favorites. He played pop. He played compositions of his own. After a couple of days, he had a following of swooning young girls and retirees and music lovers who wanted his picture and his autograph.

I took a class in vegetable carving. I read fiction. I signed up for lessons in meditation, and I did it, on deck, smelling the sea, unfrightened by the knowledge that there was absolutely nothing around the ship for hundreds of miles except changing sky and deep, deep water. I did rest. I really did.

And finally, finally, land was in sight and at four thirty in the morning, the regal *Queen Mary 2* sailed majestically into the British port of Southampton.

And even after all that resting and clearing my head, all I could think about was James.

94

Jacob, my brothers, and I boarded a plane at London Heathrow Airport and flew to Paris. Before we'd checked into the Hotel George V, we had a plan.

I would meet James privately at the appointed time and place, and then, after an hour or so, I would bring him with me to Gram Hilda's house, where we would meet up with my family to see what could be our new home.

"How do you feel?" Jacob asked as he put me in a taxi.

I felt like my skin was humming. Like everything inside me was fresh and clean and pure. I felt like anything could happen.

"Perfect," I told him succinctly.

Jacob smiled. "We'll stay in the hotel until we hear

from you, Tandy. Call. Don't forget to call. Is your phone charged?"

I nodded. Then Jacob forced money into my hand and told the driver to take me to the Louvre.

I was so deep in thought, it was as if I blinked once and the ride was over. I handed the driver some folded money and got out of the cab at the Place du Carrousel, the plaza fronting the world-famous Louvre, home of the Mona Lisa and the Venus de Milo.

There, in the plaza, near the gigantic, iconic glass-and-metal pyramid, was where I stood. Somehow, I stood still, even though every cell in my body seemed to be vibrating with anticipation.

At just before noon, there were countless people crossing the plaza: couples holding hands, dog walkers, and bicyclists.

The calm I had cultivated over the last week had vanished. My back was to La Pyramide, but in front of me was a wide cityscape with limitless hundred-and-eighty-degree views. I looked everywhere at once, my eyes flashing over the faces of strangers, searching, searching, searching for James. I must have looked insane.

And I kind of was.

Where was he? Was I in the right place? Would he show up? Oh, God, what if he didn't show up?

"Tandy!"

My heart leapt into my throat. I whirled around, scanning the throng. The world was still busy whizzing by me. With no one coming *to* me.

Of course, I'd imagined it.

Of course.

95

And then I saw him.

His hair was darker and longer than I remembered, and for a second I was sure once again that I'd hallucinated the sound of my name. He was dressed all in brown, a leather flight jacket, tan backpack, khaki-colored pants. James always wore blue. Always. At least a little bit of it.

Maybe it wasn't him.

But then the figure waved. He seemed to be haloed in sunlight. I squinted as he started across the street and the figure of this beautiful boy came into focus.

It was him. It was really, really him.

I waved back and James started to run. He dodged

traffic, leapt over a railing, and then he was with me, right in front of me, smiling his now oh-so-familiar smile.

He was exactly as I remembered him. Exactly.

"Hey," he said with a grin.

"Hi," I replied, as casually as I'd have done if we'd been meeting after school at the Starbucks on the corner of West Seventy-Sixth Street.

And then I fell hard against him, murmuring, "Oh, God, oh, God, oh, God, oh, God…" and he held me in his arms and buried his face in my hair.

It felt like we stood clutching each other like that for hours. Nothing else mattered. Not the people trying to brush by us, or the insanity of the past few weeks, or even what our parents had done to us. All that mattered was this pure connection. It was still there, exactly as it had always been. It hadn't been erased by lasers at Fern Haven. Or by time and distance.

Nothing could change this love. Nothing.

I inhaled the scents of warm leather and earthy evergreen shampoo and held him even tighter.

Finally, James pulled back. He cupped my face in his hands. "I can't believe it. I can't believe it's really you."

"Why?" I asked, my heart thumping dangerously. "Do I look different?"

He grinned and touched the streak in my hair. "I like the hair."

I reached up to the nape of his neck. "I like yours, too."

We gazed at each other for a moment, the beaming smiles on our faces full to overflowing. And at that moment, we communicated this telepathically, I know: *There is just so much to say to you right now, I don't even know where to start.*

"I'm sorry I'm late," he said instead. "I *just* got off the train and came right here."

"I don't care," I told him, looking up into his gray-blue eyes, the palm of my hand now lingering on his cheek. "I would've waited all day."

James smiled. He lifted my palm and kissed it. "You have absolutely no clue how much I missed you, Tandy."

James pulled me to him, and with my heart pounding fiercely against his chest, he kissed me, shyly first, then hungrily. At the touch of his lips, something inside me exploded. All the longing and hoping and wishing, all the confusion and anger and fear I'd been clinging to burst like fireworks.

And then, because we were in the Place du Carrousel in Paris and it couldn't have been more perfect, James lifted me off my feet and swung me around and around. I could feel tourists watching us, a few sentimental bursts of applause from the romantics, not to mention a lot of annoyed or indifferent people skirting around us, but I didn't care.

I just laughed and laughed, until I was crying.

Finally, James placed my feet firmly on the ground. "I love you," he whispered into my ear.

"I love you, too," I replied.

But when his radiant gaze flicked over my shoulder a moment later, his expression went slack.

"What's wrong?" I whirled around.

I saw that a black car had pulled up on the plaza. Three men got out, and with a sharp, visceral shock, I realized that I had seen at least one of them before.

The broad-shouldered man with clipped graying hair and a flattened nose was one of the men who had handled me so roughly in the SUV that dumped me at Fern Haven.

And I recognized another man from pictures.

He was tall, at least six-foot-two, and had thick black hair that was pure white at the temples. He wore a black trench coat and was carrying a briefcase and a camera case by a strap over his shoulder. He looked focused. And he looked mean.

"James," he called out. "We have to talk, son."

James spun me around so that I was looking only at him. "It's my father, Tandy. You have to run."

"No. Absolutely not. I'm not leaving you."

His grip on my shoulders tightened. "Where are you staying?"

I gave him the name of the hotel.

"Please. I'll find you again. I will," he said desperately. "But if he gets his hands on you, he'll hurt you. He'll crush you, Tandy. Just run."

There was no way. No possible way that after everything I'd been through, after everything we'd been through, I was going to let another psychotic parent tear us apart. I reached for James's hand and looked into his eyes.

"I have a better idea."

With that, I turned to face Royal Rampling. I stood my ground. I knew now what I was capable of. I knew who I was. I had survived Royal Rampling and worse. Maybe he could hurt me, but no one had the power to crush me. Not ever again.

I focused on James's father and shouted, "We're not afraid of you!" I pointed at him and looked around at the crowd. "Kidnapper! *Kidnapper!*"

James caught on to the plan and started yelling, too. "I'm not your property. I don't belong to you!"

Concerned citizens started to gather, streaming toward the scene we were creating. Camera phones pointed at

Royal Rampling, and I saw more than one bystander hastily dialing a phone or raising it like he or she was about to record the scene on video.

It was working. If I had to guess, I'd say the gendarmes would arrive soon.

Royal Rampling and the huge oafs who worked for him stopped cold. Rampling faked a smile, then told his henchmen to stand down. I could hear James's ragged breathing as we faced off with his father.

"*Ce n'est pas fini jusqu'à ce que je dis c'est fini,*" Rampling called out. "It's not over until I say it's over."

Then, with a wicked smile, Royal Rampling got into his car, and it peeled out into the chaotic Parisian traffic.

And I was left, for now, in the arms of his beautiful son.

FIND OUT HOW
THE CONFESSIONS
BEGAN...

AND WHAT REALLY
HAPPENED TO
MALCOLM AND
MAUD ANGEL.

TURN THE PAGE FOR A PREVIEW.

CONFESSIONS OF A MURDER SUSPECT

JAMES PATTERSON

AND MAXINE PAETRO

1

I have some really bad secrets to share with someone, and it might as well be you—a stranger, a reader of books, but most of all, a person who can't hurt me. So here goes nothing, or maybe everything. I'm not sure if I can even tell the difference anymore.

The night my parents died—after they'd been carried out in slick black body bags through the service elevator— my brother Matthew shouted at the top of his powerful lungs, "My parents were vile, but they didn't deserve to be taken out with the *trash*!"

He was right about the last part—and, as things turned out, the first part as well.

But I'm getting ahead of myself, aren't I? Please forgive me.... I do that a lot.

I'd been asleep downstairs, directly under my parents' bedroom, when it happened. So I never heard a thing—no frantic thumping, no terrified shouting, no fracas at all. I woke up to the scream of sirens speeding up Central Park West, maybe one of the most common sounds in New York City.

But that night it was different.

The sirens stopped *right downstairs*. That was what caused me to wake up with a hundred-miles-an-hour heartbeat. Was the building on fire? Did some old neighbor have a stroke?

I threw off my double layer of blankets, went to my window, and looked down to the street, nine dizzying floors below. I saw three police cruisers and what could have been an unmarked police car parked on Seventy-second Street, right at the front gates of our apartment building, the exclusive and infamous Dakota.

A moment later our intercom buzzed, a jarring *blat-blat* that punched right through my flesh and bones.

Why was the doorman paging *us*? This was *crazy*.

My bedroom was the one closest to the front door, so I bolted through the living room, hooked a right at the sharks in the aquarium coffee table, and passed between Robert and his nonstop TV.

When I reached the foyer, I stabbed at the intercom button to stop the irritating blare before it woke up the whole house.

I spoke in a loud whisper to the doorman through the speaker: "Sal? What's happening?"

"Miss Tandy? Two policemen are on the way up to your apartment right now. I couldn't stop them. They got a nine-one-one call. It's an emergency. That's what they said."

"There's been a mistake, Sal. Everyone is asleep here. It's after midnight. How could you let them up?"

Before Sal could answer, the doorbell rang, and then fists pounded the door. A harsh masculine voice called out, "This is the police."

I made sure the chain was in place and then opened the door—but just a crack.

I peered out through the opening and saw two men in the hallway. The older one was as big as a bear but kind of soft-looking and spongy. The younger one was wiry and had a sharp, expressionless face, something like a hatchet blade, or...no, a hatchet blade is exactly right.

The younger one flashed his badge and said, "Sergeant

Capricorn Caputo and Detective Ryan Hayes, NYPD. Please open the door."

Capricorn Caputo? I thought. *Seriously?* "You've got the wrong apartment," I said. "No one here called the police."

"Open the door, miss. And I mean *right now.*"

"I'll get my parents," I said through the crack. I had no idea that my parents were dead and that we would be the only serious suspects in a double homicide. I was in my last moment of innocence.

But who am I kidding? No one in the Angel family was ever innocent.

2

"*Open up*, or my partner will kick down the door!" Hatchet Face called out.

It is no exaggeration to say that my whole family was about to get a wake-up call from *hell*. But all I was thinking at that particular moment was that the police could *not* kick down the door. This was the *Dakota*. We could get *evicted* for allowing someone to disturb the peace.

I unlatched the chain and swung the door open. I was wearing pajamas, of course; chick-yellow ones with dinosaurs chasing butterflies. Not exactly what I would have chosen for a meeting with the police.

Detective Hayes, the bearish one, said, "What's your name?"

"Tandy Angel."

"Are you the daughter of Malcolm and Maud Angel?"

"I am. Can you please tell me why you're here?"

"Tandy is your real name?" he said, ignoring my question.

"I'm called Tandy. Please wait here. I'll get my parents to talk to you."

"We'll go with you," said Sergeant Caputo.

Caputo's grim expression told me that this was not a request. I turned on lights as we headed toward my parents' bedroom suite.

I was climbing the circular stairwell, thinking that my parents were going to kill me for bringing these men upstairs, when suddenly both cops pushed rudely past me. By the time I had reached my parents' room, the overhead light was on and the cops were bending over my parents' bed.

Even with Caputo and Hayes in the way, I could see that my mother and father looked all wrong. Their sheets and blankets were on the floor, and their nightclothes were bunched under their arms, as if they'd tried to take them off. My father's arm looked like it had been twisted out of its socket. My mother was lying facedown across my father's body, and her tongue was sticking out of her mouth. It had turned *black*.

I didn't need a coroner to tell me that they were dead. I knew it just moments after I saw them. Diagnosis certain.

I shrieked and ran toward them, but Hayes stopped me cold. He kept me out of the room, putting his big paws on my shoulders and forcibly walking me backward out to the hallway.

"I'm sorry to do this," he said, then shut the bedroom door in my face.

I didn't try to open it. I just stood there. Motionless. Almost not breathing.

So, you might be wondering why I wasn't bawling, screeching, or passing out from shock and horror. Or why I wasn't running to the bathroom to vomit or curling up in the fetal position, hugging my knees and sobbing. Or doing any of the things that a teenage girl who's just seen her murdered parents' bodies ought to do.

The answer is complicated, but here's the simplest way to say it: I'm not a whole lot like most girls. At least, not from what I can tell. For me, having a meltdown was seriously out of the question.

From the time I was two, when I first started speaking in paragraphs that began with topic sentences, Malcolm and Maud had told me that I was exceptionally smart. Later, they told me that I was analytical and focused, and that my detachment from watery emotion was a superb trait. They said that if I nurtured these qualities, I would achieve or even exceed my extraordinary potential, and this wasn't just a good thing, but a great thing. It was the only thing that mattered, in fact.

It was a challenge, and I had accepted it.

That's why I was more prepared for this catastrophe than most kids my age would be, or maybe *any* kids my age.

Yes, it was true that panic was shooting up and down my spine and zinging out to my fingertips. I was shocked, maybe even terrified. But I quickly tamped down the screaming voice inside my head and collected my wits, along with the few available facts.

One: My parents had died in some unspeakable way.

Two: Someone had known about their deaths and called the police.

Three: Our doors were locked, and there had been no obvious break-in. Aside from me, my brothers Harry and Hugo and my mother's personal assistant, Samantha, were the only ones home.

I went downstairs and got my phone. I called both my uncle Peter and our lawyer, Philippe Montaigne. Then I went to each of my siblings' bedrooms, and to Samantha's, too. And somehow, I told them each the inexpressibly horrible news that our mother and father were dead, and that it was possible they'd been murdered.

Can you imagine the words you'd use, dear reader, to tell your family that your parents had been murdered? I hope so, because I'm not going to be able to share those wretched moments with you right now. We're just getting to know each other, and I take a little bit of time to warm up to people. Can you be patient with me? I promise it'll be worth the wait.

After I'd completed that horrible task—perhaps the worst task of my life—I tried to focus my fractured attention back on Sergeant Capricorn Caputo. He was a rough-looking character, like a bad cop in a black-and-white film from the forties who smoked unfiltered cigarettes, had stained fingers, and was coughing up his lungs on his way to the cemetery.

Caputo looked to be about thirty-five years old. He had one continuous eyebrow, a furry ledge over his stony black eyes. His thin lips were set in a short, hard line. He had rolled up the sleeves of his shiny blue jacket, and I noted a zodiac sign tattooed on his wrist.

He looked like *exactly* the kind of detective I wanted to have working on the case of my murdered parents.

Gnarly and mean.

Detective Hayes was an entirely different cat. He had a basically pleasant, faintly lined face and wore a wedding ring, an NYPD Windbreaker, and steel-tipped boots. He looked sympathetic to us kids, sitting in a stunned semi-circle around him. But Detective Hayes wasn't in charge, and he wasn't doing the talking.

Caputo stood with his back to our massive fireplace and coughed into his fist. Then he looked around the living room with his mouth wide open.

He couldn't believe how we lived.

And I can't say I blame him.

He took in the eight-hundred-gallon aquarium coffee table with the four glowing pygmy sharks swimming circles around their bubbler.

His jaw dropped even farther when he saw the life-size merman hanging by its tail from a bloody hook and chain in the ceiling near the staircase.

He sent a glance across the white-lacquered grand piano, which we called "Pegasus" because it looked like it had wings.

And he stared at Robert, who was slumped over in a La-Z-Boy with a can of Bud in one hand and a remote control in the other, just watching the static on his TV screen.

Robert is a remarkable creation. He really is. It's next to impossible to tell that he, his La-Z-Boy, and his very own TV are all part of an incredibly lifelike, technologically advanced sculpture. He was cast from a real person, then rendered in polyvinyl and an auto-body filler composite called Bondo. Robert looks so real, you half expect him to crunch his beer can against his forehead and ask for another cold one.

"What's the point of this thing?" Detective Caputo asked.

"It's an artistic style called hyperrealism," I responded.

"Hyper-real, huh?" Detective Caputo said. "Does that mean 'over-the-top'? Because that's kind of a theme in this family, isn't it?"

No one answered him. To us, this was home.

When Detective Caputo was through taking in the décor, he fixed his eyes on each of us in turn. We just blinked at him. There were no hysterics. In fact, there was no apparent emotion at all.

"Your parents were *murdered*," he said. "Do you get that? What's the matter? No one here loved them?"

We did love them, but it wasn't a simple love. To start with, my parents were complicated: strict, generous, punishing, expansive, withholding. And as a result, we were complicated, too. I knew all of us felt what I was feeling—an internal tsunami of horror and loss and confusion. But we couldn't show it. Not even to save our lives.

Of course, Sergeant Caputo didn't see us as bereaved children going through the worst day of our tender young lives. He saw us as *suspects*, every one of us a "person of interest" in a locked-door double homicide.

He didn't try to hide his judgment, and I couldn't fault his reasoning.

I thought he was right.

My parents' killer was in that room.